Alice Fraser is an innocent young girl from the quiet Scottish countryside whose life is about to take an unimaginable turn. Soon after her eighteenth birthday, against her better judgement, she finds herself catapulted into life in London during the Roaring 20s. Through her cousin's connections, she encounters the hedonistic lifestyle of the Bright Young People. Before long, she is introduced to the intoxicating combination of jazz, alcohol, drugs and casual sex.

Accidentally gate-crashing an orgy awakens a curiosity within her, and she decides to learn more about sex. Her chosen tutor is the devilishly handsome womaniser Charlie, Lord Moorfoot. The many warnings about his reputation for being incapable of emotion do nothing to put her off. While reluctant at first, he agrees to her request, and they set off together on a sexual world of discovery. Despite numerous warnings, she finds herself falling for him, and he is shocked to discover he feels the same way. Despite their feelings for each other, untold family histories and prejudice on both sides mean they must fight to be together. Can Alice find the resolve and courage to win the fight to be with the man she loves?

The Age of Decadence
Copyright © 2022 Faye Keltie
ISBN: 978-1-4874-3320-8
Cover art by Martine Jardin

Published by eXtasy Books Inc

Look for us online at:
www.eXtasybooks.com

THE AGE OF DECADENCE
BRIGHT YOUNG PEOPLE 1

BY

FAYE KELTIE

DEDICATION

To my lovely husband, whose ability to feign interest has been invaluable, and Jim — muckle dribblings to you and yours!

Chapter One: Leaving Home

When asked to tell their stories, many people say they have no idea where to begin. I do not share that worry. Prior to June, 1926, my eighteenth birthday, I have no story to tell. Well, I do, but it is rather dull compared with what happens after.

The day after my birthday, Dad sat beside me, wearing a grave expression as though readying himself for delivering sad news. I presumed he was going to discuss a neighbour's death or illness. Although neither of us suspected, he was on the brink of suggesting something which changed my life in ways far exceeding my wildest dreams.

"Alice, I have come to terms with you showing no inclination to attend university, despite doing so well at school," he reminded me for the umpteenth time.

Dad loved telling stories about the female students at university, although men and women studied at separate times for some archaic reason. He made no secret of his hope that I would join them. Passing the academy entrance exam meant a great deal to him, almost as much as receiving my Leavers Certificate. Despite his pleas, I drew the line at sitting the university entrance exams. I knew I might pass if I applied myself, although the point of doing so escaped me. No one could explain the purpose of spending years at university learning an occupation I must forgo when I married.

"I picture myself married someday," I told him with a sigh. "Do you want me turning out a lonely, frustrated old spinster? Or married, yet unfulfilled because I abandoned my true vocation?"

I understood what being unmarried meant. The Great War consigned many young ladies into fierce competition for the attention of available young men. We had a few unmarried women over thirty living in our village, some war widows, others who had been incapable of catching an admirer's eye. Theirs looked a solitary existence, and I harboured no ambition of joining them for sake of a career.

"All I am interested in is helping you at the surgery, but you won't let me," I complained.

"I've received a letter from your Aunt Violet," he told me, ignoring my familiar grievance. "She has invited you down to stay with her in London for a wee while. I have spent some time thinking it over, and I believe it is a good idea. What do you think?"

He waited for my comments on this unexpected news, his face unreadable. A tell-tale sadness in his eyes showed he might not be as happy with the idea as he said.

"I don't want to leave here. I do not want to go to London. It means leaving you on your own, and I don't want to do that." I took his hand.

"Och, it's me that's been leaving you on your own, lass," he said, patting my hand. "I have my patients keeping me busy. You are a young lady now, and it is not right that you are on your own all the time. It is time you expanded your horizons."

"Cludenbrig is my home. I'm happy here."

"Are you?" he asked, his tone a sad one.

"Yes, I am," I replied, although I could see what he meant. My happy childhood ended abruptly when my mother died. Dad never forgave himself for missing signs of her illness, although there was nothing he could have done. Following her death, he threw himself into his work, and a long time had passed since our house could be called a happy one.

"London is so far away," I continued, changing the subject.

"You might find you love London, far away from your stuffy old faither." He smiled, waving his arm to repel my attempts at stating otherwise. "It can be a wee holiday for you, and you can visit galleries and museums. The shops are vast. You can lose yourself in them for hours. It will be a good opportunity for you to buy yourself some bonnie dresses. It has been some time since you did that. They have all sorts of fancy restaurants where you can try food from around the world . . ."

"I'll bet it won't be as nice as Mrs. McKenzie's cooking," I grumbled.

"Perhaps not," he conceded with a shrug. "But you won't know until you try. There are countless picture houses. You love the pictures, don't you? There are theatres and places for going dancing. You can do many things there that you can't do here." I did not realise then how accurate these words would prove. "If you are intent on finding yourself a husband, you may as well look for a rich one, and London is the place for that. Your Aunt Violet can introduce you to many interesting young gentlemen."

I should have expected this. When Aunt Violet last visited, she reminded Dad I was approaching marriageable age and asked how I might meet a suitable husband. At the time, I thought the question unfair as I had my eye on one boy, Robbie, eldest son of the village blacksmith. I usually walked home from school with my friend Esther, the minister's daughter. Robbie joined us when he wished, carrying our satchels. On our last day at school, he took my hand without saying a word. I found myself struck dumb by a pair of hazel eyes I now found quite striking. Esther's eyes grew huge when she realised what we were doing. She wittered on for the entire walk home, talking about everything except us holding hands. When we arrived at the manse, she left us with a wave and a sly smile.

Robbie and I walked towards my house in nervous silence, not caring if anyone saw us. Esther would have told half the village during the time taken to reach my house in any case. To my immense disappointment, he did not make any attempt to kiss me. This did not stop me becoming the envy of every girl for miles. Since that day, we had held hands and conversed at the same time. I grew convinced he might kiss me one day.

"You should think yourself lucky. Not everyone gets these opportunities," Dad continued, interrupting my reverie, "and she will look after you very well. You get along well with her, don't you?"

"I love Aunt Violet," I confirmed.

My mother's sister is a warm, generous woman. This invitation should have been predictable. Her greeting is an enveloping embrace, and picturing her frowning is impossible. Experience taught me I should avoid asking her thoughts if I might not like the answer as she gave her honest opinion, whether sought or unwanted. To everyone's annoyance, she would be correct, and she hated squandering an opportunity to remind you.

I spent the morning giving the offer some thought and, undecided, went to see Mrs. McKenzie, our housekeeper. No matter how much she had on her hands, there was always time for a chat. I would be sitting with some cocoa within minutes unless there was a lot to do, when she would rope me into peeling potatoes or chopping vegetables. When Mum died, I could always be found there or riding my horse, Bertha. The one place I avoided was the garden, where I had spent most time with Mum.

"Do you think I should stay with Aunt Violet in London?" I asked.

"You ken full well that's a question only you can answer,"

she said with a kind smile. "Ah'll say this, Ah've never been to London, and at ma stage o life, with the wee bit money Ah've saved, it's unlikely it'll happen. Ah cannae say Ah dinnae wonder what it wid be like, fae time tae time. Tae see the sights, go tae a fancy restaurant and hae someone cook fir me fir a change, then go see wan o thae big shows. Ah'm sad Ah've niver hid a chance to dae these things, but Ah micht be sadder yit if Ah had been gien a chance yit no taken it."

My friends proved of the same persuasion, Esther telling me I would be a certifiable lunatic if I passed on this opportunity, saying she would ask if she might go in my place if I refused. My objections met nothing more than further questions showing concern for my sanity. When I told Robbie I might be leaving, he stunned me with no more than a wish for a safe journey and an admission that he was a poor letter writer.

I considered their words and decided I should go to London to see if I liked it, convinced I would not. We agreed with the proviso I could return home any time I wanted.

Dad bought me a ticket later that day, giving us no chance for changing our minds. My departure day came around too soon. I said a sad goodbye to my friends, my hopes for a farewell kiss from Robbie woefully dashed.

Whereas I usually love a train journey, this one proved different. Dad wiped away a tear as he hugged me goodbye. I had only seen him cry once before, and that was when Mum died. I had the compartment to myself, leaving me alone with my weeping, which I did uninterrupted until Carlisle. My books remained unread whilst I stared at the countryside ceding into one big dirty town after another. In an attempt at passing time, I considered how long I should stay in London until I could return. I decided on at least a month to avoid hurting Aunt Violet's feelings. After four weeks, I could go home, look Dad in the eye and tell him I gave it a try.

My cousin Alfie collected me from King's Cross, guiding me through the crowds towards his car. Around us, vast throngs of people strode with determination on their busy ways.

"London's a little busier than what you're familiar with, isn't it?" Alfie asked, laughing at my expression. "Don't worry—you will get used to it."

I nodded, although I did not think that likely.

"There are so many people. I have never been further from home than Edinburgh, and here I am, being driven inside a motor car around the streets of London. Dad says cars are a capitalist indulgence. Everywhere he needs to go, he can reach by foot, horse, or train. Some farms can only be reached on foot or horseback anyway. My goodness, I thought Edinburgh was busy, yet it was nothing compared with this. I think that London is a different world altogether."

Laughing, Alfie told me he would take me the scenic way so I could see some sights. He proved a fun guide, and I relished seeing places I had read about. Despite the five years between us and the age since we last saw each other, we chatted like old friends as we flew along broad city streets.

Our house is among the biggest in our village, yet it was dwarfed by the townhouse Alfie parked outside. Although just Aunt Violet, Alfie and his wife, Caroline, or Lonnie as everyone knew her, lived there, the white-painted house stretched four storeys high. I understood Aunt Violet, or the Dowager Lady Lyndsey if giving her proper title, was wealthy. Until then, I did not realise how wealthy.

"Welcome to your new home, Cousin Alice," he said, declaring our arrival with a peep of the horn.

Aunt Violet ran outside, greeting me with another of her all-enveloping hugs. "Lovely to see you. I am delighted you will be staying with us."

Taking my arm, she led me inside, where I met an

obeisance of servants who spirited away with my bags. The grand wood-lined interior seemed even bigger inside, and my beautiful new bedroom was much larger than my room back home. My room overlooked Holland Park, and I felt thankful to look at grass and trees, helping me remember London included more than bricks and concrete.

Though seriously tempted, I refrained from jumping onto the enormous bed with its plump cushions. What stopped me was the presence of Dawson, Lonnie's lady's maid, and mine for the duration of my stay. I did not have the first idea what a lady's maid did. Reluctant to ask, I hoped it would become apparent. She had already unpacked my cases and helped me freshen up. It felt strange having someone other than Mum do these things for me, although being looked after made a pleasant change.

Feeling pampered, I entered the dining room, where I met Lonnie. Some years older than me, she was the prettiest woman I had ever seen and proved unlike any woman I met before. Her blonde hair was worn in a Dutch bob, beautifully framing her smiley, expressive face. The red lipstick and nail varnish would be met with many disapproving looks in Cludenbrig. I supposed her a flapper, although I never heard anyone in London using that word.

"It's delightful to meet you. I have heard wonderful things about you. I do hope you enjoy London," she said, kissing my cheek.

"I hope so," I answered, although she spotted my hesitation.

"I do imagine it is all a bit strange but don't worry. We are a friendly bunch,"

She pushed a drink in my hand. I had no inkling what it might be, though I could tell it contained alcohol. Unfamiliar with the taste, I struggled to keep from screwing my face as the liquid burned its way towards my stomach. She lighted a

French cigarette on a long holder. I could not avoid staring, as I had never seen a woman smoke. Then, with a giggle, she offered me a puff.

I was recovering from my coughing fit when I decided I should quit smoking. "I love your dress. I've never seen such a pretty one," I told her once I retrieved my ability to speak. The dress was stunning, with a sapphire blue crushed velvet body and lace sleeves lined with pale blue satin. I wondered how much such a fantastic dress would cost, as it looked expensive.

"Do you like it?" she asked with another dazzling smile. "It's a princess line. Picked this up for a song in Paris. You must try it on. It will look fabulous with your shape." She put her hands onto my waist, judging my form.

The manhandling from someone I had just met left me speechless.

"Oh, most definitely. I must take you shopping. I can show you the best places. How are you fixed for tomorrow?"

I looked at Aunt Violet, who nodded and accepted her invitation.

"Great, it's a date, as the Yanks say. There is some fabulous stuff around, cannot wait to show you. I adore what is in right now and am glad to see the end of the boyish look. It isn't meant for anyone who has even a hint of a bosom, and I cannot be jiggered bandaging these babies." She pointed at her chest and laughed. "I have a side-lacing brassiere that works beautifully, but I cannot breathe wearing it."

No one minded her discussing these topics with a man present. Mum only mentioned underwear when alone. We would be mortified if Dad had overheard. Looking at her cleavage, I saw why she might find underwear a problem. My breasts were a shade smaller, yet I shared her concerns. I did not fancy substituting my restrictive underwear with another limiting set.

"Abso-bloody-lutely," Alfie agreed, "imprisoning such magnificent jubes is indeed the most heinous of crimes."

Everyone laughed, including me. Life in London did not appear to be anything like home.

"Now," Aunt Violet interjected, "we are responsible for helping our Alice here find a husband."

I began to object, wary of being tied to London by a husband, but thought better of admitting that.

Resolute, Violet persevered. "You haven't come out. Your father had little truck with such matters, and dear Mary's death did not help matters. She might have changed his mind. Sadly, we will never know. I could present you. It's far too late this season, but there is always next year." She gave the idea some thought, although a scowl appeared when she considered the consequences. "Although, I fear your father would never speak to us again if he found out. Perhaps we oughtn't after all."

I showed my agreement with a nod, although she showed no interest. We both knew I would not do anything Dad disapproved of behind his back. My dad and Aunt Violet are fond of each other, despite the fact he has no time for the concept of nobility. She likes teasing him about his dislike not preventing him from marrying an earl's daughter. He is a staunch socialist and a Labour party member from the beginning. To him, titles, privilege, and organised religion are anathemas that must be questioned and distrusted. My great-great-grandfather emigrated to Canada, returning to marry my great-great-grandmother after making his fortune. The money was spent by the time Dad, the youngest of seven, was born, yet my grandparents made sure their children attended school beyond their thirteenth birthdays.

Dad had been first in his family to attend university after winning a scholarship. He studied in Edinburgh, where he met Mum at a ball. It sounded romantic, although their courtship appeared a difficult one. Judging by information I pieced together, mostly overheard conversations, my parents had been shunned by some friends and relatives who disapproved of their marriage. Dad was trade, which became their word for Dad's work, a running joke between them. It explained why we lived nearer Dad's family than Mum's.

"Still, coming out is not such a great deal these days," Aunt Violet continued.

"Thank your lucky heavens for that, believe me," Lonnie interrupted. "It is a never-ending succession of unbelievably dull balls where unbelievably dull girls seek unbelievably dull boys for dancing or possibly marriage."

"Yes, well, there are many events you may still attend," Aunt Violet continued, ignoring her. "Things haven't been the same since . . ."

Her voice faltered, and I understood why. Her thoughts had turned to the war and my cousin Bertie, Alfie's older brother, who died in Amiens. She gave herself a shake before addressing Alfie and Lonnie.

"You two know many young eligible bachelors, and therefore it is your responsibility. I want a steady queue of handsome young suitors at our door first thing tomorrow."

"Wouldn't we all." Lonnie said with a giggle. A married woman making such a proclamation surprised me, although everyone laughed again.

"What about an introduction to young Charlie? It is high time he settled down." She watched Alfie's face before giving Lonnie a cheeky wink.

"I don't think he is the settling down type," Alfie countered with an impish smile. "Besides, do you think there is a chance in hell the Duchess would give her approval?"

"Nonsense," she brayed, batting the idea into the distance with a hand. "It merely takes the right woman to make a man desire domestication. He clearly has not met her yet. The

Duchess' blessing, though, is damn near impossible. Still, Charlie is a grown man, more than old enough to make his own decisions, although her reaction would be delightful," she said, laughing at the idea. "I think an introduction might be on the cards purely so I can see the look upon her face. He is your closest friend, Alfie. It is inevitable they will chance upon each other at some point."

"Yes, I suppose it may be," he said through thin lips.

"Hugo Crawford?" Aunt Violet suggested, not conceding without a fight.

"You haven't heard? Most unlike you. He put a handcuff on Hetty Symington's finger."

"The eldest Symington girl? It has not been in the newspapers. Terribly disappointing. He could do much better, lovely looking girl, yet no manners."

"This might not be quite as easy as you thought," Lonnie said, teasing.

Undeterred, Aunt Violet continued, "Arthur Brewster?"

"Do you wish to bore poor Alice to death?" Lonnie asked. "What on heaven or earth might you have done to deserve that?" she asked me, an eyebrow raised.

"Oh, my goodness, yes, excellent point. Unless you have a deep, enthusiastic love for Egyptology?" she asked, looking hopeful.

I shook my head.

"No, thought not. Ever since he attended that damned talk, the poor man can barely speak of anything else. What about Freddie Evesham?"

"The lift doesn't stop on all floors any longer," Lonnie answered, making a swigging motion.

"Pity. Waste of a marvellous mind. Gilbert Bradshaw-Jones?"

In response, Alfie put a finger on his nostril and inhaled. I did not know what the mime meant, but I did not want to ask, considering everyone except me understood.

Aunt Violet turned towards me, her smile undiminished. "Never fear, we will find you a husband yet. These two have so many friends, I cannot begin keeping up."

"Thank you, Aunt Violet. There is no rush," I told her, although I doubted she would pay me the slightest heed.

After a day's dress shopping, Lonnie invited me to accompany her on a night on the town. We spent our evening in London's fantastic clubs, where my love affair with Jazz started. Jazz proved wild and energetic, poles apart from anything I had ever heard before. I adored it from the moment I stepped into the first club.

We visited many clubs and met Lonnie's friends everywhere we went. I met lords, ladies, writers, artists, and an assortment of fascinating characters. One chap had a pet mongoose straddling his shoulder as a living stole. A slight-built young man named Bernie Ambrose was a gossip columnist who wrote stories about his friend's antics for the newspapers, yet no one minded in the slightest.

It took a shameful amount of time before I realised who these people were. Curious, I investigated my suspicions.

"These people you are introducing me to, are these the Bright Young People I keep reading about in the newspapers?" I asked Lonnie the first opportunity I got.

"Well, yes and no. Some are, although most are horrified at the very idea of being associated with them. Many of our friends utterly resent that title, although I suppose you might call us a subsect. The ones who revel in it are not necessarily as wild living as the papers would have you think. Most will not take anything stronger than booze and no heavy petting before marriage. Some might undertake the odd fling with a West Indian jazz musician or two. Who hasn't?"

"So, it is made up? The stuff in the papers?"

"No, it is mostly true, some much worse than what gets printed," she said, shrugging. "You can trust Bernie. He knows what he should write and what he must omit. They can be marvellous fun in small doses but are not people you want to spend much time with. At times, they can make Bertie Wooster seem sophisticated and urbane. It is comparable with the nursery when Nanny pops out. Theirs is a ridiculous babyish language, and they think playing ceaseless practical jokes on each other is endlessly hilarious. If you spend time at their houses, it is all midnight feasts and watching out for someone hiding your pyjamas or apple pie your bed and the like."

"They put apple pies in your beds?"

"No, sweetie," she said with a laugh, explaining the trick with the folded over sheets that prevented you getting into bed.

Bernie introduced me to Leslie, his girlfriend, who wore a fabulous black silk tulle dress with delicate beading. They proceeded to tell me some wild gossip. I heard about events at treasure hunts, balls, and something called freak parties. Their tales were of scandalous affairs involving people whose fathers were MPs, lords, and royals. Not content with that, they then shared stories of their parent's antics. Some of their stories shocked me, although some left me confused. Not keen on admitting my ignorance, I acted what I thought looked an appropriate level of shock in response to their cues.

"Oh, fabulous, Tabby's here," Lonnie said, pointing towards the doors where an attractive young woman was entering the club on the arm of a handsome gentleman. She spotted us and gave us a wave. "You will adore Tabby. I can't wait to introduce you. She is fabulously wealthy, a fascinating character, and excellent company. She is the sole heiress to the Consolidated Electrical Cable fortune, and her allowance could keep a small country afloat. Her family died in a tragic house fire years ago, though she was too young to remember. She lives with her Aunt Agatha, who is of advanced years and has been quite senile for some time, leaving Tabby free to come and go as she very much pleases. She's loaded now, although when she comes of age or Agatha dies, she'll be richer than Croesus."

"Poor thing," I said, disliking the sound of being so alone.

"Most people are incredibly envious of her. Some would kill their entire families to change places with her or merely be allowed inside her inner sanctum. She has entertained kings, queens, movie stars, politicians, writers, and artists. She has no title, yet in our circle, is practically royalty."

"Must I mind my P's and Q's? I mean if she entertains royalty —"

"Be yourself, honey. Tabs is simply interested in how fascinating you are. She is a great hostess but is no collector."

"Collector?"

"A society hostess whose whole reason for living is inviting the most impressive guest list to their functions. Each one favours a particular group, for some, artists and writers. Statesmen for others, and some prefer royalty. Whatever the field, the higher the status, the better. Tabby does not care about those things. If she finds you interesting, you receive an invitation to some event or other. If she likes you, you are invited to her country home, which is always cluttered with the great and the good. If not, you are silently yet definitely blackballed. She has cut off a few people with impressive social standings. For some, being blackballed by her is abject horror, just social suicide, but don't worry. She will adore you."

This unwelcome and somewhat intimidating information scared me. I disliked the sound of being blackballed by Tabby.

"Who is that with her? Is he her paramour? He's rather handsome."

"Can't say I know him, although that is no surprise. There

is a never-ending supply of ridiculously handsome young men adorning her arm. Christ alone knows where she finds them all. Rarely, if ever, the same one twice."

The beautiful young woman approaching wore a gorgeous embroidered dress and expensive-looking jewellery, topped with a flamboyant beaded headdress. Greeting Lonnie with a hug, she flashed me a welcoming smile.

"You must be Alice. It's heavenly to meet you." She kissed both cheeks and gave me a warm smile. "Do hope the gang are treating you well."

I told her my treatment had been exemplary, and she introduced us to Miles, her companion, who towered over her. We talked about how I was finding London and discussed the finest clubs. We chatted easily, our conversation peppered with her infectious giggles.

"The Black Bottom," she cried with a squeal, hearing the band strike a new number. Grabbing Miles' hand, she jumped to her feet. "This is the most wonderful of most wonderful things, an absolute hoot. Madly love this, absolutely must dance. Will you?" she asked, her voice full of enthusiasm.

I admitted my ignorance, and Lonnie told her she would keep me company. Bottom lip protruding at our slight to her favourite dance, Tabby left with an enthusiastic Miles.

"She's a little dynamo," Lonnie commented, watching Tabby run towards the dance floor, pulling Miles with her.

"I can see how she'd be a lot of fun."

"Fun and Tabby go hand in hand. She is wholly committed to the most hedonistic life possible. As you will undoubtedly discover, she enjoys a high life involving varied male companionship, drink, drugs, and parties. Can you believe she's a year younger than you?"

"Really? She is so elegant and graceful. I felt a dowdy, backwards country yokel standing beside her."

"Oh, believe me, at times, I do too, sweetie," Lonnie said

with a smile. "Theoretically, she's too young to purchase alcohol. Not that Tabs will ever let the law stop her from doing whatever she wants, whenever she wants. There is not a beak or copper she cannot sweet-talk into letting her have her way. She liked you. I think you've gained approval."

"Do you think so?"

"It is most unusual for her to stay still enough to talk to anyone so long when there is music playing."

"How will I know if she approves of me?"

"If you never receive an invite, you're not in," she said with a shrug.

CHAPTER TWO: ANGELS AND DEVILS

Aunt Violet received many visitors, taking their turns to scrutinise her mysterious Scottish niece. She ordered beautiful visiting cards for me, insisting they be engraved, not printed. If not visiting with Aunt Violet, Lonnie took me shopping or to cinemas, cocktail bars, and tea houses. Alfie took me to the Jubilee Championships at the All England Club, where I became infatuated with tennis. Weekends meant avoiding London's crowds, taking turns visiting each other's country houses. At times, the invitations caused a tyranny of choice.

My love for jazz continued unabated. I saw Layton and Johnstone perform and bored everyone with my endless professions of love for them. With practice, I learned the Black Bottom and Heebie-Jeebies, although I struggled with the Shimmy, giving it up as a bad lot.

I received an invitation to Tabby's country house for the weekend, the absence of a blackball coming as a relief. Despite my invitation, I felt a wee bit nervous during the drive along a terraced cul-de-sac. The spectacular modern villa stood at the end, overlooking a sandy beach. We were shown into a drawing room, the bay windows offering stunning sea views.

Tabby greeted me with a kiss, and we chitchatted until she noticed Leslie dancing.

"Look at Leslie's outfit. It's bloody gorgeous. Just too envy-inducing. Wish he'd tell where he has them made." Shocked at hearing such language, I did not linger on what was said.

"I have asked many, many times, but it is a secret he will

17

take to his grave," Lonnie said with a glum expression.

"Did you say he?" I asked, arriving at a late understanding.

"Yes. Leslie is a man," Lonnie told me.

I giggled, thinking it another of their jokes until I realised she was not laughing.

"You're not joking?"

"No, sweetheart," she said, smiling. "No matter how he dresses, he's still very much a man and requests addressing as such."

"She, I mean he, is so feminine looking. The clothes he is wearing, his voice, manner, and make-up, he is stunning. I thought you were joking."

Tabby thought my admission hilarious, her laugh proving infectious.

Back in London, Lonnie invited me to spend a morning at a beauty salon. She was preparing for a rather exclusive party, and although not invited, I joined her. I had never been to a beauty salon before. I found myself having my hair cut and finger waves put in. I asked if I should dye my hair, which is a shocking deep red. Lonnie and the hairstylist looked horrified, telling me many would commit murder for my Titian colour. They would not be as enthusiastic if they endured the teasing I had experienced at school for being ginger.

Aunt Violet was enthusiastic in complimenting my new look. With scarce time for breath, she turned as though asking a question that had just struck her, although it had most likely been planned.

"Why don't you take Alice with you tonight? You must allow her an opportunity to show off her fabulous fresh look. Charlie will just adore her," she said with a wink in my direction.

Lonnie gave the idea some consideration. "Isn't that what we are supposed to fear most?"

"How can you possibly go off and have fun while leaving your poor cousin stuck at home with no admirers except crusty old me?" Aunt Violet cajoled, determined to have her way.

"You know she isn't invited," Lonnie said with a firm tone.

She opposed me attending this party, which hurt. I thought we had been getting on well. My curiosity was firmly piqued, making me desperate to investigate this Charlie and why we must be kept apart.

"How could Charlie possibly invite her if he has no idea she exists?" Aunt Violet persisted. "There will be many gate-crashers there, and I am certain he will not mind in the slightest." Their discussion continued as though they forgot I happened to be present.

"That is not what is concerning me, as you well know."

"As we have both said, it is merely postponing the inevitable," said Aunt Violet in one of her resolute tones.

Lonnie thought it over. "Oh, okay, why the hell not? There will be a few of your eligible bachelors, I suppose. I will be your alarm clock, but you must leave before midnight."

"Midnight? Am I Cinderella? Are you worried I will turn into a pumpkin?"

My joke fell flat.

"Events after midnight are definitely by invitation only. It can be a little wild," she answered without smiling.

Lonnie left to consult Dawson. Confused, I asked Aunt Violet, "What did she mean by alarm clock?"

"A chaperone, dear."

After a few minutes, Lonnie entered the room, her expression serious. "We had better get ready. The theme is angels and devils. I think I know what you can wear. Dawson is sorting everything."

Lips pursed, she took my hand and led me upstairs.

Lonnie wore a devil costume with a short red fringed taffeta skirt and a tiara with two shiny red horns attached. I wore an incredible angel costume of such cleverness it did not look like a last-minute construction. Lonnie loaned me a fringed white dress which revealed my bare thighs over my white stockings when I swayed. Dawson finished it with lacy wings salvaged from a fairy costume and a halo fashioned from a tiara wrapped in tinsel.

I sat beside Alfie during the drive to Cyneset House. He did not say a word during the entire journey. Their sullen expressions told me they had quarrelled, although they did not discuss it, and I felt disinclined to pry. We arrived at an enormous residence situated on Park Lane, although built back from the busy road. Tall walls prevented all except those on top decks of omnibuses from viewing it. Driving through massive wooden gates revealed a house with a stark Palladian exterior giving no clue to its opulent interior.

I gasped at the impressive hallway and its magnificent staircase with white marble steps, posts, and handrails. Servants collected our coats and showed us inside an enormous ballroom, already full of people. The high ceiling covered with ancient, gilded frescoes made the jazz band playing in the corner appear strangely out of time.

Tabby joined us, handing me a drink containing fruit juices and gin. Finding it pleasant, I took a big sip, causing Lonnie to give me an anxious look.

"Do be careful, darling. You're still not used to the giggle water."

"Now, don't be such a mother hen, Lonnie," Tabby scolded. "It's too, too tedious. Alice will be fine. Let her spread her angel wings and have some fun."

Lonnie did not say anything, although she kept a close eye on me. Tabby spent some time preoccupied with Jolyon, a new and fascinating acquaintance. Looking at him, I understood her preoccupation.

When I finished my third or fourth drink, I felt warm. Fanning myself with my hand, I looked for somewhere I could find some fresh air. Unfortunately, I could not see if the windows were open due to some heavy black damask curtains. The door nearest me stood ajar, the room behind it dark and empty. No one stopped me, so I pushed the door open, discovering an extensive library. Shelves heaved with an impressive collection of leather-bound books, although I struggled to see the titles in the gloom.

As my eyes adjusted to the dim light, I noticed a set of French doors. After further investigation, I found they opened onto a terrace. The doors were locked, but there was a key in the keyhole. I turned it and opened the door, welcoming the instant coolness of the summer evening air. I stood on the terrace looking over the rear garden, which I thought tiny for such a substantial house. Rehearsing what I could say if it happened, I stood for a time, summoning the courage to approach one of Aunt Violet's bachelors.

I retraced my steps back to the ballroom, almost colliding with Lonnie.

"There you are. I was looking for you," she said with palpable relief.

"I wanted some fresh air," I told her, taking a drink from a convenient passing servant.

"Are you feeling all right?" she asked, looking concerned again.

"I am fine," I insisted. "Now, I can see a few attractive looking young gentlemen. Why don't we find an unattached one?"

I did not leave the dancefloor until the band stopped playing at midnight. Lights came on, and guests gathered their possessions as they made their way outside. Lonnie led me to the front door with a strange urgency, guiding me away from the people saying their goodbyes in the hallway.

"Aren't you coming, too?" I asked, although she clearly was not. She did not have her coat.

"No, I'm staying. I will catch you at home. Forgive me for abandoning you. Do you mind terribly going back on your own?"

"Of course not," I lied, hiding my envy as I climbed into one of many cabs waiting outside.

"Cheers, darling. Goodnight," she said, dashing back inside without looking back.

Sitting in the cab, I pondered the wild party continuing without me. I had not met Charlie, I presumed because of my gate-crasher status. He must be frightening if they thought I should hide from him, although I could not imagine them being friends with someone so scary. The dangerous combination of alcohol and my annoyance at missing out on some fun provoked a rash decision. I stopped the cabbie after a few minutes, a few streets away. He was more annoyed at forgoing his full fare, such as it was, than concerned for my safety. I gave him double to stop him complaining.

I walked towards the house, feeling glad it was a simple route. All that was necessary was following the park until I found the place again. Some people were chatting beside the closed main gate. To my increased annoyance, they said their goodbyes, then struck up another conversation many times. I waited until they left, growing more impatient with each minute.

After a lengthy wait, I was alone, and I became aware of my heart thumping in the quiet street. Taking a slow deep breath, I walked towards the smaller gate and pushed it open. There was a path, but I stayed clear, creeping along the darkest wall, thinking it best for avoiding detection. Cursing at the deafening sound of my shoes upon the gravel, I tiptoed my way towards the house.

In my excitement, I had not considered my strategy for getting inside. It was not as though I could let myself in. However, a stone archway looked as though it led towards the rear garden, so I went through, finding myself at the foot of some stairs leading to the terrace I had stood on earlier. I could not remember locking the library door, so thought I would check. Fumbling in the moonlight, I found my way upstairs. The library was still dark, although light shone in through the ballroom doorway.

Crossing my fingers, I grasped the door handle and stood motionless, holding it whilst willing my hand to move. Heart racing, I stood immobile, summoning my courage before I turned the knob. The door swung open, and I took a deep breath before tiptoeing inside. I made my way towards the ballroom before realising the band had started again. I had no need to worry about anyone overhearing me.

Trembling, I pulled the door open as wide as I dared, peering into the ballroom. There were dozens of people rather than the hundreds who'd attended earlier. The band had gone, and in their place was the biggest gramophone I have ever seen. My gaze was drawn towards the people dancing, more frenzied this time. After a moment or two, I realised some had no clothes on! I stared open-mouthed. Two half-dressed women engaged in a long passionate kiss with a handsome man kneeling before them, kissing and caressing their bodies one after the other. Two men lay on a sofa, one with a mop of grey hair, the other half his age. The grey-haired man undid the other man's trousers and extracted his organ. It looked enormous, yet I watched him lick it from one end to the other before taking the entirety in his mouth. Realising my mouth was still agape, I closed it with a gulp.

At first, I marvelled at how he did so without gagging. After further viewing, I considered if a more appropriate reaction would be shock. The exquisite happiness upon the younger man's face struck me with awe. I studied his face, enjoying his enjoyment. Scared to move lest it drew any attention, I surveyed the scenes of sexual pleasure.

On another sofa lay a naked woman, her face obscured by a man leaning over her, circling a breast with his tongue. He tickled a pert nipple as another man kneeled before her, licking between her legs. Overcome with a warm, pleasant sensation, my body tingled everywhere. I did not feel scared or revolted, more excited. My enjoyment worried me. I knew many would consider such activities immoral and a sin, or at least something they presumed wrong.

The woman arched her body, giving a low moan when he stopped licking. He put a hand under her bottom and raised her as he pushed himself between her legs. Her head was thrown back as her mouth formed a groan. I watched, transfixed, imagining how she was feeling. When the other man stood to put his organ in her mouth, I realised the woman was Lonnie!

Chapter Three: Meet the Devil

I stood stock-still for a moment or two before making a slow, gradual retreat towards the library's shadows. Lonnie had not been exaggerating when she said things turned wild. Whilst I had enjoyed watching, I knew I should leave. I had no idea what I could say to Lonnie if she saw me, and disrespecting her privacy this way felt wrong.

I did not see Alfie and had no idea if he could be aware of what I saw his wife engaging in. I presumed he must be performing similar acts with other women, out my view. It struck me as an unusual situation for a married couple, although having seen them interact, their love for each other was evident. Whatever their reasons for attending such a party, it worked for them. I suppose many would deem their actions as wrong, yet I did not want to judge them. I adored them both. What they did behind what they thought were closed doors was their business, categorically none of mine.

Everyone looked preoccupied and had not observed me, or so I thought. As I turned towards the French doors, an overhead light snapped on. To my horror, an unfamiliar voice called after me.

"I say. You are not thinking of leaving us already, are you?"

Caught! Heart thumping, freezing for a moment, I considered running towards the door. I knew it would be futile. If he chased me, he could beat me with ease. He might think pursuing me inelegant, although I thought running might make my situation worse for some bizarre reason.

For the first time, I regretted the immediacy of electric lighting. I might have made it outside during the time taken to strike a match. Cursing my luck, I turned to see a gentleman I did not recognise. Mortified, I opened my mouth, but with no idea what I could say, I curbed my tongue.

The man was so handsome I found myself incapable of doing anything more than staring at his jet-black wavy hair and amused smile. Luscious thick black eyelashes outlined captivating cobalt blue eyes I could swim in forever. My heart pounded at an alarming rate. I could not be sure whether the cause was his good looks or the situation I had gotten myself into. Panicking, I pondered what the penalty might be for being both a trespasser and a peeping Tom.

"No, I mean yes, I mean . . . look, I am deeply sorry. I am not actually supposed to be here. I wasn't invited," I said in what came out as a meek voice.

He looked at me in a most peculiar fashion, making me squirm under his intense stare. To avoid looking at him, I tried fixing my gaze at an ugly portrait of a man astride a grey horse.

"I surmised that when I saw you sneaking in," he confirmed with an alluring smile.

I scolded myself for turning my gaze from the portrait, although he proved a more delightful view.

"You lost your nerve, I take it?"

I allowed myself my much-delayed exhalation.

"Oh no, I wisnae sneaking in. Honestly, I wisn . . . wasn't. If anything, I was sneaking out. I was curious about what was happening. You see, I genuinely did not know, because if I had, I promise you, I would never have dreamed of coming back. Now I know what I know, I do know I shouldn't have, but I did, and I cannot change that. I am really, really sorry. I was leaving when you called me back. Please do not tell anyone you spotted me, especially the host. He mustn't know I was here," I babbled. I cursed myself for being incapable of constructing a coherent sentence.

"Ah, right. Yes, I see," he said with a chuckle.

There could be no way he did. I could not be sure I understood much myself. I felt thankful that he did not seek any further explanation.

"I am certain the host would not mind in the slightest, but I promise I will not tell a soul, do not worry. You have a charming accent. You are from Scotland, the south, I presume?"

The unexpected compliment put me at ease. He seemed more amused than angry.

"Cludenbrig, a tiny wee village in Dumfriesshire, five miles from Dumfries."

"Ah, Burns country. *My love is like a red, red rose* and all that."

"Yes, but I think you'll find *and a' that* is called *Is There for Honest Poverty*," I said, teasing him, delighted when I received a chuckle in response. "Which is my favourite Burns poem as it goes."

"The rank is but the guinea's stamp. The Man's the gowd for a' that," he quoted with a smile.

"Correct," I said, applauding. He gave a quick bow.

"The scenery of your homeland is undoubtedly the inspiration for some great poetry. Dumfries is the Queen of the South if I remember rightly?" he asked.

I nodded. "Yes, you do. I am impressed by your knowledge. So many people here have no idea where Dumfriesshire is. Those who do know recall it as a place they travelled through. They do remember it being stunningly beautiful, of course."

"It is a beautiful part of the country. It is rather apt, a beautiful young woman from such a beautiful place. An angel sneaking away from a house full of devils, eh? You do not

27

wish to join in the fun?" he asked with a raised eyebrow, teasing me.

"You neither, judging by your attire," I replied, surprised at my newfound forthrightness.

Unlike most partygoers, he remained fully dressed, although his undone red bowtie gave him a rakish air. He made an attractive devil.

I gave a thankful sigh when he laughed, then lost my bravado, thinking I owed him a proper explanation. "I'm sorry. I came here for the party earlier. I should have gone home at midnight but came back because I knew something secret was happening. It seemed so mysterious. I don't think I'd normally do that, but I have had a drink or two. It appears to have erased my usual timorousness. I was curious or being a nosy parker, as my dad would say."

"Curiosity in itself is not always a terrible thing. However, it did kill the cat and sometimes can lead to people seeing things they are not supposed to see. Not ready to see. How old are you?" I studied his face, but his expression was genial.

"I am eighteen, and I am not as naïve as you think I am," I blurted, wincing at my own words.

He looked unconvinced, although I sounded unconvincing, and he raised an eyebrow, although he did not say anything. My annoyance at his teasing became side-lined by how his eyes twinkled in such a fascinating way. He looked me directly in the eye in an intense manner I found daunting, although I found it near impossible to make myself look anywhere else. A shiver overtook me, leaving me with goosepimples making every hair stand on end. For a second or two, I thought he would kiss me, but the moment passed.

"I grew up in the country," I continued, trying to hide my disappointment, although I should have kept quiet. I preferred hearing him speak anyhow. "I know a wee bit more than you might think regarding hochmagandy." I turned my head with a blush, conscious of how ridiculously childish I sounded.

"Hochmagandy," he said with a laugh, causing a flutter in my chest. "A tremendous word I have not heard for years. I do not hear it enough. I should use it more often, although I could never make it sound anything near as lovely as it did coming from your lips."

His compliments came so frequently and effortlessly I doubted their sincerity, although it proved pleasant listening. He smiled, indicating I sit on the sofa. I obeyed, transfixed.

"Yes, I suppose it is somewhat apt. Sex is a wonderful and natural phenomenon. It drives and, of course, continues our species, therefore it is the most primal force around, yet it is hidden, shut away behind firmly closed doors. It is one of our society's greatest taboos, yet still permeates our culture and our art."

"It does? I don't think I am entirely sure what type of art you are referring to."

"Why, all of it. From cave paintings to the works of Mr. Picasso. Take a walk around any art gallery, although anything considered shocking is hidden from the public gaze. Literature also, although a surprising amount does pass the prurient bowdlerising of the censor. Burns was a particular fan. A friend owns a rare edition of *The Merry Muses of Caledonia*. Have you read it?"

"No, I've never heard of it."

"Of course not. I must see if he will lend it to you. There are some parts I do not understand. Perhaps you might translate for me?" he asked.

I nodded with enthusiasm at the prospect of seeing him again.

"It is scarce, and copies are extremely valuable. Other sexual references are hidden in plain sight. Shakespeare's Pompey talked of *groping for trouts in a peculiar river*, Othello made *the beast with two backs,* Marvel begged his coy mistress for it, and Rochester wanted Jane to *come to him entirely*. There are many more examples, of course, some more explicit than others. Listing them would take some time."

"You appear rather an expert on sexual representations in art," I told him. "I admit ignorance in such matters. Nevertheless, I am taken aback by your incredible knowledge."

Despite my ignorance, I agreed with everything he said. I was altogether taken with him and might possibly have concurred if he told me the sun and moon were meeting in the night sky for drinks and gin rummy.

"Me? Why no, I am but a mere enthusiastic amateur," he said with a chuckle. "I ought to introduce you to my good friend, Effy Evesham. If there is such a thing as a sexpert, as Mr. Fabian calls them, it would certainly be him. He possesses the largest collection of pornographic art I know of, perhaps the second biggest in the world, if what I hear regarding the Vatican is true. Some exhibits are many thousands of years old, intended to be on display for all to see."

"It sounds impressive. I'd like to see it."

He made the collection sound fantastic, and I did want to see it. Although, if he described a stinking cesspit, I would still like him to take me there.

"You and many others, I think. It is an absolute crying pity that it must be hidden away in shame, yet possessing it is illegal. Here we are in supposedly enlightened modern times, yet we are told we must be ashamed of our sexual urges, hiding our bodies and desires. Our antediluvian laws forbid acts which hurt no one and make many incredibly happy."

He stopped, leaving space for interjection. I said nothing, so he continued.

"And there are the newspapers, who make the most of everyone's peccadillos, spreading them over their front pages. Everyone tutting, pretending they are shocked and horrified, yet secretly thrilled and titillated. Lord knows many are engaging in similar or perhaps even worse acts behind their own closed doors."

"I do know about sexual intercourse. Well, I know how it works in theory. Mother explained after we saw horses on an afternoon walk . . ." I trailed off, deciding embarrassing myself any more would be silly.

He nodded, giving me a benign smile. "I expect you were told sex should be confined to the marital bed, though?"

"Yes, quite firmly. Until just a few minutes ago, I supposed it purely a device for having babies. Mum didn't give the impression it'd be anything I should look forward to," I conceded. "Or dread either, if I am being fair," I added, feeling I should defend her.

"When I saw you open that door, I expected you would turn and run or scream the place down. Instead, you stood there with a remarkable expression on your face — captivation, fascination perhaps," he told me, sitting beside me. He gave off a mesmerising sweet yet musky scent I could happily breathe forever.

"That is, without a doubt, not something you see every day," I said with a smile. "On reflection, what surprises me most is how envious I feel. The people looked joyful, and I wanted to experience what they are experiencing. I *want* to experience what they are experiencing," I admitted. I wondered if he would take the hint, yet his face remained so inscrutable it was infuriating. An eternity followed until he broke the silence.

"My dear, you are an innocent soul. I would wager with confidence that you have never been kissed. Doubtless, you are in the blessed state called virginity." He paused.

I stayed silent, disinclined to confirm his suspicions. He did not press me for an answer. There was no need. I was aware I was blushing.

"Such a special, tender status should not be smashed in a crowd at an event of this fashion. It warrants being given in a gentle act of love. This," he said with a wave towards the other room, "is not for you right now."

I could not believe how excited his words made me feel. It might happen one day.

"It may well be. You have no idea. You don't know me or what I need." I said, spurred on by my excitement, unable to stop the words bursting from my lips.

"Now steady on, little kitten, why the haste to become a cat? What is the reason for this urgency? Sex should never be taken too lightly. There can be severe, long-lasting consequences. It can be an incredibly powerful and dangerous business for the innocent to play with."

I recognised truth in his words, try as I might to think of a way I could argue with him.

"I'd like you to do something," he told me.

He scrutinised my eyes again, setting butterflies in motion over my body. I would comply with anything he asked.

"I doubt you have ever done this, but do not feel you must tell me either way. Before you consider giving yourself to someone, learn about yourself first. Explore your body, stand naked before a looking glass, watch as you touch yourself. Learn where you like and do not like being touched. Study between your legs until you know every quarter inch exceptionally well. Bring yourself to climax, considering how it makes you feel. Love both your body and your sensual self. Then we will discuss you attending these parties." Standing, he offered me his hand. "Come, I will see you get home."

Disappointed at our short meeting ending, I took his hand, trying to ignore the electric jolt accompanying it. I could not help wondering if he also felt it. He did not acknowledge it as he took my arm, leading me via the terrace. At the gate, he waved over a driver waiting in a massive motor car, giving me a smile and a nod goodbye as we drove off.

I cursed my cowardice with the stranger, realising I did not even know his name. As asking his name would have meant revealing mine, that was probably a good thing. My more significant concern was whether I could have instigated a kiss myself if I had leaned closer. Waiting for him to make a move towards me had been stupid. My solitary hope lay in seeing him again and having more bravado if the opportunity presented itself.

A nagging voice told me it was evident he was not interested in me. If he liked me, he might have spent more time with me, not sent me home after a few minutes. Although I made no secret of being keen to experience sex, he baulked at fulfilling my desire, albeit in a charming way. His disinterest was understandable. There could be no reason someone that handsome and clever would be interested in me. The horrible truth remained. Someone waiting next door interested him more. Someone better looking, more experienced, and mature than me, a regular girlfriend or wife, perhaps.

The melancholia accompanying that thought proved instant. I sat looking at the empty streets when a realisation gave me hope. If he did have someone waiting, he did not give the impression of being in any great hurry to return to them. I recollected how he looked at me with such intensity that I thought my insides had melted and my heart might explode. Might it be possible that look meant nothing at all? In the time I spent with Robbie, I never once saw him look at me that way.

CHAPTER FOUR AN AWAKENING

I lay on my bed, considering the handsome devil and replaying our conversation. Following his suggestion, I stood naked before a looking glass, staring at my body. To my annoyance, it had been a good guess, as it was the first time I had done this.

Looking with a critical eye, I would say my body might be considered passible, I suppose. My breasts are overlarge yet firm, my waist slim, the curve of my hips excessive. My gaze moved towards my pubic hair, which is a few shades darker than that on my head.

Sighing, I gazed at my thighs. With my feet close together, my thighs look what I can best describe as chunky. Parting my legs proved an unnatural pose, although it made my thighs look slimmer. I hated seeing myself in stockings, convinced they drew unwelcome attention. My hips and thighs are my least favourite body parts.

I stroked and cupped my breasts, thinking over the stranger's words. The feeling proved pleasant, so I continued. I touched my nipple, delighting in the increased sensitivity when it hardened under my fingertips. Slipping my hand downwards, I headed for between my legs. I explored the lips, separating them so I could feel around.

Sitting on my bed, I pulled the looking glass closer, tilting it in pursuit of an unobstructed view. Finding the results inadequate, I fetched my compact, examining myself at close range. It felt strange, naughty, yet at the same time intriguing.

I felt myself getting wetter in response to my finger. After some fumbling, I discovered a wee lump beneath a wee hood of skin. Touching it brought on an immediate warm shudder. My finger lingered, building speed until I found myself rubbing harder and faster. I felt overcome with new sensations as it opened under my touch, exposing a pearl-sized bump. My legs trembled when I increased the intensity. I found myself alternating between holding my breath and panting to concentrate on these fantastic sensations. Thousands of fireworks went off inside me, ending with a tremendous climax. Each slight touch brought another pleasure wave, each one diminishing in intensity. I relished the fantastic experience, my entire body buzzing and tingling.

Overwhelmed, I lay naked on my bed. I took a rest to gather my thoughts before trying again, watching myself in a meticulous fashion. With reluctance, I aborted my third attempt. I felt too tender, caused by my earlier enthusiasm. Feeling everything except sleepy, I visited the kitchens for a snack. The dawn light meant I found my way without much difficulty.

I crept into the kitchen, nervous about disturbing the housekeeper sleeping next door. She and Simpson, Alfie's valet, were the only servants living in. As I walked back upstairs, the front door opened behind me, almost causing me to lose my grip on my sandwiches. Catching them in time, I turned to see Lonnie walk in the door. My heart thumped as though caught in a naughty act. She started when she saw me.

"Oh fuck, you gave me such a fright," she said with a squeal. I had heard that word twice before, neither time said by a woman, although I doubted I could find anything shocking any more. "What the hell are you doing up and about at this ungodly hour? I thought you would be off in the Land of Nod by now. Ooh, sandwiches, how super," she exclaimed, looking at my plate. "What a fabulous idea, darling. I am entirely famished. Be an absolute doll and grab a couple for me.

I'll see you in your room imminently. I'll have a quick wash and jump into my pyjamas."

While I waited, I considered mentioning my meeting with the stranger. I needed to talk with her, although it meant admitting I had not followed her instructions. Worse, it meant confessing I had seen her with those other men.

My share of the feast had gone when she entered my room wearing gorgeous turquoise silk pyjamas. She sat beside me, producing a bottle of wine, a corkscrew and two glasses from behind her back. She opened the wine, handing me a glass and taking a sandwich.

"Well, did you have a wonderful time tonight, darling?" she asked between mouthfuls of cheese and cucumber.

"Yes, I did. Thank you for taking me."

Try as I might, I struggled to fathom how I could broach the subject of my encounter. We chatted for a time, telling tales of our fellow guests. By the time we had almost finished the wine, my secret refused to stay a secret any longer.

"Lonnie, there's something I have to tell you. After I left you, I did not come straight back. Instead, I snuck back to the party."

Her glass froze for a moment midway to her mouth. "Ah, you did, did you?" She gave me a nonchalant shrug and sipped her drink. "I admit I am rather impressed. I did not have you down as the adventurous type. I suppose it must be those detective novels you read. Spill the beans. What exactly did you see?"

"A lot," I admitted, ashamed. "I watched from the reading room for a few minutes. I got more than a smidgen of a fright. I have no idea what I expected to see, although I don't think it was that."

"Oh, bloody hell, petal, are you completely terrified and horribly traumatised? Disgusted and sickened down to the absolute core?" she asked, finishing her sandwich.

"No, which did surprise me a wee bit. I felt intrigued, curious, fascinated, aroused even."

"Really?" she asked with a raised eyebrow, studying my face. "Darling, that is quite a relief. I am awfully glad you do not think the worst of us."

"Why on earth would I?"

"I have not the slightest idea, but believe me, many would. Many have. Look, I suppose it is only fair you know the reason we attend these parties. Alfie and I have a lavender marriage, as he is a homosexual."

"A what?" I asked, confused. I had never heard that term before.

She giggled until she looked at my face. "Oh, God, you are serious, aren't you? A homosexual is a fruit, a fairy, a tapette, an unnaturalist, a sodomite, a buggerer, a queer, a poof, or lavender boy. I believe our cousins over the pond call them faggots, although how fried offal is concerned is frankly beyond me. Put simply, a man who is physically and romantically attracted to other men rather than women."

"Oh," I said, digesting this latest information. "I had no idea Alfie is attracted to other men. Until this evening, I did not know it could be possible for a man to like other men that way. I am learning so much tonight."

"Of course you didn't know, as he would be imprisoned if he expressed love for another man. Therefore it is top secret, hush-hush. We were planning to tell you but were waiting for the right time. Please do not think we did not trust you. Whole thing is such a bloody stupid state of affairs. Might have been the same for us girls, but thank goodness, the Lords saw sense."

"Does Aunt Violet know?"

"Of course," she said with another giggle. "Have you tried keeping a secret from her?"

"Did you know when you married him?" I asked, curious.

"Oh, my God, yes. We have been friends since our cradle days, and I have known as long as he has. Years ago, I was engaged to Edgar, love of my life and dear old Bertie's closest friend. By the time they called him up, the fighting was almost over. He had only been home for a few weeks when he died of Spanish flu. Absolutely fine when I said goodnight on the telephone but dead by morning. Life is a real bugger sometimes," she said with a sad smile.

"My goodness, how dreadful. I have no idea what that must have been like for you," I said, upset by her story. "I do know the agony of losing someone you love. It does still hurt, no matter what lies people tell about it getting better with time."

"You're right, sweetie. It hurts a little less, although I do not think the pain will ever go away. Alfie proved invaluable when Edgar died. He helped me through, kept me sane. I had done the same for him when he lost poor Bertie. We became inseparable, have been ever since. Alfie needed to put up a show of happily married life for appearance's sake. We realised we actually love each other to pieces, so here I am. We do most things married couples do except sleep together, meaning have sex. We always sleep in the same bed when we're together, as we both hate sleeping alone."

"What will you do if you find another love of your life?"

"Then I will consider myself fortunate indeed. Alfie and I will apply for a quick divorce. I will be free to marry the love of my life, and he can play the role of the gay divorcé. Until then? Well, I swing both ways, what you might call a free lover, I suppose. I do love a fabulous fucking, but I am not at all averse to a bit of sapphic passion. Charlie's licentious parties are how we blow off some steam, satisfy some urges." She looked at me, her forehead wrinkled. "Oh, lovey, have I shocked you?"

"No, you haven't, although I think I might possibly be

shocked if I knew what sapphic meant."

"Lesbian, darling," she said with a laugh. "Woman to woman. I mean, there is a chance the love of my life may be a woman. I do sometimes forget what a complete innocent you are."

"Oh no, not you, too. Why does everyone think me innocent?" I said with a groan.

She raised another curious eyebrow. "Someone spoke with you?"

I related the story of my surprise encounter with the gentleman at the party. She nodded as she listened, raising an occasional eyebrow.

"Did this handsome mystery man tell you his name?"

"No, he didn't. I did not think to ask, although he did not ask mine either," I admitted, feeling sheepish.

"So, what did he look like?" she asked, rolling her eyes at my stupidity.

"He wore a devil costume, maybe around Alfie's age and almost as tall, broader across the shoulders perhaps, but narrower at the waist. He had a handsome face, hair the colour of varnished ebony, sparkly blue eyes that were just astounding and the most incredible eyelashes I have ever seen on either man or woman. He was quite bonnie."

I stopped talking, realising Lonnie was laughing at me.

"Someone is completely and utterly smitten. However, I cannot blame you in the slightest. If it is the person I think, he is quite bonnie indeed."

"I am not smitten. I merely found him interesting. He was incredibly attentive, extremely charming, and inordinately clever."

"From the description you are giving, I'd say you have had the pleasure of meeting the infamous Marquess of Moorfoot. Moorfoot to some, although the title sits uneasily with him. Those who have known him longest call him Charlie. If it is him, you are not the first, or perhaps thousandth, woman to find him interesting. He is a charming and handsome chap, a great conversationalist, and a most fantastic fuck. His incredibly talented tongue is an experience not to be missed."

I gasped, and for a moment, I found myself fighting intense envy. "You've lain with him?"

"Sweetheart, who hasn't? Apart from you and Violet," she said, laughing at her joke. I did not join her. "He is by a substantial chalk, one of the best lovers around, but I must warn you he is a once in a lifetime opportunity as a rule. He is an aristocratic robot, an automaton by royal appointment, utterly incapable of loving anyone other than himself. It is all in the inbreeding, I think. Alfie is right. Charlie is anything but the sort to tie himself down to just one solitary woman. He is guilty of breaking countless hearts, male and female. He loses interest in someone the minute after he sleeps with them. He's into women for the challenge as much as the fuck."

"So, you only experienced him once?" I asked, feeling comforted.

"No," she admitted, "I am the exception testing the rule, I think. I can count myself among the favoured few who have had the fortune of being permitted more than one ride on his fabulous cock. Lack of numbers, you see, although that is not usually a problem for him. Believe me, he has many notches on his bedpost. Not that he is one to boast or any such thing, his discretion is legendary. Never been so much as a whisper of a hint of a scandal. Once was the time when hundreds attended his parties. Numbers have dwindled a bit, what with people marrying off and such. Unfortunately, we experienced a serious lack of interesting women tonight, and I quite literally had my fill of men. Charlie seemed off-form in any case. Hence, I am home earlier than I expected. In the old days, his parties went on all night and well into the following days on at least a couple of memorable near riotous occasions."

"I thought it appeared incredibly well attended," I told her, bemused.

"It has been better and worse. Problem is something does not add up. You said you allowed him the opportunity of taking full advantage of you?"

"Most definitely yes," I affirmed, nodding.

"Yet, he didn't touch you?"

"He took my arm as we walked. Apart from that, no."

"You'd put up no resistance?"

"Oh, God, absolutely, definitely not, no."

"Then it does not describe the Charlie I know. Catch is, from your incredibly detailed description, I can't see how it could be anyone but him." She looked confused.

"I pretty much declared myself ready and very willing to lay with him right there and then. He did not seem at all interested."

"Are you sure?"

"He told me I should go home and explore my own body first."

"Did you?" She put her hand beneath her chin, leaning towards me. I nodded my confirmation, causing an eyebrow raise. "How'd you find it?"

"Exciting, thrilling. I cannot believe I have never done that before."

"What, never?" she asked, eyes widening.

"Mum told me good girls keep themselves clean down there, but the hand must never linger."

She laughed at the idea. "You are no longer a good girl?"

I could not help sharing her laughter. "No, I suppose I am a bad girl now. I do not feel bad, because *it* did not feel bad. It felt good and natural. I liked it a lot. I want to experience those sensations many times, repeatedly."

"I know what you mean."

I considered something she said that made me curious.

"Earlier, when you said you make love with women, how does it, em, work?"

She caught my gaze, perhaps seeing the longing. With a gentle touch, she put her hand on my leg. I felt astonished at how much excitement this gesture caused, trembling in response.

"I can show you, if you want?" Her smile meant I could not be sure if it were meant as a joke. It might be the wine doing the talking, but she had given the answer I hoped for. I felt myself tingling at the idea.

"Yes, I would," I replied, deciding the best way to discover if she was joking would be calling her bluff.

"Are you sure?"

"Absolutely certain."

Lonnie looked surprised, although she recovered in quick time. She placed her finger under my chin, leaning forward to kiss me. The warm tingle in my stomach returned. With an incredible light touch, she caressed my back. I shivered, enjoying how it made me feel. Kissing me again, she raised my nightdress, and I lifted myself as it was pulled over my head. I wore nothing underneath and, as a result, sat naked before someone for the first time.

She stepped out of her pyjama bottoms, and I unbuttoned the top, revealing her fantastic bosom with dark, burgundy nipples complimenting her teardrop-shaped breasts. We fell onto the bed, our breasts brushing, my nipples hardening whilst we kissed and caressed each other's bodies. She stroked my breast with her finger before taking it into her mouth, tickling my nipple with her tongue. The sensation felt divine!

With a long sensual stroke, Lonnie moved her hands towards my mound. My lips were parted, and a finger darted inside me. Unable to do more than moan, I basked in the incredible sensations overtaking me.

Taking my hips, she pushed me onto my back, pulling my pelvis towards her. She rubbed her mound against my leg, her tongue exploring me the same thorough way my fingers did earlier.

"Relax, honey, why so tense?" she asked, an irritating interruption to the glorious work she was conducting.

"My God, this is amazing." I managed to say as she licked my lips with a swirl of her tongue.

She settled upon my pearl, causing a louder moan, and triggering delightful feelings, making me feel I might climax within seconds. Short flicks with her tongue were alternated with gentle sucking until her pace quickened, causing my legs to tremble. In no time, my entire body tingled, climaxing with a flood of electricity taking over me. After a slight pause, she applied more pressure, stimulating another current. This continued until, unable to stand it any longer, I pushed her head away, squealing.

She stroked my back whilst I took her nipple in my mouth, exploring it with my tongue. Satisfied, she gave out a moan as I took it between my teeth, giving it a gentle press. Wanting her experience to resemble how good she made me feel, I kissed her smooth, soft stomach and fabulous curves. I reached the wet hair between her legs and opened her lips. Although tentative, I moved in, savouring the softness of her skin along with the scent and flavour of her sweet, tangy essence.

I attempted to reproduce what she had done, flattening my tongue, and exploring until I reached her hood. As my tongue brushed it, her legs tensed. I circled her emerging pearl with my tongue, settling to a steady rhythm.

"My God, have you done this before? How the hell are you this good?" She panted, arching her body with another deep moan.

Fighting the temptation to rush for fear my tongue might

not maintain the pace, I kept going, spurred on by her encouragement. Her legs trembled, and her hands tightened on my head, pushing me deeper. She squealed as her body tensed with a shudder before falling limp.

For a few minutes, we lay kissing. It felt strange and exciting tasting my juices on Lonnie's lips. We held each other until tiredness overcame us, when we pulled the covers over us, falling asleep naked in each other's arms.

CHAPTER FIVE: OPPRESSIVE AUGUST

It felt strange waking beside Lonnie. I had never seen her without cosmetics, yet she looked beautiful despite that and her exertions of the previous evening.

"You're awake," she said with another gorgeous smile.

"I most certainly am. Thank you for last night, for everything. I had a lovely time."

"My pleasure, sweetie, glad you enjoyed it. Any time you desire a repeat experience, let me know." She gave me a cheeky wink.

"That may be sooner than you think. Last night opened my eyes to a whole new sexuality inside me. This is a beginning, and I know that I must explore this side of me much, much further."

"My God, you are keen," she said with a chuckle. "What kind of monster have I unleashed?"

"I think I woke as a different Alice Fraser," I told her, feeling solemn.

"Not too different, I hope. You're adorable as you are."

She kissed my cheek and climbed out of bed. I watched her dress, reflecting on the events of the previous evening. Despite waking naked beside her, I could not remove the strange doubt that I had dreamt what happened between us in a state of intense arousal.

Lonnie snuck back to her room before Dawson appeared to collect my laundry, as she did on Aunt Violet's instructions at ten every morning, no matter what time I crawled into bed. Some mornings I chased her away if coming round after a heavy evening. She always knew the precise time to reappear with a pot of tea and toast with jam, my usual recovery breakfast.

The following day was spent reading some books Lonnie gave me and exploring and enjoying my body. I touched myself, thinking of my handsome stranger, imagining his hands stroking me. I proved an enthusiastic, inquisitive student on the subject. Having conducted many experiments, I felt confident I understood everything regarding bringing myself to climax.

I found playing with myself delightful, although I enjoyed it more with Lonnie. We repeated the experience now and then. I found it pleasurable, yet it always woke my new curiosity. No matter how much I strove to dismiss the idea, I yearned to discover what sex with a man would be like.

The days passed in a whirl, with numerous social events with Aunt Violet and nights with Lonnie. Our evenings meant visiting as many places as possible. Nursing a drink always proved a bad idea, because you would never know when the call might come to move on to the next club or party.

One afternoon Aunt Violet announced August was approaching, causing immediate suspicion. Her idle chit-chat, by and large, usually preceded a request for some favour. In this case, she had made plans for the month and intended I should be part of them.

"August is by far the most oppressive month in London. Damned ruthless and positively relentless," she grumbled.

I nodded, thinking it for the best, even though I had never spent August in London, although July had been bloody hot at times.

"When I was wee, you always spent August in Scotland, didn't you?" I asked, thinking that was what she had in mind,

"Yes, dear, for the shooting. Every August for years. When

your Uncle Ernest died, I decided it would be a frosty day in Hell before I returned, having hated every blasted second."

"You don't like Scotland?" I asked, stunned by this revelation.

"My dear, do not get me wrong. I love Scotland, but I refuse to visit during August or any month those blasted midges are out for my blood. Winter, early spring and the fantastic colours of autumn, yes, but never, ever August. My consolation after Ernest died was never suffering a Scottish August again. I vowed I would not pass another day fighting those satanic buggers. Always stayed close by the ghillie who smoked a filthy great pipe. I was almost tempted to adopt pipe-smoking myself."

"Where do you spend August?" I asked, unsure. There had to be a point coming, although she appeared in no rush to get there.

"Foxcotte, of course. Alfie and Lonnie cannot join us for the entire month, but I am certain you won't be too bored."

She gave me what I presume was meant as a reassuring smile. I did not feel reassured, yet I considered myself in no position to refuse the invitation. I smiled, telling her I could hardly wait.

Foxcotte House was the Hampshire family home, located near a wee village on the edge of the New Forrest. The reason Alfie and Lonnie declined the invitation became apparent when I found myself spending a pleasant yet dull few weeks meeting friends and relatives. I found them all agreeable, although a good many were three or more times my age. A few turned out to be in the convenient position of having unmarried sons, although I was not left alone with any of them. Anything more than polite conversation proved impossible. I spent my free time reading or walking in the gardens, dwelling on my handsome stranger, jazz, clubs, movies, and London in its entirety.

At the close of a few long weeks, Alfie and Lonnie joined us.

"To make amends for your isolation . . ." Alfie managed to say before Aunt Violet cut him off.

"Isolation? What isolation? She has been kept company by Hampshire's best society."

"To atone for you having been kept company by Hampshire's best society," he continued, giving Aunt Violet a defiant look. "Some of the gang will be joining us here for the weekend."

"Thank you for consulting me," Aunt Violet said, not as cross as she pretended. "I am off to hide the good booze, minus the few stiff sherries I will need if I am to be invaded by young things for the weekend."

She went off to do so, and Lonnie turned to me with an apologetic expression.

"How bored have you been?"

"It hasn't been very bad," I lied.

"No need to be untruthful. You do not have to save my feelings. I apologise for leaving you on your own with Mother," Alfie said with a laugh, "but when you are given the opportunity to attend the Grand Prix at Brooklands, it proves too good to pass up."

"For you, perhaps," Lonnie interrupted. "If it is any consolation, Alice, watching cars go round a racing track for hours on end is an exercise in mindless boredom."

"Yes, but Charlie is a fantastic host. If he invites you to stay at Hornbeam when his parents are away, then you would be a halfwit if you consider turning the offer down," Alfie reminded her before asking me, "What have you been doing to stop yourself from dying of tediousness?"

"I've met everyone Aunt Violet knows with an unmarried son within a fifty-mile radius."

"Any take your fancy?" Alfie asked, although I suspected

he had guessed.

"Not really," I admitted.

"Any exciting adventures?"

"The gardens are beautiful. I've explored them thoroughly. I brought books but finished them all. My thoughts kept turning to the library at home."

"Sounds tedious, apologies for deserting you, peaches, but wait a moment, did you say home?" Lonnie asked.

Until then, I only used the word when meaning Cludenbrig. "Yes," I confirmed, having thought it over. "It's strange thinking of London as home, but it is beginning to feel that way."

Lonnie put her arm around me.

"Do you hate us?" Alfie asked. I assured them I did not. They told me stories of the fun and games I missed, including a shocking scavenger hunt which made most newspapers and a costume ball attended by royalty and film stars. I informed them that I had changed my mind and now thoroughly detested them both.

As the month neared its end, Aunt Violet asked if I minded extending my stay for a few more days. Desperately longing for London, I did mind, yet I felt unable to refuse. Lonnie and Alfie apologised but declined the invitation citing prior commitments. Violet expected a friend who, as I expected, would be accompanied by her unmarried son. She informed me without a hint of subtlety that he was my age and a decent young man with marvellous prospects.

The young man, whose name was Gerald, turned out to be more handsome than I had expected. He had lovely brown eyes behind his thick glasses and out-of-control curly brown hair. For the longest time, he proved mute. I spent a frustrating few hours smiling at him as we listened in on our relatives chatting without pause. Every attempt at instigating conversation met with a nod or a curt answer inviting no further discussion.

At Aunt Violet's prompting, we took a stroll in the gardens. She hoped separating him from his mother might encourage conversation.

"Camellias are my favourite, and our gardeners are experimenting with some late flowering varieties. Some of them are coming into bloom," I told him, mustering forced enthusiasm. "We can go there first if you want."

"Right." He examined the ground as though looking for dropped coins.

"We can head along the lavender walkway. The scent is fabulous."

"Certainly."

The rest of our walk remained silent and took longer than usual.

"Here we are," I told him, stating the obvious as we surveyed camellia bushes of many colours and types. He appeared unimpressed. I attempted to pick a flower, but it proved impossible with my bare hands. He produced a pocketknife and cut it, offering it to me with an averted gaze. Appreciating his gesture for its potential romance, I held it to his nose for him to smell. His face went a darker crimson than the flower.

"Thank you. Isn't it beautiful?"

"Qu-qu-quite," he stammered.

I had not read many romance novels, but when seducing the heroine, the hero tells her something about how she overshadows a flower's beauty. It did not seem an appropriate compliment for a heroine to say when making an attempt at seducing a hero. I felt sure he would not appreciate such a compliment.

He appeared no more comfortable discussing topiary and shrubs. I accidentally brushed his hand at the walled garden gate and thought he might shatter into many pieces.

"Can you hear my mother calling?" he asked, looking towards the house. He looked at me with a gulp before breaking into a run towards the house.

I walked back to the house, meeting Aunt Violet on my way.

"Ah, there you are. I was coming to fetch you for lunch. I thought I would have a rest from Daphne's constant chattering. My goodness, that woman can talk."

I thought better of mentioning she had been more than holding her own when I left her.

"Where's Gerald? What have you done with him?" she asked, looking around as she became aware of his absence.

"He thought he heard his mother call. I'm surprised you didn't pass him en route."

"No, I didn't see him. I did not hear Daphne either. Why would she be calling him? Aren't we too far from the house to hear her in any case?"

I shrugged.

"Are you two getting along?" she asked, glancing at the flower in my hand. Her voice incorporated a hopeful tone, despite the lack of Gerald stating the contrary.

"Aunt Violet, will you promise me something?" I asked, putting my arm through hers.

"Of course, my dear. What is it?"

"Please swear you will never, ever leave me alone with Gerald again."

"I promise, dear," she said solemnly. "Perhaps we should introduce Gerald to Alfie?"

She stuck to her word, although the rest of their visit proved no more agreeable.

Glad to set foot in London again, I took a deep breath of the marvellous dirty city air. Lonnie treated me to dinner at Boulestin, and I insisted we visit the Kit Kat, never leaving the dance floor. In desperate need of fun, I embraced any opportunity for dusting off the cobwebs, catching up with friends and making up for an awful lot of lost time.

I spent one rainy afternoon reading a French novel Lonnie loaned me. Unfortunately, my French is not what it could be, and few people required directions to the train station, causing much time spent consulting a phrasebook. It did not always prove much help, and I found myself guessing the meanings of many words, my imagination going wild.

When the clock showed it was nearly lunchtime, I went to the drawing-room. I found Aunt Violet sitting with a dark-haired young man I presumed to be Alfie. If I had looked closer, I might have discerned our visitor's hair was darker in colour.

Aunt Violet greeted me with a smile. "There you are Alice. Hiding away from the world again, always with your head in a book."

The visitor stood, turning to greet me and I realised that he was my handsome stranger! He smiled at me, causing a flip in my stomach.

"Charlie is collecting Alfie for some undoubtably rambunctious, drunken escapade at their boy's club. Another night in the cells is looming for either or both of you, no doubt." She raised her eyes skyward, although her smile betrayed any pretend annoyance.

Realising my mouth hung open, I closed it. My mystery man was the infamous Charlie! I cursed myself for not having consulted the looking glass, hoping on everything that was holy and some things that were not, that I looked presentable.

"I believe you two have never been introduced," Aunt Violet said, giving Charlie an accusatory glare. After the party, she had quizzed me for some time over the men I had met. It left her surprised and beyond disappointed that he had not been among them. I had not told her about my encounter with my mystery man. It seemed the best course of action.

"Why no, you are correct, that particular pleasure, unfortunately, passed me by," he answered.

I must admit he told the truth.

"I understand your paths did not cross at your house party, although I cannot for the life of me imagine why. Absolute criminal neglect on the part of the host. While I am aware I will sound like my mother, that would never happen in my day."

"You are correct, Lady Lyndsey. I can but apologise. I am most heartily ashamed. I will take myself outside and have myself soundly whipped." He winked at me. I fought an attack of the collywobbles as I told myself I must stop staring at those gorgeous eyes.

"Charlie," she continued, ignoring him in her determination to ensure we received a formal introduction, "this is Alice Fraser, the only child of my late sister, Lady Mary Fraser and Dr. Alasdair Fraser from Dumfriesshire. She is staying with us. Alice, meet Charlie, Marquess of Moorfoot, son of the Duke and Duchess of Cyneset, Alfie's oldest and dearest friend."

My first thought was how Dad would not be pleased. Staring at him, I decided there was no reason Dad need know. Although, in theory, he should be happy, as meeting rich men had been the motivation for me being in London in the first place.

"It appears I am most certainly the worse off for my negligence. I am certain that spending some time in the company of this lovely lady would be an absolute delight. How d'you do?"

He took my hand, brushing my fingers with his lips in a gentle kiss. My knees responded with a wobble. I could not tell if Aunt Violet noticed, although he did, judging by how he smiled at me. My cheeks burned from my nose to my ears.

"How d'you do?" I managed to mumble.

"Charlie and Alfie have been friends since their naughty schooldays. Individually they were hellions, but together demons fresh from Hell itself. I don't think either of them has grown up a jot since then."

I struggled to decide what I should say, and Charlie laughed too hard to refute her allegations. To my intense relief, Alfie chose that moment to charge through the door.

"You didn't need collect me, old boy," he said, tying his tie. "I would never be late for this one." As he saw me, the smile disappeared, his face darkening.

"Not at all. I happened to be passing. Spending time in the company of the charming Lady Lindsey and your beautiful cousin has been a pleasure. For some reason, you neglected to tell me she is staying with you."

"Ah, yes, we had better run, Charlie. It's getting on," Alfie answered. He looked embarrassed.

"Indeed, I must say my goodbyes. It was lovely meeting you, Alice," he said with a nod towards me.

"You, too, Lord Moorfoot."

"Charlie, please," he said with a smile.

As they approached the door, he stopped and turned. I looked away, but he could not have missed me staring at him.

"I nearly forgot. How terribly remiss of me. I am having a house party on Friday week. Now we are introduced, I would be delighted if you could come. The theme is scarlet. I am sure you look enchanting in red."

"I'd be delighted," I replied, cursing myself for my hastiness.

"You, too, Lady Lyndsey, of course," he added, giving Aunt Violet a nod.

I deflated.

"Far too old for those sort of things," she grumbled, waving her hand at him in a dismissive manner.

When the door closed, Aunt Violet gave me a huge grin.

"You made an impression. He likes you."

I studied her face to see if she might be teasing. I had reason for my caution—she loved teasing at every opportunity, and it was unclear when she was playing with you.

"Do you think so?" I asked, the speed of my reply betraying my eagerness.

"I think you like him, too."

"He seems nice, and I cannot deny he is incredibly handsome," I said, avoiding telling a lie.

Aunt Violet resembled the cat who got the cream. "It is up to you to turn his head at his party. I don't think that will prove difficult."

"I am not so sure. I don't think scarlet suits me."

"Nonsense, it is merely a case of finding the right shade. Trust Lonnie, as she has an eye for these things. She will be back soon, and you can descend on London's dressmakers and shopkeepers. I feel rather sorry for them—they have no idea what they are in for."

I considered my fleeting encounter with Charlie. He invited me to his party, but what did that mean? Did he think I should stay after midnight this time? Might this be my chance to sleep with him? My solitary chance? The more critical questions was would he think me ready this time? Did *I* think me ready? I possessed few answers for my myriad questions. Two thoughts occupied my mind—wanting to experience my first time with a man, and hoping above all that man would be Charlie.

I consulted Lonnie later when we were alone.

"What are you in desperate need of sharing with me?"

"The man from the party came around. It turns out it *was* Charlie."

"You met him? Does Alfie know?" she asked, giggling.

"Yes, Aunt Violet introduced us before Alfie came in," I

told her. Her giggle became an uproarious laugh. "What's so funny?"

She shook off her giggling fit so she could speak. "Sugar, Alfie has tried his damnedest to prevent you two from meeting from the minute you arrived. We kept telling him it was inevitable that you would meet eventually, but he felt he must try. I do wish I had seen his face when he realised."

"Charlie did seem surprised Alfie never mentioned me."

"He was furious with me for taking you to Charlie's party. He worked incredibly hard at keeping you from bumping into each other. It was desperately funny, like some ridiculous farce. He didn't relax for a single second until I told him you had left."

"He must have known we might meet someday?"

"We have been living in a real-life Wodehouse story. Simpson is a marvellous valet, but he is no Jeeves, and Alfie would surely mess up sooner or later. I could have told him you had already met, but it proved too much fun watching him try keeping you apart. He thought it possible to do so long enough for you to meet and fall for someone who is not Charlie. He feared an affiliation between his cousin and his best friend because precious few of Charlie's previous affiliations ended at all well for the women involved. I was not kidding about those broken hearts. Alfie doesn't want him to break yours, too."

"He seemed nice. He invited me to his party," I told her, with an attempt at nonchalance.

"What party?"

"The scarlet party he's having on Friday week."

"I had no idea he planned a scarlet party on Friday week or any other time. It looks like a jolly recent, or perhaps spur of the moment decision. Curious."

"Do you think the invitation includes events after midnight?" I blabbed without thinking.

She leaned her head to one side. "I don't know. Is that what you want?"

"Yes—no. I genuinely don't know. I think so." The question rattled me.

"Look, pumpkin, there is categorically no need for rushing into these matters. You are young, gorgeous, and so damn sweet it is almost nauseating, although I believe many men are somewhat lured by that. I will swear on a hillock of Bibles that there will be many, many other opportunities for you to give away that precious virginity of yours. No doubt to someone special, possibly Charlie. Who knows? Perhaps you ought to wait until you feel you are more prepared, you know, ready."

"It isn't that. I am ready, more than ready. Having him as my first lover is what I want more than anything, and I have done since the party. My concern is the idea that my first time would be so . . ." I searched for the word.

"Public?" Lonnie suggested.

"Yes, public, the very word. That idea is frightening. I don't think I'm ready for that."

"It was scary for me first time, and believe me, I was no virgin. If that is your problem, then discuss your issues with him. Ask if he will agree to take his part in making your dream come true. I'm certain you will find him more than obliging."

"I couldn't," I stated, finding the idea dreadful.

"I can ask him?"

"Oh, God no, please don't," I pleaded, thinking that idea much worse.

"Darling, perhaps you aren't as ready as you think. You're contemplating fucking a man, yet you're petrified by the idea of merely conversing with him about it?"

"No, I can do it. I can, and I will," I told her, feeling more determined. I was scared by the idea of visiting, Charlie but more scared of missing my chance.

Lonnie insisted we shop for my outfit the next day. Tabby happened to be at a loose end and volunteered to join us. I avoided wearing red, thinking it a bad idea with hair the colour of mine. Some intense searching resulted in us finding a dress that proved me wrong, a beautiful dark scarlet satin gown. It had a cowl front and plunging back with a stunning fishtail effect. The seamstress concocted an ingenious elastic contraption that flattened my chest at the front, although invisible from the back. The design made wearing any underwear impossible, and I doubted I possessed the confidence to wear this figure-hugging outfit in public. Nonetheless, I loved how it made me feel. Pushing my shoulders back and chest forward, I ran my fingers over the soft fabric.

"It's perfect, sweetheart," Lonnie told me with an accompanying whoop from Tabby.

I bought the dress.

The following morning, I took Lonnie aside.

"I have made up my mind. I will visit Charlie. I have one question, however. How do I ensure there will be no consequences?"

"Ah, yes, excellent question—come with me."

We went to her room, and she handed me a book called "Wise Parenthood." Dawson drew me a bath, where I read it from cover to cover, re-reading specific passages for certainty. Lonnie informed me she had made me an appointment with her doctor while I was in the tub.

I attended the clinic where I spent a humiliating half-hour having a cervical cap fitted. The doctor and nurse acted in a professional manner, although I knew my notes said Miss Alice Fraser.

Installing the cap myself proved a tricky manoeuvre, requiring many attempts, as it kept slipping from my fingers.

He gave me a longwinded lecture, telling me completely relying on it would be lunacy. I crossed my fingers, hoping my experience might be more positive.

In my room, I unpacked the package. It contained a diaphragm, a douche, and spermicidal jelly. Satisfied, I found Lonnie to report my progress.

"After my intensely mortifying experience, I now possess the tools for the job."

"Good for you. So, when will you visit him?"

"Why not tonight?" I blurted without thinking. "Before I change my mind, strike while the iron is hot. Fortune favours the brave and all that. Aunt Violet wants to listen to a Dvorak concert on the wireless and has invited me to join her. I like the sound of visiting Charlie better."

She poured me a stiff drink. "Fabulous darling, here, have a drop or two of Dutch courage. Be careful, do not go falling for him or anything. Remember that to him, this is no more than a bit of fun. It would be best if you looked at this the same way. Look, if he finds someone no challenge, he is famous for losing interest with indecent haste. Why don't you procrastinate around the bush for a time? Are you absolutely, positively, definitely certain you don't want to play a long game on this one?"

It was a good point, and I gave it some consideration. In endless romantic stories, the heroine wins her beau through acting aloof and disinterested. I felt reluctant to play that game, doubting I possessed the acting prowess that could convince anyone I was indifferent about Charlie.

"No, I am absolutely, positively, definitely certain I cannot wait, but don't worry. I heard you warn me. No falling in love."

It was far beyond that point, although I could not acknowledge that yet.

After my bath, I inserted the appliance, albeit with the

added difficulty of my impatience.

I told Aunt Violet I had a headache and would be in my room until it passed. Telling me I did not know what I was missing, she went to claim the wireless for the evening. My feet got colder the more dressed I got, telling Lonnie I thought he might not be home. Smiling, she informed me she had telephoned him. Assuring me she had not mentioned my name, she was nonetheless quite confident he would be home.

Panic built when I realised I had no more excuses. Lonnie asked me for what she promised was the last time if I felt sure I wanted to go through with it. I took a deep breath and nodded. She hugged me, wished me good luck, and told me yet again that I must be careful.

CHAPTER SIX: THE VISIT

After fifteen short minutes, the cab dropped me in the street outside Charlie's house. I walked towards the gate and stood there, watching people walk past. After an embarrassingly long wait, I gave myself a talking to and stepped through, striding in the boldest manner I could feign towards the house, which someone had relocated a mile from the gate. The newly emboldened me found my boldness diminishing the closer I got to the entrance. The unwelcome thought that I might be making a complete and utter fool of myself proved a recurring one.

By the time I arrived at the front door, my courage had deserted me. I turned for home a few times, although I stopped myself, realising how stupid I would look if Charlie could see me. The idea that he could be watching me, however improbable, made my knees knock. My heart pounding, I stood staring at the door, wishing I could go through it and run from it at the same time.

I found the courage necessary for pushing the doorbell, my hands shaking. To calm myself, I tried telling myself it did not matter as he would not be home in any case. It felt strange, but I was not sure I wanted him to be. If he had gone out, I suspected I might be more relieved than disappointed.

After a wait that was anything from a minute to an hour, Charlie's valet opened the door. His face remained impassive, although I swear I saw a slight lift of a pointed eyebrow when he caught sight of me.

"Good evening, miss. How may I help you?"

"Is Lord Moorfoot at home? He isn't expecting me, but I would like to see him, if possible," I asked, attempting a casual air.

"Sir is bathing. I can ask if he can see you if you want to wait," he said with another slight eyebrow raise.

I told him that I would, and he opened the door. He took my card and led me inside to the drawing room. I wondered if many women had sat in my place, experiencing this mixture of emotions. After a few minutes, he interrupted my musings to tell me Lord Moorfoot would be with me imminently. He offered me a refreshment, and I accepted with gratitude, in desperate need of a top-up of Lonnie's Dutch courage.

I have little idea how long I waited, although I have passed hours, perhaps entire days, quicker. In an attempt at killing time, I studied the heavy-framed paintings. They were primarily landscapes, one reminding me of home. The more time passed, the more I berated myself for coming. Every time I felt myself beginning to panic, I tried focussing on the painting's fine detail, like the curve of the horns of a stag or the crops in the fields. I sat in silence, my heartbeat becoming more erratic, my hands trembling, my mouth getting drier and drier. My glass had been quite empty for some time, but the valet had disappeared, and I saw no other servants.

By the time Charlie entered the room, I had persuaded myself that I should leave and talked myself out of it at least three times. He was wearing a navy-blue smoking jacket over a tieless shirt. My heart stopped for a moment, jolting back into action at double speed. The butterflies in my stomach chose that moment to migrate towards my chest and throat. I stood, which proved a terrible mistake. My legs trembled so much I worried my knees might give way.

"I say. Why it is you, Kitten. I thought Watkins misheard until I saw your card, although it would not be typical of him," he exclaimed. "It is lovely to see you again. This is a rather unexpected yet delightful surprise. I presume this is what Lonnie hinted at on the telephone earlier. Does Alfie know where you are?"

Surprised by the question, I shook my head, unsure if my voice would work.

"Ah, right. What can I do for you?"

I made the stupid mistake of looking at those eyes again. For days I had rehearsed what I should say ad nauseam. Looking at him made the words I had carefully memorised melt away. I stood tongue-tied and dumbstruck, waiting until I found my voice. Thankfully, he waited so he could hear me out rather than presume me a lunatic and usher me towards the door.

"Over the past few weeks, I have given a great deal of consideration to what you said at your party," I admitted, looking to see his reaction. If he was surprised, his impassive face hid it.

"You have? I'd love to hear your thoughts and conclusions. I am certain it will be fascinating, if you are inclined to tell me, that is. May I fetch you a drink? I see your glass is empty. I do apologise. Lonnie suggested I give the staff the night off so I could give a mysterious visitor some privacy. Only Watkins remains, and I apologise for having somewhat monopolised him since you arrived." He indicated I sit on the sofa.

"A gin and orange, please."

He poured the drinks and handed me one, getting close enough that I could smell his intoxicating scent again. My heart sank as he took the seat opposite mine.

"What are your thoughts? That is if you want to tell me, of course. You are under no obligation. If doing so will make you in any way uncomfortable, then do not feel you need share them."

"I'd like to tell you," I confirmed, taking a much-needed sip of gin. "I explored my body and learned where I like and don't like being touched. I know every quarter inch of what is between my legs. I have brought myself to climax many times and considered how I feel. I know I love my body. I am aware of my sensual self. I must thank you for your instructions as it has been an interesting experience." With a sigh of relief, I readied myself for the words approaching my mouth. "I think—no—I know, I am ready to make love with a man. I want that man to be you. I want you as my first lover," I whispered.

"What, now?" he asked, raising an eyebrow, smiling a mischievous smile. The idea tickled him for a second or two before his face took on an unwelcome darker expression.

"Why not? I am ready mentally, physically, and medically if you know what I mean. That is if you want to and have no other plans, of course," I told him, unsure whether I had the courage for returning by appointment. I had depleted my courage supplies and doubted I had any in reserve.

"I see." He raised both eyebrows, not saying anything for an age. "I do not have plans as it happens." "However . . ." he said in a stern tone, then sipped his drink.

I did the same, incapable of thinking of anything else to do. My heart beat faster, knowing I was hearing what I dreaded, him rejecting me one more time.

"Kitten, believe me when I say I am incredibly flattered you thought of me. This offer is an honour indeed, but I do not think I am the man for you, and that is telling you nothing but the unvarnished truth. I assure you I could never be the slightest bit worthy of the honour."

"But I . . ." I began my objection, but he shook his head.

"Your first time should be a sweet act of love. I am not in the slightest bit capable of such a performance. You are offering an extremely precious gift to the most unworthy recipient."

The tears welled, despite my efforts at fighting them.

Under no circumstances would he see me crying. He stared at me without saying a word. I met his gaze, enthralled by those gorgeous eyes. The only sounds were the loud ticking of the grandfather clock and the noise my heart was making as it sunk to my boots.

"What if I do not want my first time to be sweet and romantic? What if I give my gift to someone experienced, someone who knows about giving satisfaction? Someone who can make my first time a pleasurable one rather than an embarrassing fumble."

I endured a long pause. Nevertheless, he was giving my argument some consideration, and I took hope from that.

"I am certain there is someone capable of giving you pleasure as an act of love. I am most definitely not that person. I do hope you find him. I am certain you will."

"I am making a fool of myself. I am sorry I came. I should not have. I have only succeeded in embarrassing us both. I should go." I endeavoured to stand, although my legs remained inert.

"You could never appear foolish. Please do not be embarrassed. Any sane man would kill for the mere opportunity to take you up on your tremendous proposal. Nevertheless, you deserve far better than me. You must find someone who will adore you every bit as much as you deserve and will treat you accordingly. Come on—I will drive you home," he said, taking a drink.

Arguing would be pointless. He did not find me attractive, as I had feared. He stood, offering me his hand. I accepted it, however once upright, I leaned towards him to kiss him. Having missed my chance last time, I felt determined I would not miss my opportunity again. This time I might at least possess the memory of a kiss throughout my eternal embarrassment.

His lips were unresponsive, and I panicked. I had done the wrong thing again. I pulled back to break the kiss, ready for copious apologies. Instead, his arm pulled me closer as he reacted to my lips. It became a long, passionate embrace, my feet leaving the floor, my insides melting. He broke the kiss and stroked my face.

"Oh, Kitten, you make saying no so damn difficult. What black magic is this you are performing on me?" He leaned in for another kiss, giving me no chance for an answer. "Are you categorically sure this is what you want?"

"Absolutely certain. I think, despite what you say, you want it, too."

"Denying it would be pointless," he said with a sexy half-smile.

He held out his hand to take mine, leading me towards his bedroom. It was a dark room with beautiful modernist, walnut furniture, in contrast with the baroque rooms downstairs. He closed the door and took both my hands as he looked me in the eye.

"You must tell me if there is anything you are uncomfortable with or you find unpleasant. If you want me to stop, say stop, and I will. Do you understand?" he asked in an earnest tone, giving me a scrutinising stare.

I nodded, although I could not imagine him doing anything I might want to stop. We kissed again, and I turned so he could unzip my dress. He pulled the zip in an unhurried manner, setting in motion a medley of tingles. It dropped onto the floor, leaving me wearing my pink lace step-in slip. I faced him and slipped the straps over my shoulders as it joined my dress.

Feeling self-conscious, I stood naked before him. I parted my legs, keeping my thighs apart as he looked me over for an age. His impassive face only made me feel more vulnerable. I put my arms behind my back to conceal my trembling, hoping he would not reject me for seeming too innocent again. Consequently, I did nothing to cover my nudity.

"Why, Kitten, you are exquisite, quite breath-taking."

"Thank you," I replied when I could breathe. "I'd reciprocate with some praise myself, were it not for the fact I am not in a position to." I cocked my head, astonished at my audacity. I had no idea where that voice came from.

The serene expression slipped. He looked flustered, although his composure recovered within a blink or two. Apologising charmingly, he unbuttoned his shirt. Underneath it was a smooth but toned chest, his muscles defined, although not to an excessive extent. I grew impatient to see more.

He removed the rest of his clothes and stood naked. I studied his body in the same slow, careful way he had looked at me. Before the party, the only unclothed man I had seen was a picture of Michelangelo's David. Charlie also looked magnificent, albeit with more substantial parts. His organ also looked more substantial than the ones I had seen at the party. The size of it startled me, yet I wanted it inside me. We stood in silence, staring at each other.

"You look rather splendid disrobed yourself," I confirmed. The desire to lick, kiss, and touch that smooth, contoured chest built, yet I stood rooted to the floor. I grew more nervous as I waited for him to initiate contact again.

"May I touch you?" he asked.

The question surprised me, as I had presumed permission was implied. I ached with the exhilaration of anticipation. "Yes, please," I whispered. Inside I screamed a sarcastic response, although I kept it to myself. I wanted him to touch me everywhere.

He stepped towards me, taking me in an embrace to kiss me. Our naked bodies touching initiated a succession of new sensations. I gave an involuntary gasp, pressing myself against him to disguise my trembling. Something tickled me from inside, travelling through my veins at a tremendous speed. I took a deep breath, inhaling his potent scent. His organ grew more substantial and harder against my thigh, and I felt alarmed at the idea of accommodating it. I had only the haziest of notions of what I was doing but decided I should concentrate on enjoying the experience. He was supposedly an expert—I considered myself in good hands. He picked me off my feet and lay me supine on the bed.

His every touch electrified my skin as he nuzzled and kissed my neck, caressing me along my arm in one continuous gesture. I shivered and moaned as my earlobe was given a gentle suck. He smiled and kissed me again as I stroked his chest, running my hands along the contours.

I trembled as he kissed the underside of my breast, working his way around my nipple giving a gentle blow. Goosepimples rose in response to the glorious sensual feelings enveloping me. He enclosed it in his mouth, sucking and flicking my hardening nipple with his tongue. I moaned, welcoming the pleasant sensations. An incredible gentle bite sent me over the edge.

Meanwhile, his hand stroked the wet hair between my legs. His proved the gentlest of touches, probing me until he found and stroked my pearl in a subtle, teasing way. He applied more pressure, and I gasped at the resulting sensations. He kissed my stomach until his lips replaced his finger on my pearl.

I gave a strange yelping noise when he circled it with his tongue, alternating delicious sucks and delicate flicks. With his head immobile, the slow and steady rhythm made my body arch and my legs tremble as I clutched his hair. I considered pushing his head deeper inside me, although I felt scared to interfere. He increased the pressure, causing delightful surges of pleasure. My legs shuddered then my whole body joined them, melting in an exquisite climax. He did not stop, and my body convulsed with a series of aftershocks.

I lay panting as he lay by my side, giving me my chance to

discover his body. I intended another exploration of his hypnotic cock. I held it, incredulous at how it felt firm, yet the skin so soft. It was as long as my hand's span, and my finger and thumb did not quite meet around the broadest part. I ran my finger along its length, watching him shiver when I circled the head. There were a few drops of the pre-seminal fluid I had read about, and, without thinking, I stuck out my tongue and licked it, causing another shiver. It proved an indescribable flavour, sweet yet a trifle salty, though not disagreeable.

He rolled us over, so he lay on top of me, kissing me again as I parted my legs. He pushed the head of his cock inside me, causing a pained gasp.

"Am I hurting you?" he asked, with a look of alarm.

"No," I lied.

It did hurt, although I knew it would and had expected much worse. I moaned, which he took as permission to proceed, pushing himself inside me a wee bit at a time. Each time I felt sure he could not go any further, he proved me wrong. When he was all the way inside, he held me so tight it proved tricky moving much more than my arms and legs. I relaxed, finding myself lifting my legs to allow him in deeper.

"Does this feel good?"

The feelings proved different to anything I had experienced before. I was tingling all over and losing myself in how what he was doing was making me feel. Incapable of articulating that, I nodded.

Driving harder, he pushed me into the bed, pulling my arm above my head as we locked our fingers together. I caressed his muscular bottom with my free hand, feeling it tense with each powerful thrust. Bodies intertwined, we pushed ourselves in unison, grinding ourselves together until my sudden climax. My orgasm brought happiness tinged with sadness. I wanted these feelings to last forever. I floated atop warm water, wave upon sensual wave hitting my body.

His soft moans deepened as he climaxed, his thrusting becoming long and slow. He took my head in both hands, kissing me for an age before withdrawing. We lay in an embrace, his arm around my shoulders, my head laying on his chest, our breathing all I could hear.

"Well, Kitten, it appears you are ready after all. I hope you found the experience lived up to your expectations," he said, looking somewhat anxious.

"Oh, my goodness, yes. It exceeded them, thank you. So that is what sex is like?"

"Well, one type of sex," he replied with an amused smile.

"You mean there are more? Several types? Then I want to experience different types. I want to try everything," I exclaimed, feeling giddy.

"I don't think I could manage with such meagre notification," he said, raising an eyebrow. "You are absolutely fascinating."

"I think I am fascinated by you too, you handsome cluitie."

"A handsome what?"

"Sorry, Mum always told me off for breaking into Scots when I am excited. It means devil."

"Excellent. Devil — I like it," he said with a hearty laugh.

We lay embracing until I felt his cock growing against my thigh again. The prospect of him being ready for more thrilled me as I was keen to go again. I traced my way around his chest with my nail, working my way towards his hardening cock, stroking it until it was fully reinvigorated. He pulled me towards him, and within minutes we were making love again, face to face and legs intertwined, kissing each other throughout. We lay holding each other until I heard the clock chime nine.

"Oh, Christ, is that the time? I had better be getting home," I told him, sitting up.

"Must you go?"

His disappointment appeared genuine, giving me hope he might want to see me again.

"The Dvorak concert on the wireless will be ending soon. Aunt Violet has no idea I am not in my room with a headache. I will not be missed until it is over. Everything will be fine if I can make sure I am back before then. Thank you for this evening. I am awfully glad you didn't have plans."

"I did as it happens, although what I had planned would never have lived up to the evening I have just experienced. Don't worry—it was nowhere I might be missed."

As we dressed, he offered to drive me home. Any other day I would walk on such a pleasant evening, but I agreed with gratitude. We addressed the lovely weather and other pleasantries without discussing what happened.

Outside my house, which we reached despite a mere two minutes passing since we left his, he kissed me, keeping one eye upon the door. He climbed out of the car and opened my door.

"Goodbye," I said in a cheery tone. "I suppose I will see you at your party."

"Oh, yes, I cannot wait," he said, although his lips were pursed, and a slight crease appeared between his eyebrows. He watched the front door looking as though he expected Aunt Violet to emerge and thrash him for daring to kiss her niece. I could not understand the cautious expression—it was more probable she might shake his hand or hug him. I was the one who had to avoid seeing her or else have much explaining to do.

CHAPTER SEVEN: COLD FEET

The wireless was playing in the drawing room as I dashed upstairs, removing my coat en route. Safe in my room, I fumbled into my pyjamas, expecting Aunt Violet to charge in and interrogate me about where I had been. I was sure her reaction to hearing where I spent the evening could only be a happy one, although having no chaperone might give her cause for concern. To be fair, she would have a right to feel concerned, considering what we had just done. Although she would, without a doubt, pretend otherwise, I felt sure keeping her from a secret might be the biggest sin in her eyes.

I caught sight of myself passing the looking glass, although it was only me looking back. Silly though it may sound, I expected to see a full-grown woman reflected there. I felt disappointed that I did not look different. I felt different.

I could still smell Charlie's scent on me, and I swore I would relish the aroma as long as I was able. Never bathing again was a distinct possibility. Throwing myself on my bed, I lay grinning at the memories of the evening. I marvelled at how our bodies harmonised, mine curiously knowing what it should do. I loved the way he touched me and how he made me feel. I could not help wondering if he had felt as good. I thanked the heavens for the fifth or sixth time that I had found the courage for that kiss.

My euphoria evaporated when an unwelcome thought dealt me an uppercut. Lonnie warned me an experience with Charlie would be an unrepeatable one. Despite her caution, in the fantasy situation I had imagined, we would make love at his party. Considering his face when I mentioned the party, I realised it was unlikely. The idea had troubled him — he did not want us to make love again. This realisation made me dissolve in tears. I longed to experience him day in, day out for the rest of my life.

Lonnie did not press me for details, although I related an edited version of events to her, admittedly omitting my indulgence in self-pitying weeping. Despite my attempt at my best enthusiastic voice, she could tell I was keeping something from her. I was loath to explain the reason for my upset. She warned me I should not expect more and had been more than explicit in her warning.

I denied it when she asked if anything was wrong, and the subject was not raised again. She told me that it would be best if we did not discuss Charlie when Alfie was present, telling me we should keep it a secret between us girls. I agreed without question — I did not feel like discussing my visit with Alfie in any case.

The next few days dragged by at a tedious rate, no matter how I kept myself occupied. Lonnie and Alfie were visiting her parents, leaving lots of time with Aunt Violet. I read, although every book reminded me of my situation or failed to distract me from it. Despite everything Lonnie told me, every day commenced with the hope this might be the day Charlie would get in touch. Every night I lay in bed feeling more despondent than the night before.

When Lonnie returned, she made a valiant attempt at distracting me, dragging me to the cinema. We watched a tedious melodrama whose name I cannot recall. She chose it — I had not heard of it or the actors in it. It featured a woman forced into a ridiculous choice between her mind-numbing boredom inducing husband and dreary lover.

"Well, it is evident you did not enjoy the flick, judging by the faces you were pulling," Lonnie said as we left the picture house. As was our custom, we headed to Claridge's to discuss the film we had just watched.

"It was stupid," I protested. "Incredibly stupid woman makes a series of implausibly stupid choices and — it goes without saying — spends her time paying a terrible price for her decisions."

"Why don't you tell me how you really feel? That is interesting. I did not think it entirely without merit. I take it you disagreed with her decision. Would you go off with the lover, leaving the tedious, dull husband behind?"

"My preference is neither. Both were horribly flawed. She'd be better off alone."

"She'd finish in the poorhouse. How on earth could that in any way be better? You appear to have woken on the wrong side of the bed again this morning, and the film has not improved your mood one jot. I presumed you annoyed at me for deserting you again, but there is plainly more to it. Will you tell me what's wrong, or must I drag that information from you, either literally or figuratively?"

I knew I should talk about my worries, although it meant admitting my failure to heed her warning. We sat at a quiet corner table where we had no chance of anyone overhearing, yet I lowered my voice in case.

"I've thought it over, and I'm not sure if I should go on Friday," I said, seeking a circuitous route into the conversation.

"I see," she said, lighting her cigarette and taking a long, deep drag, indifferent to public view.

"To Charlie's party, I mean," I added unnecessarily.

"Obviously. Look, it is completely up to you, darling. It must be your decision and your decision alone. If this type of thing is not for you, it is the absolute berries. It is not for everyone, à chacun son gout, etcetera. I categorically swear no one will hold anything against you or think any the worst of you. Why don't you leave at midnight as you did last time? If you decide you would rather not stay behind for this one, then there's always next time."

I gave it some thought for a moment or two.

"No, the party looked such fun. I know I want to experience it for myself. Anyways, how would I know if that kind of thing is my kind of thing if I don't take part in the thing in the first place?"

"Right, bloody good point. So, go." She took another drag, waiting for my reaction.

"I know, I know, you're right, I should go. I want to go. When I recollect watching you at the last party, I remember how I wished I could be a part of it. I thought about tearing off my clothes and getting involved before remembering that I had no idea what I would be doing. I could not believe how incredibly aroused I felt. I felt more than a wee bit envious of you. The thing is, it's . . ." I paused, determining the right way to tell her, although it was unnecessary.

"For crying out bloody loud. Is this by chance about bonnie Marquis Charlie?" She pronounced his name in an exaggerated Scottish accent and gave a melodramatic sigh.

"Yes," I answered. Lying was pointless. "He didn't say he wished to see me again, so I know I should not expect it. Despite that, I hoped he would. I had such an enjoyable time the other evening, and I thought he did, too. I know you warned me, but I hoped there might be a chance he might want to see me again one day."

I averted my gaze. I knew she would be disappointed in me, and I did not want to see it on her face. When I met her gaze, she gave me a sympathetic smile.

"Oh, darling, you unfortunate thing. I did try to tell you not to fall for him. and believe me—it was for your own good." She gave my hand a squeeze.

"I know, but I think it was too late, as I had already fallen for him. Despite my best efforts, I cannot stop coming over all Cathy Earnshaw. I might end up marrying someone else, but I would be thinking about Heathcliff."

"Need I remind you that particular infatuation did not end well for your particular lovestruck antiheroes? Unless you have a fantasy where you both enter tedious marriages to someone else that make each other envious until he ends up digging up your corpse?"

"No, they were both miserable all the time, and I am not. I suppose I am merely an amateur moper in comparison to those two. I must throw myself wholeheartedly into some serious moping. If I am honest, what concerns me most is the possibility that I might see Charlie make love to someone else. I dislike the thought of watching him do as much as simply having a conversation with another woman."

"Ah," she said, narrowing her lips. "Well, I admit there is a high possibility unless your intention is keeping your eyes closed throughout the entire evening. You can go for a blindfold if you think it will help. You might even find you enjoy it," she said with an encouraging smile. "If you fear a visit from the green-eyed monster, you are in for a rather miserable time."

"I know. The thought is eating away at me incessantly. I know I have no right to be envious, although I cannot deny I am. Beyond envious, in fact. Ridiculous though it may be, I find myself insanely envious of a hypothetical woman in a hypothetical situation."

"You can pine for Charlie all you like, but think of the other experiences you will be sacrificing. Consider all those other cocks you are yet to encounter, and the amazing men attached to them. Perhaps you will meet someone at the party — there undoubtedly were a few handsome men at the last one. There are one or two fellows I can introduce you to who can prove a fascinating if temporary distraction."

"If making love to another man proves half as good, then it will be a lovely and sensual experience, but how can I know until I have a similar experience I can compare it with?"

"Tremendous news, the girl has got it. Trust me, poodle — a few men out there can run him incredibly close. We will find you one, two, or more if that is what will float your boat. You absolutely must get all thoughts of Charlie from your head."

"I know you're right. Believe me, I am trying my utmost, but . . ." I said no more, lacking a defence.

"That tongue, those hips, that cock?" she said with a wink, reading my thoughts.

I remembered she had made love to him and became envious of her for a moment or two. Recalling that it happened on multiple occasions was heartening. I hoped there might be a shortage of women at this party so I could also join the fortunate few.

"That's just the beginning," I added, dreaming again. "Don't forget that smile, those fingertips, his charisma, and those eyes. He may well be incapable of love, yet he is capable of some red-hot passion. If he is what automatons are like, I welcome the future. I know I have no excuse. You warned me I would be allowed one turn on the once-in-a-lifetime roller coaster. I knew that, yet I let my impatience get the better of me. I could not wait. Deep down, I am aware that I have had my turn, and now it is time for moving on with someone else. He probably already has."

"That's the spirit," Lonnie said with a smile.

"Thing is, I wish I could have one more turn or more even."

"Well, darling," she said with a laugh. "Who knows what the future might bring? He might have already fallen head over heels for your Scottish charms. He may be counting the hours until he sees you again, for all you know. Even if he miraculously managed to resist your charms, this party is your opportunity to show him what he is missing. You look stunning in your dress. Chaps will be queueing for a chance to be the one you choose. You are bound to turn his head, making him envy whomever you end with."

"I can try," I agreed, although I was lying. I felt sure making him envious would be impossible, but what could I lose?

"I will tell you something for absolutely nothing, sweetie. Whether by accident or design, you have dabbled in the fabulous world of free and easy sex. For some, this world proves more than enough to send them running screaming into a world of marriage, children, and cosy domesticity. For others, and I believe we can unquestionably include you in this particular circle, once that Jack is let out of the box, it can never, ever go back in. Do you intend to end up a withered, bitter Miss Havisham type?"

"No, I don't," I told her, shaking my head.

"I almost said fuck Charlie, although I realise in the circumstances that is the wrong thing to say. So let us say to hell with Charlie. It is your decision, but if you do go, then you can leave at any time. If you do stay after midnight, you can take part as much or as little as you want. I am convinced there will be a long queue of incredibly willing young men who will be champing at the bit for a chance to fulfil your every wish. If you would prefer not getting involved, you can watch. I promise you I will not leave your side for a second – unless you tell me I should fuck off and leave you with some fabulous bit of stuff, that is."

"I think with you by my side, I may make it through the evening without too much heartache," I told her, feeling buoyed and more assured. "If nothing else, then we can have some fun together, if you are willing. This may well be the beginning of a whole new chapter in my tale of sexual discovery. To hell with Charlie indeed."

I hugged her, feeling optimistic again, and we headed

towards what we hoped was the direction of some fun. Giving myself a shake, I determined I would throw myself, heart and soul, into relentless gaiety. A few cocktails helped.

We saw Easy Virtue at the Duke of York's, which proved an excellent choice, with its witty, sharp dialogue. I could not help but enjoy myself. Afterwards, we visited the Embassy Club. We sat some distance from the stage because your place in the seating arrangement depended upon your social status. The sofa at the front was reserved for the Prince of Wales, although it remained unoccupied during our visit. Had I been alone, I would be further towards the back, which stung, although Lonnie reminded me I had been granted membership when many had been refused. We spent the rest of our evening and most of the morning drinking until it became a blur.

CHAPTER EIGHT: THE SCARLET BALL

After a few prolonged days of waiting, I found myself on my way to one of Charlie's parties again. I did not dare discuss him with Alfie present, although he had been the solitary occupier of my mind for some time. Alfie looked uncomfortable, although less sullen than on the drive to the first party. Lonnie told me he opposed me attending this party but had been overruled again. She convinced him I was far from the innocent he thought I was and gained his accord after promising she would always keep me under her wing.

Lonnie took my hand, giving me an encouraging smile as we arrived at the ballroom. I looked around, trying hard not to make it evident I was doing so. The curtains were a luxurious red, the frescoes covered with scarlet drapes hanging from the ceiling. The lady's frocks looked incredible, with many wearing red wigs. I permitted myself to feel smug because mine was natural. The gents opted for red ties and waistcoats, although some went the whole hog, wearing red suits. Tomato salad, lobster and caviar were served along with desserts of strawberries, berry jellies, and trifles. The drinks choices were cocktails, red wine, or vodka with tomato juice, annoying some spirit drinkers.

I spotted Charlie, who looked fantastic in scarlet, making him look more of a cluitie than when we'd met. My treacherous heart betrayed my enforced calmness, beating in syncopation with the jazz drum. He looked in my direction but did not return the smile I gave him. Convincing myself he did not see me, I turned my head in an attempt at hiding my disappointment.

He chatted to a group standing beside the window, everyone smiling and looking happy. I attempted to establish
whether any of the women might be with him, although I
could not be certain. One trollop stood too close, gazing at
him with obvious intent and playing with her hair. I hated
her, although he did not pay her the same attention. Tabby
put her hand upon my shoulder, interrupting my reverie.

"Oh, you have fallen hard for him, haven't you?" she asked
in a sympathetic tone.

I did not know whether Lonnie told her or she had
guessed, although it did not matter. We looked at an oblivious
Charlie, and I gave my best attempt at a smile.

"The old unrequited. Total misery-making."

"You have loved someone who did not feel the same way
about you?" I asked, surprised by her admission.

"Why, yes. Everyone has at one stage or another. Fell for
our first footman, practically lay naked at his feet. He said it
was more than his job was worth. Spent some time getting
over that one. Was only fifteen at the time. Still think about
him now and again, wonder what might have been."

"Does he still work for you?"

"No, he left to work in some factory. That made it worse.
Wasn't as though he needed good references to continue in
service or anything."

"Ow," I said, not sure if our conversation was doing much
to improve my mood.

"Ow, indeed. Hurts like fucking hell, doesn't it?"

I nodded my agreement.

"Let's do something about it — why not have some local an-
aesthetic?"

She handed me a short drink, and I downed it in one go.
"How about another?" I asked with a smile, ignoring the
burning sensation as it made its way down my throat.

"Abso-fucking-lutely," she agreed, downing her drink.

We approached a servant carrying a tray of drinks, each taking another two.

I knew more people than at the last party, and I enjoyed myself more than I thought. After realising Charlie was keeping his distance, I stopped myself looking for him. That only confirmed what I feared and what Lonnie had told me, bringing on a fresh feeling of disappointment.

By way of a distraction, Lonnie introduced me to an attractive young man named Julian Carmichael, Jolly to his friends. He was what was known as a gigglemug, smiling so much I wondered if his jaws hurt. We danced many dances together, chatting with ease between dances. He stayed at my side for the rest of the evening.

He was pleasant, although a touch dim. I doubted him capable of telling me the prime minister's name, although I fought the temptation to ask him. However, I was confident he could name England's first eleven against Australia in the last test match. Mrs. McKenzie would describe him as not the sharpest knife in the drawer.

An inch taller than me, he had a stocky, athletic-looking build. His sandy blond hair fell in a Gary Cooper type kiss-curl over his forehead. I could not help staring at his hazel eyes, with fair lashes invisible in a particular light. He moved with surprising grace for such a heavily built man, lifting me as though I weighed nothing. My thoughts were turning to the upcoming part of the evening, and I hoped he might be my partner after midnight. If he proved happy to participate, we might have some fun together.

During an infrequent rest, he went to fetch us drinks. Unimpressed by the red offerings, he topped up his drinks from a secreted spirit selection in the next room. He went to help himself, and I took the chance of catching my breath. Alfie watched him leave with an approving nod.

"You're doing well for yourself, I think. Jolly is a salty bit of a dish."

"Do you know him?"

"Met him once or twice. Always found him a thoroughly decent chap."

"He does seem nice, although not too sharp, I think. He told me he gave up playing cricket when a wicked fast bowl knocked him out of his stuffing. He is incredibly well built, isn't he? Do you think he likes me?" I asked, uncertain. At one time, I had thought Charlie liked me.

"I'd say so, judging by the rather impressive basket when you were dancing."

His implication sounded positive, and I took it as such, despite having no idea what it meant. It was some time before I discovered he had been referring to Jolly's erection, which I had not noticed.

"I think he is a wee bit gin-soaked," I confessed, concerned.

"But clearly not plastered enough to impede his performance. I think you will be all right. Stick with this one, and we will all be happy tonight, what?"

He gave me a wink and a snorting laugh. Jolly was not the only one guilty of being in a gin-soaked state.

Jolly did not return. At midnight the band stopped playing, overhead lights came on, and guests made their way towards the door, just as before. I gave up looking for him and slipped off so I could freshen up.

I returned to the ballroom, still pondering the option of finding and fucking Jolly. Feeling anxious, I scanned the faces for his in vain, bumping into Lonnie instead.

"Have you seen Jolly?" I asked, looking for him, my hope becoming a forlorn one.

"No, not for some time. Perhaps he has gone home?"

"I didn't see him leave, and he didn't say goodbye. Does he normally stay behind at these parties?"

"No idea. I've never seen him at one before," she said with a shrug. "Well, despite the lack of the delectable Jolly, fortunately for you, there is quite a masculine majority this evening."

"Yes, many of them are attractive, although I know some of the most handsome chaps are homosexual. You must tell me which."

"No need. It will soon become quite apparent," she said with a smile. "Are you sure you want to continue?"

I nodded, and she took my hand.

The clock struck half past the hour, and the lights dimmed as the needle fell on a frenzied number. We sat in the corner, pulling a screen across so we could hide ourselves away from the crowd. She took her silver locket and pressed a hidden button. The top sprung open, revealing a lid with a tiny spoon, which lifted to uncover a white powder. Scooping some powder onto the spoon, she held it to her nose and inhaled, shuddering.

I knew what it was—newspapers talked about it all the time. They described it as a deprived evil, yet I took it without question when she offered me some. I had read the people taking it had an enjoyable time, and who does not want an enjoyable time?

I inhaled as she had—the effects almost instantaneous. I got over the bizarre sensation assaulting my nose and, in an instant, felt euphoric, confident, and alive with a vibrant energy.

"Wow, this is amazing. My god, I feel fantastic. Why, it is just bloody remarkable. Everything is incredibly intense. This is amazing, absolutely amazing. Why on earth have you never given me this before? I cannot believe the way it makes me feel. It is so fantastic, and the excitation is continuing to build."

"Divine, isn't it? Believe it or not, it gets better. This will be an incredibly sensualistic experience," Lonnie said, smiling.

For the first time, I became aware of the naked people opposite us, aroused by the sights and smells. Lonnie took my hand, and I thrilled at how different the sensation turned out.

"Wow, your touch on my skin, it's softer, yet somehow it's more strong, stronger? No, more powerful, is that the word I mean? Anyhow, it is completely amazing. Everything around me, lights, sounds, even the smells, seems more intense. It is as though every sense has been switched on. No, that is wrong, as they were not actually off in the first place. Intensified? No, amplified, that is the very word. It is incredible, fantastic. Is it always this good?"

"Usually, poodle, although you will need to top it up now and again when the buzz wears off. Darling, would you mind terribly if I were to ask you to stop talking long enough to kiss you?"

I giggled at the tingle as our lips met.

We unzipped each other's dresses and lay back. Because my backless dress did not allow for underwear, I sat with my naked body on show for anyone to see, yet I did not care. Lonnie looked incredible, her gorgeous breasts peeking through the silky black fabric of her chemise. I straddled her, and we continued kissing, caressing each other as we rubbed our hips together.

I pulled her slip away, and she lifted her legs so I could remove it, allowing me to kiss her glorious breasts. Kneeling before her, I let my tongue explore what she called her pussy, savouring the fabulous tastes and smells. I pushed my tongue inside her before teasing her pearl with short licks as she shivered with pleasure. I took a nipple and rolled it between my fingers, which always made her give out a low, moaning noise.

As I did, I felt someone kissing and caressing my bottom. I wiggled it in appreciation. Jolly had found me after all!

I could not greet him without disappointing Lonnie, although I appreciated the pleasant sensations set off as he slipped a finger inside me. I continued licking Lonnie's pearl, gauging her expression. She gave me a big smile with a wink, indicating our new participant met her approval.

Another finger found my pearl, causing me to utter a sonorous moan. It proved an unexpected yet welcome introduction for us both, Lonnie letting off a whimper of her own. I increased the pressure, and she stretched her trembling legs while grabbing at my head. I sucked hard until she came with a shuddering climax.

"Hello, Kitten," whispered a familiar voice in my ear.

My heart leapt. That was what the wink meant! I turned around to see Charlie's gorgeous face and that fantastic twinkle. Without a thought, I threw my arms around his neck and kissed him. Having him hold me as he responded to my kiss felt like bliss. Lonnie kissed the top of my head, mouthed good luck, and left us alone.

"Do you want me?" I asked him, not taking his presence for granted. Again, I found myself captivated by his eyes.

"My God, yes, I want you. I crave you. I need you," he said, stroking my cheek and looking into my eyes.

I shuddered at the intensity of his words, gaze, and touch.

His delectable fingers caressed my nipples, and he took one in his mouth, playing with it with his tongue. He lifted me onto the sofa, kneeling before me to caress my pearl. I shuddered in response to the teasing light touch, savouring the sight of him. He applied more pressure, giving it a gentle suck. My climax was immediate, the exhilarating thrill overwhelming me again.

He held my leg against his waist, and I wrapped it around him. I expected he would enter me, but he used the head of his cock to stroke my pearl, making me melt into the sofa. He pushed himself inside me, pulling himself back out straight away. I sighed with slight disappointment. Every time I thought he might fill me, he drove himself further inside before withdrawing again.

"Oh, please don't tease me," I begged.

He smiled and thrust his fantastic cock up to the hilt inside me, leaving me panting.

"Oh, yes, that feels really good. Don't stop, please," I said. He obliged.

He lifted my legs, placing my feet against his shoulders and entering me deeper and deeper. Before long, I quivered as my climax hit me. It lasted much longer and felt more potent than any of my previous experiences. I collapsed, shaking, as I recovered my breath, feeling as if my entire body had been swapped with blancmange. My orgasm brought him to climax, shuddering when I stroked his face as it contorted with his ejaculation.

My body tingled for a spell, although I admit it might have been partly because of the cocaine. We lay entwined in a long embrace.

"You are indeed rather extraordinary," he murmured.

"It was wonderful. You were wonderful. It was a wonderful experience. I'm sorry, I cannot think of any adjective but wonderful right now." I stopped babbling and started crying, uselessly wiping my eyes with the back of my hand.

"If you found it wonderful, why are you crying?" he asked.

"Because it was wonderful," I said, thinking that explained everything.

"Then I take your tears as somewhat unlikely compliments," he said, taking me in his arms.

"I must look a fright. My tears have ruined my make-up," I grumbled.

"No, you are beautiful, as always. More so," he said, kissing my forehead. He retrieved a handkerchief from his jacket, which was placed on a folded pile. I cleaned the smeared mascara, ruining it in the process. I apologised, but he gave an unconcerned shrug.

"Why didn't you talk to me earlier? I thought you weren't interested in me," I said, stroking his face, finally asking the question that had been buzzing around my head.

He looked embarrassed, and I thought he might not answer. "It was not easy," he admitted. "You looked stunning in that dress, although you also look fabulous out of it."

"So, why stay away?" I asked, ignoring the compliments because I was cross at him changing the subject.

"I rather feared venturing too close in case my attraction became apparent to everyone." He smiled then saw I was not pleased with his explanation. "Well, at first, I assumed you were with Jolly and thought it best to keep my distance. Honestly, I felt more than a tad envious until I saw Jolly passed out in the drawing room. When I saw you with Lonnie, I could not resist being with you again."

Did I hear him say he was envious?

"Is that where Jolly went? Is he all right?"

"Perfectly. He is next door sleeping it off, snoring at a decibel level that would shame a pneumatic drill. If you listen closely between dances, you may be able to hear him. Despite his build, he is not much of a drinker. Poor fellow cannot accept that a couple of drinks will knock him for six."

"Well, since he is not in a bad way, I am happy he did pass out. I thought you'd never come over. I have been told many times by many different people that you never swim in the same river twice."

"Ah, according to Heraclitus, that would be impossible." He pulled me closer for a kiss without giving me a chance to ask him what he meant.

We lay watching what we could see of the other partygoers. The party was in full swing, with guests performing different forms of sex. Activity continued in every direction. A woman sucked the cock of one man as another took her from behind. The grey-haired man from the first party lay on another sofa with a different man, sucking each other's cocks with enthusiasm. Charlie explained the older man was a King's Counsel, a convenient friend to have.

"All this is going on, and all I want to do is go upstairs with you, take you to bed, and spend the whole night lying with you in my arms," he said with a happy sigh.

"Well, why don't you?" I asked, taking his hand.

We left the party and our clothes behind us. When we reached the door, he took a last look around, and I worried he regretted his choice. A concerned look vanished as he looked at me and smiled. We walked to his bedroom and climbed into bed.

I stroked his chest, leaning towards him for a long, lingering kiss. He nuzzled my neck, and before long, we were kissing each other's bodies with increasing passion.

"Why, Kitten, you are utterly insatiable."

"You appear rather ravenous yourself," I said, indicating his growing cock. I stroked it until it reached its full glory.

"When it comes to you, I can never be satisfied," he said as I sat on his lap with my knees astride his hips.

I guided him inside me, lowering myself onto his magnificent cock. Putting my hands around his neck, I leaned in and kissed him. Moving my hips in a steady circular motion meant I felt his cock rub against my insides. I enjoyed having total control over my pleasure and the freedom it gave me. The sound of my breasts hitting together, combined with our bodies slapping against each other, filled the room. He pushed himself deeper, and I rocked myself until my pearl pressed against his pubic bone, causing an electrifying new wave of sensations.

I kept pace as long as I could until I started flagging. Sensing my fatigue, he took firm hold of my hips, lifting me up and down his cock. I squeezed my knees together, encouraging him deeper inside, filling me. Trembling with bliss, I could not stop myself squealing louder than I expected. He continued for a few more minutes, tensing in his climax. We kissed as we fell back on the bed.

I rested my head on his shoulder until, feeling sleepy, I turned onto my side. He turned with me, his breath on my neck causing goosepimples everywhere. I put my arm upon the arm around me, pulling him closer. I fought sleep until I could do so no longer, savouring every moment.

I woke with enough time to dress and return home, not enough to contemplate what had happened. Aunt Violet would be breakfasting at the Goring, as per her daily routine. She had decided preparing breakfast at home was an unnecessary extravagance as most mornings Alfie and Lonnie were dead to the world until lunchtime. Francois, her cook, was a culinary maestro, although Violet complained that because he was French, he had no concept of what made a good breakfast in any case. She would be home before long. I had to beat her back.

Charlie retrieved my clothes and drove me home, asking if he might see me again when he stopped the car. I nodded, kissed him, and ran inside. In my rush, I almost collided with Lonnie on the stairs. She asked how I felt before seeing my smile, telling me the coast was clear without waiting for a response.

I ran upstairs, yet despite my lack of sleep, I felt anything but tired as I fell onto my bed in a state of utter bliss. No way would I cry this time. I had no reason. I spent a fantastic evening with Charlie, and he wanted to see me again.

Though I was reluctant to acknowledge it, he was not disposed to do much more than have sex with me. Pretty delightful sex, I must admit. I had long stopped pretending lust kept my interest alive. I was in love with Charlie. My uncertainty about which of these applied to him bothered me. Did mere desire drive him, or might there be a chance he loved me? Despite everything, I loved him, and I celebrated the idea he loved me, at least in a physical way. Whatever he offered, I would take it. If all I would be to him was an occasional fuck, then I would be the best occasional fuck possible.

CHAPTER NINE: HERE BE DRAGONS

One evening, Lonnie and I had tea at Claridge's discussing Don Juan. We thought it a spectacular flick, although neither of us found Don Juan attractive. I admitted that I had found myself more taken by Leandro. Lonnie giggled and opened her mouth, on the verge of refuting my assertion but froze when something caught her eye.

"Well, I'll be jiggered."

She looked pleased for a second before her smile vanished. "Oh, buggering bugger," she exclaimed with an exasperated sigh.

"What is it?" Unable to see what she was looking at, I started turning around.

"For God's sake, petal, do not turn around," she said through clenched teeth. I froze, desperate to look. "It is Charlie, and he is coming this way."

"Honestly? Are you kidding me?" I asked, not understanding why she thought this unwelcome news. An accidental meeting was what I had longed for since we met.

"No, I'm not teasing. He is here, but please do not get too excited. He is with his mother, and as you are almost certainly about to discover, she is an absolute first-class harridan. I could not see them at first—that enormous floral display hid them from view. Get ready to don your best bogus smile."

"Good afternoon, Your Grace, Moorfoot," Lonnie said, standing to give them a charming smile. Taking Lonnie's lead, I stood too. Charlie approached the table accompanied by a cross looking grey-haired woman wearing a dark, old-fashioned flock woollen coat with a high neck. She reminded me of old Queen Victoria, although I thought her younger than she dressed.

"Why, it's Lonnie," Charlie exclaimed, "and the lovely Miss Fraser." He looked at me with an alluring smile. Yet again, my knees trembled, and I hoped no one observed my wobble. There did not appear the slightest chance, judging by the intense way the Duchess stared at me.

"Mother, may I introduce Alice Fraser from Dumfriesshire? She is the daughter of Lady Mary Fraser and Doctor Alasdair Fraser. Alice, this is my mother, Her Grace, the Duchess of Cyneset."

"How d'you do," she said, looking down her nose at me.

"How d'you do, Your Grace."

"One was so sorry to hear about your mother."

She looked human for a brief spell until the hard features reappeared. I was surprised to discover they knew each other. It seemed unlikely that Mum would ever be friends with this hard-faced woman.

"Thank you, Your Grace, that is kind of you to say. I do miss her still."

She had once been handsome, although her face showed the result of the years carving a scowling expression. Her eyes were lighter than Charlie's, more of an icy blue. If they ever contained his twinkle, it had long extinguished.

"Mother and I are off to see Don Giovanni," he said, consulting his watch.

"How ironic, we have just come from there," Lonnie said, smiling.

I smiled too, although our visitors looked confused. I thought it better to leave her in her confusion, doubting the Duchess would approve of the cinema. She gave the look of someone whose approval would be hard to gain.

"Unfortunately, we cannot tarry. Goodbye, ladies," his

mother boomed, with particular emphasis on the last word accompanying a nod in my direction.

He gave a rueful smile, his mother's tone wounding us both.

"It is delightful to see you both again. Some other time, hopefully soon." He glanced at his mother's retreating form and kissed my hand. With a sad smile, he followed his mother, who had made her way halfway towards the door.

I watched them until unable to see him anymore. Lonnie rolled her eyes.

"Where the hell is Sir bloody George when you need him?"

"She does seem dragon-like," I agreed.

"She is a dragon of the highest order. Old Cyneset, Charlie's father, is an absolute darling, just the cat's meow. Heaven only knows what he saw in Duchess Dragonbreath there, yet he is well and truly under her thumb. If I were trying to see things as you see them, I'd point out she has a reason for her miserable demeanour. She lost her eldest, and Charlie is the first to admit her favourite son, in the war. However, I knew her before dear Moorfoot died, and I found her no less horrible then."

"Poor Charlie. I always thought being an only child was sad, yet it is worse if you have a brother and lose him."

"He also lost his sister, Louisa," she said, shaking her head. "I don't mean she's dead," she added, seeing my concern. "She lives in Palestine now after a few years in Persia. She is the eldest child and could not wait to escape from under her mother's nose. She felt her mother's disappointment for failing to be a boy and believed her mother was practising on her until the boys came along. Away from her mother, Louisa became the life and soul of every party, the most vivacious person you have ever met. She had a lengthy list of willing suitors and could have married any man she chose. In the end, she married some mousy little man from the Diplomatic

Service. A few days after the honeymoon, they went off abroad. I miss her terribly, but I understand. Her mother disapproved of her lifestyle and practically suffocated her."

"I would go halfway around the world if she were my mother. She looked at me as though troubled by a foul smell immediately under her nose."

"Oh, no, that is permanent. Please do not take it personally."

"No, I just know she didn't think much of me."

"She can tell Charlie has feelings for you. She's not blind," she said with a shrug.

I tried without success to keep my excitement under my hat. "Don't be silly. He cannot have feelings for me. He is incapable of love, an automaton by royal appointment, you said," I reminded her. In response, she gave me a scathing look as though amazed by my stupidity.

"I could agree with you, but then we would both be in the position of being demonstrably lacking a brain. It is bloody obvious he has bloody feelings for you. He did not take his eyes off you once the entire time he was here. How could you fail to see that? In the many years I have known him, I have never known him as anything other than last man still standing at any party, far less first to leave. You have made quite the impression on him."

"Do you honestly think so?" I asked with my hopes raised. I was unfamiliar with her appearing at all optimistic regarding my prospects.

"Oh, bloody hell, there you go getting soppy looking again. I swear, the two of you utterly deserve each other, wandering around doe-eyed like a pair of lovestruck bunny rabbits."

"Much as I don't want to admit it, I fear he is becoming somewhat of an obsession. I think I am completely, utterly, and totally in love with him," I said with a sigh and an attempt at a smile.

"Yes, sugar. I rather think you are. Good luck to you, though, because I fear you will need it."

"Why? I thought you said he has feelings for me?" I did not like her introducing a dark cloud to my otherwise sunny outlook.

"Your solitary, yet regrettably major problem is his mother there. Charlie is her sole living son and heir, and she will not release him from her talons for just anyone. She will demand that whoever contemplates marrying her son must be nothing less than the most impressive thoroughbred. Unfortunately, my darling, that unashamed virago will inevitably regard your family pedigree as inferior. Earl's granddaughter or not, your family tree must be equally impressive on both sides. The aristocracy are like horses. It is all about their bloodlines."

Although Lonnie had not meant to be unkind, her words hurt, despite my seeing the truth in them. My pedigree fell short of the requirements necessary for being a permanent part of his life.

"I thought I had been catapulted into the twentieth century, yet all of a sudden, I find I am living in some Jane Austen novel."

"I know, a century later, and so much yet so little has changed. That supercilious old witch stands between you and a happy-ever-after with Charlie. No way in heaven or earth would she approve of your match. Violet tells me she violently disapproves of your father."

This news proved more surprising than discovering she had met my mother.

As the weeks passed, Aunt Violet retreated to Foxcotte more often. She had long stopped inviting me there, understanding London's lights held more attraction than the quiet of Hampshire, no matter how lovely. Lonnie and Alfie became my official chaperones, leaving me free to come and go as I pleased. I knew it was pathetic, but I did not please to come or go anywhere.

"Right, Heathcliff, it's time for you to get yourself outside into the wide world again," Lonnie instructed, utilising a firm tone. "Come on, Dawson is on her way, and she will help you freshen up and put your best party frock on. After that, you and I are going to hit the town as though today were the last day before prohibition. Since Claridge's, you have spent all your time moping around thinking of eternal gas and gaiters with Charlie, and it must end."

"I like spending my time moping around thinking of eternal gas and gaiters with Charlie," I said, giving her a pretend smile. "Or gas and gaiters with Charlie for any duration of time. Look, I am incredibly aware the Duchess will never give her permission for us to get married. I cannot say I put such thoughts out of my mind as such thoughts were never in there in the first place. I mean, can you imagine me a duchess someday? I am not cut from that particular cloth, and Dad will disown me if I as much as consider it. All I am concerned with is having any type of affiliation with him right now. I am not thinking about the future at all."

"There have been many duchesses lower born than you, and there will be many more. You are not thinking about together forever with Charlie? Honestly?" she asked, not hiding her disbelief.

"Cross my heart, hope to die. I promise you my feet are firmly on the ground when thinking of marriage. I will doubtless end up settling for one of Aunt Violet's bachelors one day. Perhaps Gerald and I will settle into eternal monosyllabic bliss with our brood of monosyllabic children."

"Wouldn't you have to make him communicate with you before that could happen?"

"Yes, although I must devise a plan that stops him running away first. He may be more of a writer than a talker. Perhaps we may be the first married couple to communicate completely by post. Until then, the absolute best I can hope is seeing Charlie when I attend his parties. Have you any idea when the next one will be?"

"Who knows? Not even he knows sometimes. His parties are held whenever he feels like having one. The next one may be in a few days, a few weeks, or a few months. Meantime, may I suggest you make sure you keep yourself as busy as possible? Attend every single occasion you are invited to and a few you are not."

With a lack of any other options available, I decided to heed her advice. One evening, dancing in an unfamiliar club, I sat catching my breath. I grew convinced I could see Charlie talking to some friends in a far corner. He faced another direction, and I stood for a better view. He looked so handsome I found myself giving a pathetic sigh as my stomach flipped. I considered talking to him, although I had no idea what I should say.

I stood staring when Tabby grabbed me, spinning me to face her.

"What are you doing?" I asked, confused. "I was just . . ."

"Know what you were doing. Know exactly what your axe is. Do you want him looking over and seeing you staring at him like some lovesick puppy?"

"No," I said with a sigh.

"Quite right. However, he would most probably adore you. You do resemble one of those delightful doe-eyed breeds, a spaniel or something. In any case, understand you want to know what is going on," she said, on tiptoes so she could peek over my shoulder. "He looks every bit as pathetic as you do. Everyone is laughing, only his smile is not as wide. The conversation's going on around him a bit."

"Is he looking this way? Do you think he knows I am here?"

"No, don't think so," she answered after another peek.

"He's standing away from the group, staring off in the far distance, can't see what or who he's looking at. He looks not necessarily sad, yet not happy either. Never seen him so distracted. He is normally the life and soul. Think he's missing you."

"Oh, please don't build my hopes up, Tabs."

"Just telling what the eyes are informing the brain. Oh, Alfie's gone over now. They're talking." She paused, face creased in concentration as she observed their conversation. I waited anxiously for her report. "Rather intense chat, by the looks. Not sure they are having an enjoyable time. Do not think you will either if you hang around here any longer. Perhaps moving on would be a clever idea. Try somewhere else?"

"That is probably wise."

As we were leaving, my gaze met Charlie's. Frozen, we stared at each other until Alfie spotted Charlie was not paying him any attention. He followed his gaze in my direction and glowered. He recovered himself, giving me a smile and a perfunctory wave. Seemingly in response to something Alfie said, Charlie nodded towards me before turning his back. A nod, with not even a hint of a smile, he had grown bored with me. I felt devastated.

Giving it some thought in the cab en route to our next stop, I looked at events a different way. Alfie wanted Charlie and I kept apart. Might Alfie be responsible for his recent silence? My rational mind advised me I read too much into what I saw, but the fanciful part informed me there was hope for us yet.

Lonnie knew something was amiss and wrung the story from me. She promised me she would discuss it with Alfie, who remained convinced any affiliation between us would end with heartbreak. Lonnie proved true to her word, and Alfie took me aside the following day.

"I've had a chat with Lonnie, who tells me I am

mollycoddling you when it comes to Charlie. I must admit I have tried keeping you two separated. Still, I am given to understand I am merely closing the barn door after the horse has bolted."

"We have strong feelings for each other, Alfie, well I certainly do. I don't think there is anything you could have done to prevent it happening."

"Perhaps I am being overprotective, but believe me, I have excellent reasons. I have known him since junior school, and over the years, there have been many, many women. He is my friend, and I love him as a brother, but if I can be frank, when it comes to women, he is not just a cad. He is an outright bastard. Many of them he merely used and tossed aside when he grew bored with them. I'd hate to see him use you the way he used those women."

"Lonnie warned me, although it was too late. I fell for him the first time I saw him."

"He informs me he has fallen for you, too."

My heart thumped on hearing this news.

"He talks in a way I have never heard him talk before, and I want to believe him, I honestly do. I do rather feel I ought to warn you that you must be careful, although I will not stand in your way. I want everything to end up nothing but well for you both. I really do."

He looked uncertain. I gave him a hug, thanking him repeatedly.

The day proved hectic, giving me no chance of dwelling on the hope the conversation with Alfie instilled. Smiling, I crashed into bed and did not wake until late afternoon. I enjoyed partying with Lonnie and her friends, but I did not share their stamina. Despite the assistance of a quantity of cocaine, keeping pace was a struggle at times.

It had gone two before I could leave my bedroom. I

ventured downstairs and found I had the house to myself. My headache made reading impossible. I took an aspirin powder and switched on the wireless, searching for something gentle that might mitigate my extended hangover. I happened across what the Radio Times identified as a Bach Violin Concerto. It was an unusual choice, although soothing.

My headache was abating when the footman informed me Charlie was at the door, asking if he could see me. I queried it, and he told me in a level tone Lord Moorfoot was at the door and had asked for Miss Fraser. Panicking, I told him to show him in, rushing through the other door so I could freshen myself up.

The results in the looking glass proved unpleasant. Fortunately, news of my visitor had reached Dawson, who rushed upstairs to help.

"Oh, Dawson, I'm so glad you're here. Can you work your miracles?" I asked, brushing my fingers through my hair.

She was way ahead of me, having picked out a green chemise cut dress with a hip wrap.

"I think this dress if you want to make an impact on your visitor?"

"Oh, is it obvious?" I asked. Her response was a knowing smile. Taking her up on her excellent suggestion, I changed my clothes. "I don't know why he is asking for me. What on earth does he want to say? What might he possibly want?" I asked in a garbled fashion.

"I think it is likely his lordship is here for the very reason you are hoping. The thing is, you won't know until you go downstairs and talk to him."

"You're right, Dawson, as always." An application of cosmetics, a brush of my hair and a cross of my fingers left me ready as I could be. "How do I look?"

"You look beautiful, Miss Alice. He won't be able to resist you."

Thanking her for her kind words, I gave myself a shake and ran downstairs. With every step, my heart thumped harder. Charlie greeted me with a smile, and I heard my heart pounding in my head.

"Hello, Kitten. It is lovely to see you again. How are you?"

"I am well, thank you. It's lovely to see you, too," I said, telling the truth. Putting him out of my mind had proved a colossal failure. More than one gentleman had tried wooing me but was sent on their way because he did not compare. Who would? We stood still, enduring an awkward silence until I found my voice again. "May I fetch you a drink?"

"No, thank you. I am afraid this must be a short visit."

My heart sank. I had hoped he might whisk me away somewhere. He paced the floor, stopping a few feet away, staring as he ran his fingers through his hair. The resulting tousled fringe flopped over his forehead in a sexy manner, instigating another wobble.

"Will you not sit down?" I asked him, taking a seat on the sofa.

"Thank you, I will, yes."

He sat beside me, making my heart skip a beat.

"Some people are waiting for me, but I needed to speak with you. Alfie and I have had a frank and earnest discussion. He knows what I have done in my past, and admittedly, some of it is shameful, my moral compass in great need of recalibration. Alfie made me promise I would not touch you because he does not trust me, and he is right to. He adores you, and he is protecting you, and I understand that. If I were him, I would feel I must protect you from me, too. That was the old me, although I do not think I quite succeeded in convincing him. I will tell you what I told him — that my intentions regarding you are entirely honourable. I would never willingly do anything that would hurt you. You believe me, don't you, Kitten?" He took my hand and stared into my eyes. If what he said was lies, he was disguising them well.

"I admit I heard some disturbing opinions, but I am a wee bit reassured in hearing that. Is that why you kept your distance?"

"Yes, although it proved ridiculously challenging. I gave my oath I would keep away, yet I could not. Alfie is my dearest friend, and I did try. I felt I owed him that. I thought I was capable of that until the wonderful evening you visited. I had determined I would send you away, but I wrestled with my conscience when I saw you. I strove to find the will needed for sending you away yet could not bring myself to do so. Alfie has not caused me any physical harm, so I assume he remains ignorant of what has happened between us?"

"Yes, I haven't told him. Lonnie warned me not to. What about your party? Weren't you scared he might see us together?"

"Yes, and that is why I did not approach you earlier, much as staying away was killing me."

"What you said about staying away because you were envious of Jolly was not true?"

"No, that part is true. I was terribly envious, especially as it was interfering with my plan,"

"Your plan?"

"I wanted to be with you, so Lonnie and I hatched a plan that would distract Alfie. I dreaded him refusing the blindfold. Thankfully he went for it. I thought that I might have to knock Jolly down to get to you, and I was seriously considering the prospect."

"Then again, I thank the heavens for Jolly's low tolerance to alcohol."

"I had to hope he had drunk enough, and thankfully he had. Lonnie told me she panicked when she saw us going upstairs, although by then Alfie's attention lay elsewhere. When he asked for you later, she told him you had gone home."

"I'm glad he believed her," I told him with a smile.

"Not as glad as I am. Lonnie reckons he might have killed me had he seen us, and I believe her. Alfie warned me to keep my distance. I only dared do so because I knew him to be otherwise engaged. We talked at considerable length last night, and we have come to an agreement. I am permitted to see you with the further understanding that if I ever do anything to hurt you in any way, I will spend the rest of my life sans testes. I do not take this as mere badinage in any way. With everything resolved, I wondered if you are interested in spending some time with me? Or was our lengthy and hypothetically painful conversation entirely hypothetical?"

"No," I said with a laugh. "Spending some more time with you would be delightful."

"That is a relief." He did look more reassured.

"I don't believe any man ever staked his testes for me before. It is reassuring, I think." I could not help but giggle.

"Well, let's make it worth it," he said, leaning for a delightful kiss. "Do you have any plans for tomorrow?" he asked, with a cheeky-looking smile.

"No, I don't." It was the truth, although I would have cancelled anything I had planned.

"Capital. What do you say to accompanying me on a picnic?"

"A picnic in November? It is a lovely idea, but don't you think it a bit chilly for that?"

"Don't worry. This will be an indoor picnic." I did not have the first idea what he meant, although I would agree to anything if it meant I could spend more time with him.

"Oh, I've never done that. It sounds fun."

"I am certain it will be. Shall I collect you at noon tomorrow?"

"Yes, please," I answered, without disguising my eagerness.

"Until tomorrow." He looked at me and stroked my face. I put my hand on his, and he smiled, giving me a quick kiss before leaving without a word.

I sat, taking in what had just happened. Although brief, his visit had cheered me no end and made my headache disappear. Ignoring Bach, I performed a quick Charleston around the room.

Chapter Ten: Expanding My Education

Half-past eleven the following morning found me sitting with my hat and coat on, ready to leave. Lonnie had not yet emerged from her bed. That was a relief, as I had no doubt she would think the sight of me hilarious.

My overactive mind saw me lying awake to greet the dawn. I do not pay much attention to my dreams, but I experienced a vivid one where I sat waiting for Charlie. In it, I listened to an endless amount of people telling me he would not keep our appointment. The creepiest part was one of them was my mum. She came into view now and again, although always some distance away. I have no idea what she would say. I woke before she reached me, although I begged the crowd to allow her to the front.

I found myself awake when Dawson came in, and for once, I did not plead for more sleep. Panicking, I begged for help mitigating the effects of my insomnia. All that occupied my mind was spending time with Charlie, and now we were free to do so. This thought brought another worry, might my new availability cool his interest?

To distract me from my fears, I wondered where he would take me. I hoped wherever we went that we might have an opportunity for making love. I would be happy if we did nothing but make love. For an entire half-hour, I paced the floor, periodically looking out the window, convincing myself my dream would prove accurate. I felt great relief when his car arrived just before twelve.

"Good afternoon, Kitten," he said, raising his hat. Giving me a smile and a quick kiss, he ran to open the door of his sporty green motor car.

"Good afternoon, Cluitie. This is a nice car," I told him, climbing inside.

"Isn't it? It is a three Litre Bentley green label four-seater with custom all-weather tourer coachwork. This model won Le Mans in '24. I can make a hundred and two miles per hour on the right road," he told me, sounding excited. "Possibly more in the right conditions."

"You can? That sounds incredibly fast," I said, cringing at the banality of my statement.

"I can see cars are not a great subject for you," he said with a laugh.

"I don't know anything about motor cars. I have no idea what the greater part of what you said actually meant," I admitted. "I can't drive. I had never even sat in a car until I came down here."

"You cannot drive? Well, perhaps one day, I will teach you."

"Yes, please. Controlling tons of complicated machinery as you are flying along a wide, open road must be amazing. I would love to try it. Alfie keeps saying he will teach me, but he is always busy. There's Aunt Violet's driver, although she never seems able to spare him long enough for lessons. Lonnie tells me she is not the best person to learn from unless I want to pick up some bad habits."

"That is wise counsel. Being a passenger when Lonnie is driving can be a hair-raising experience," he confirmed. "If not cars, what is an appropriate topic of conversation?"

"Well, there's cinema, any type of film really, but I especially love Douglas Fairbanks, Harold Lloyd, and Buster Keaton. I love detective novels, especially Sherlock Holmes and

Hercule Poirot. I enjoyed the first Father Brown stories, although I did not enjoy the recent ones as much. There are many Scottish writers and, of course, our land and history. Do not forget jazz music, especially Layton and Johnstone, and I adore dancing and cabaret."

"I reckon we will be capable of finding a conversation topic in there somewhere," he said with a chuckle.

As we drove through Pimlico, I realised I still had no idea where we were going. London seemed enormous, and I had yet to learn much of its geography, although I could tell we were heading south of the river. I hadn't asked him, as I decided it more fun going along with the surprise.

The journey passed in no time as we chatted about London, Aunt Violet, and cinema. He listened when I told him my sadness on hearing of the death of Rudolph Valentino, blethering on about a double-bill retrospective I saw a few days previous. He drove for over an hour until we arrived in a pretty wee village in Kent.

We drove through the gates of a sizable country estate, following a long driveway that seemed to go on for miles. Eventually, we could see a massive house that looked as though it had stood there for many centuries. A grey-haired servant greeted us, and I expected he would take us to the master of the house. Instead, he retreated with a bow.

"Is this house yours, too?" I asked, confused.

"My goodness, no, it belongs to a friend. He has gone off for the start of the ski season in Austria. We were playing cards the other night, and he said we should drop in. Well, not quite, but I offered to write off his debt in return for a loan of a key while he is away. His name is—"

"Effy Evesham?" I understood where he had brought me.

"However did you guess?" he asked. He looked worried, doubting whether bringing me had been a good idea. Most men take their girlfriends to lunch at a Lyons, the cinema, or a walk in the park if short of a few bob. I suppose a pornography collection would be far from an ideal venue for a romantic encounter for most people.

He had not promised romance, and I had no reason to expect it. I told him that I would like to see the collection, and he took me at my word. He had talked with such passion I felt I was being allowed in on a huge secret.

"Excellent," I exclaimed.

"Please, come this way," he said, relief apparent in his smile.

He led me through to a sizeable wood-panelled library. The bookshelves looked ordinary, the titles fairly standard, and I was puzzled. Seeing my expression, he gave me a smile and a wink. With a flourish, he produced a chain with two large keys from a pocket. I looked around to see the doors they unlocked. All I saw were bookshelves everywhere, apart from an ordinary-looking fireplace.

"I don't understand. Where is the lock it opens?"

"A secret room, very well hidden. Watch this."

He pushed a panel on the fireplace, and it came away, revealing a hidden lever. With a smile, he indicated I should pull it. A section of the bookcase swung forward as I did, exposing a solid looking recessed wooden door. He unlocked it and flicked a switch, illuminating stone stairs which led down to another door. After taking my hand, he climbed down the steps with me. He unlocked the door with the other key, and it swung open with a slight creak. It was far too dark to see much beyond the arc illuminated by light from the staircase. He switched on the lights, revealing an enormous windowless room as large as the ballroom at Cyneset House. I gasped as I perceived my surroundings. White-painted walls were filled with pornographic art. Man-sized statues with enormous phalluses stood beside shelves loaded with curios and numerous glass-fronted cabinets.

The only wall not covered with prints and paintings had a cinema screen with a projector pointed at it. Two sofas faced each other in the middle of the room, a sheepskin rug with a low table between them. A picnic basket, bottle of champagne, and two glasses sat upon the table.

"This is beautiful. It is not at all like I expected. It's like a museum."

"It is a museum, a museum of sexuality. You said you wished to know about sex. Believe me, if it is not here, it does not exist. The collection is rather impressive, isn't it?"

"It is huge. I mean, I know you said it was enormous, but this is impressive."

"Isn't it? This is the first and possibly the only time ever I have visited without Effy watching over me, warning me I must be incredibly careful. By the way, we must be incredibly careful."

We examined the many objects and exhibits, losing track of time as we looked over the collection. Ancient Greek and Roman sexual aids sat on shelves alongside statues of Egyptian gods and fertility statues from around the world. Many of the exhibits were beautiful, some fascinating, some stimulating, and some plain terrifying.

Bookcases in a corner explored erotic literature, and we read a fascinating story from Japan. We became engrossed in a beautiful, illustrated Kama Sutra we could only handle wearing gloves. He stood beside me now and again, putting a hand upon my shoulder or taking my hand. I trembled with each of these simple touches.

"Well, Kitten, are you sure you still want to try everything?" he said with a mischievous smile, waving his hand to indicate the exhibits. He poured two glasses of champagne, handing one to me.

"Oh, my God, yes. Well, mostly yes, with one or two maybes along with a most definite couple of when-Hell-freezes-overs."

He laughed. Making him laugh gave me the same pride as having turned him on.

"Excellent. Here's to expanding your education and finding your limits." he said, raising his glass.

"Are you offering to be my tutor?" I asked, hoping for a positive response.

"It would be an absolute honour. If you are happy to assume the role of my pupil, I promise to do my tutor duties to the absolute best of my capabilities."

"Excellent. I am rather interested in finding your limits, too," I said, raising my glass in our toast.

"I think you might not be the only one who receives an education," he said with a rakish smile.

He moved the table and pulled me to the floor in a kiss. We lay embracing and kissing until he reached beneath the table, producing a chest. Inside I saw several dildoes of different shapes and sizes, geisha balls, dilators, and a box labelled Vibro-Electra Massage Unit. We kissed and undressed each other as he laid me on the rug, stroking my naked body with his delicious light touch. He took the geisha balls and applied some lubricant before inserting one inside me. After a slight pause, the second ball popped inside.

I enjoyed it at first, although nothing happened. He pulled a rocking chair forward, indicating I should sit. My initial puzzlement vanished when I stood and it gave a pleasant but strange sensation. They contained some type of weight, and rocking the chair produced some delightful vibrations. I had wondered about the rocking chair, as it looked out of place, although it clearly served a purpose.

Charlie switched on the massage unit, which resembled Lonnie's electric hairdryer. The room filled with a loud buzzing noise. The vibrating rubber attachment looked intimidating, so I raised an apprehensive eyebrow. In reply, he lifted my hand, applying the rubber brush. The pulsating incited a pleasant sensation, making me relax into my rocking. He brushed his way along my arm, working his way to my breasts.

The tingles continued until he placed the machine upon my pearl. The wonderful sensations brought me to climax. The warm vibrations surged through my body, ending with my toes. I took the machine from him. It proved heavier than I expected. Standing, I tensed my muscles, pushed him onto the chair and kneeled before him. Lifting the machine, I brushed his nipples. He gave a smile, and I massaged his stomach. I tickled the head of his cock, making his mouth form an O shape before creasing in concern. I moved the machine to his balls and took his cock in my mouth, leaving a moment or two before switching it off.

He withdrew from my mouth and pulled me onto his lap. I kissed him as I guided his cock inside me. The sensation the geisha balls provoked was adorable. Now and again, they would clang together, causing many fits of giggles. We sat facing each other, me riding his cock, him kissing and nibbling my nipples. He took my bottom in both hands, thrusting upwards. We rocked together, our climaxes building, him kissing my neck as I enjoyed the fuzzy feelings ravaging my entire body. I reciprocated when his ejaculation came.

"Well, just when I think it cannot be any better, you prove me delightfully wrong," he told me, kissing my forehead.

"It cannot be better every time, can it? Surely, there will come a time when it's as good as it will ever be?" I asked, cursing myself for my pessimism. "Although, if this is as good as it ever gets, it will be good enough for me," I added without giving him opportunity to speak.

"And for me, also," he said with a laugh. "Although having a target to aim for is helpful."

We decided it time to pause for the delicious-looking

picnic. We dimmed the lights and selected a film from an enormous collection to watch as we ate. We settled on a French stag film based on the Madame Butterfly story. It featured explicit sex between men and women, women and women, and men with men. There was a strange undertone to it with sex between men performed as an act of punishment. The men I witnessed at the party did not treat it that way. The opposite seemed more the case.

"Shall we peruse the exhibits once more?" he suggested with a smile when the film ended. I nodded. It felt warm, so we continued our investigations without dressing, taking time over everything. He led me to the bookshelf, producing "The Merry Muses of Caledonia." He had me read some of the poems, translating what I could. It proved an eye-opening anthology, putting Rabbie Burns in a whole new light. I must admit to a struggle when I reached *"O lease me on my Charlie lad, I'll ne'er forget my Charlie! Tway roaring handfus and a daud, He nidge't it in fu' rarely."* I had to admit that I had no idea what *lease me on* meant. The rest I explained with a giggle.

Whenever I examined an exhibit or took an interest in a display, he asked what I did or did not find stimulating. I stopped to admire a Japanese painting, and he stood behind me, his arm enveloping me, sucking my earlobe the way I found irresistible. Reaching behind me, I stroked his face, his cock hardening against my back.

We went over to the rug, where he pulled me down on all fours. After a slight pause, I felt something pushing against my back entrance. A slight panic welled, yet I trusted him as I felt myself open without the pain I expected. I presumed it was the anal plug I saw earlier. It looked wee in its box, although I thought it enormous as it stretched me. After a few gradual pushes, it was in place.

I gave a long moan when he entered me, a rhythmical slapping noise echoing around the room. It felt fabulous having two holes filled, and I came with a yelp, shuddering with the intensity. Not long after, his moan and long slow thrusts indicated his climax. He removed himself and the plug before lying beside me.

"This has been an incredible experience," I told him, giving him a grateful kiss. "Thank you."

"Oh, no, I think I ought to thank you." He smiled his gorgeous smile, accompanying that captivating twinkle.

"Do you think Effy brings women here?"

"No, it serves as more of a temple of onanism, if I'm honest. A masterbatorium if you like."

We tidied after ourselves because the staff were forbidden to enter. He double-checked that he had locked both doors, and we left for London. When we neared home, I thought to ask who organised the picnic. He admitted he arranged the delivery of the hamper from Fortnum's and made a trip first thing to set everything up. I felt touched he had gone to such an effort, although he declared everything worth it.

The trip whizzed by much quicker than the trip down. Mere minutes later, we arrived at my house, where he stopped the car and kissed me.

"May I see you again?"

"I'd like that very much," I told him, grinning.

"That is wonderful news as I would also like that very much. Unfortunately, I have some events I cannot shift this week. Does Friday suit you?"

"Friday is perfect." Although ages away.

"What would you like to do?"

"Absolutely anything."

"Well, that leaves me many options, I suppose. Shall I pick you up at three o'clock?" he said, offering me his arm.

I agreed without pausing.

As we walked to my door, he kissed me goodbye. I danced a jig to my room.

CHAPTER ELEVEN: ON THE TOWN

Friday took an absolute age to arrive. When I complained for the hundredth time that my boredom had reached the limits of measure, Lonnie and Tabby dragged me uptown. For reasons I cannot remember, we found ourselves visiting the American Bar at the Ritz. In a mischievous mood, Tabby convinced some American tourists that Lonnie was the much-loved daughter of our own dear King George, and we were her ladies-in-waiting.

I marvelled at how she kept a straight face as I struggled to do the same. Leaning towards them in a conspiratorial manner, she informed them that Lonnie was a code name when the princess needed to remain incognito whilst letting her hair down.

To my utter shock, they fell for it hook, line, and sinker, not questioning why we let complete strangers into our secret. We swore them to secrecy, and they promised to keep our true identities under their hats. I bit my bottom lip when Tabby told them the king would be livid if he heard of his daughter visiting such a lowly establishment. If what I heard was correct, many places worse than this enjoyed the patronage of members of the royal family. Admittedly, I had not witnessed that with my own eyes.

We kept the entire charade going until our new friends left, despite having to stifle a tell-tale giggle from time to time. We did not pay for a drink, our acquaintances insisting everything must be on them.

At the end of the evening, Tabby and Lonnie left with two

gorgeous men. I went home alone, having literally beaten off the attentions of their friend. Despite being a good looking and pleasant fellow, he was not Charlie.

Friday dragged itself into existence, and Charlie met me with a kiss, handing me a blue wallet wrapped in a red ribbon tied with a bow. As I untied it, the words 'County of London Driver's Licence' revealed themselves. Confused, I opened it, discovering my name written inside.

"Shall we go for a drive? Or, more specifically, shall you go for a drive?" he asked, laughing at my reaction.

"You are going to teach me to drive a motor car?" I shrieked. He nodded with a grin. "Your car?" I asked, unsure. Another nod. "Oh, my goodness, how fantastic. Thank you." Throwing my arms around him, I gave him an appreciative hug.

Sitting in the driver's seat for the first time proved a thrill. He loved this car, and I felt honoured he trusted me to drive it. He explained the controls until convinced I understood. I started the engine and flew off, squealing as I put my foot on the accelerator with excessive enthusiasm. I drove several trips around the square, each one a wee bit smoother than the previous circuit.

When satisfied I had the hang of it, he directed me towards Hyde Park. Trying to hide my nervousness, I followed the road, avoiding omnibuses, carts, bicycles, and a thousand other cars. He proved a calm, patient teacher, making my anxiety vanish. By my fifth or perhaps sixth lap, I had gained enough confidence to press my foot a wee bit harder. Although still a bit nervous, I loved driving.

"Why, you are a natural, Kitten. There is no stopping you now. Someday we can hit the wide-open road where you will be getting this thing towards a ton. It feels magnificent. I just know you will adore it."

I felt determined I would prove him right one day. The idea

of driving fast was exciting, although impossible in central London in mid-afternoon. At his suggestion, I drove along Piccadilly. We had afternoon tea at the Criterion Restaurant, which I remembered from a Sherlock Holmes story I loved as a child. He confirmed he chose it for that reason.

We went to the Embassy club, sitting nearer the front because I was with Charlie. We met some familiar faces and a few new ones. As I said my hellos, someone pressed a Tom Collins into my hand.

I recognised Jolly from the party and went over to say hello. The second he saw me, he went a conspicuous red.

"Why hullo, Alice. Before you say anything, I feel I ought to apologise for abandoning you at Charlie's party. Please forgive me. I fell asleep."

"There is nothing I need forgive, Jolly. I don't hold anything against you."

"That is incredibly decent of you," he said, cheering. "Must have been more fagged out than I thought. Only meant to lie down for five minutes, didn't wake until noon. My aunt says the sole purpose of my existence on this earth is serving as an example of what not to do. At times such as these, I think she may be right."

As we chatted, Charlie joined us, handing me a drink and giving Jolly a warm greeting. A look from me to Charlie informed him he had missed his chance, and I fancied he gave a rueful smile.

Charlie introduced me to some more friends, including Simone, an artist who divided her time between Paris and London. A gorgeous Frenchwoman, she had jet black hair, razorblade cheekbones, and dark red lips. I adored her energy and no-nonsense air. She wore an elegant navy pinstripe suit with a lilac silk shirt and a spectacular orchid in her buttonhole. Like most of the clientele, she looked stunning. Despite wearing my newest dress, I felt dowdy standing beside her.

Tabby arrived without a man in tow. On entering the club, she surveyed the room for talent, striking up a conversation with Jolly. Bernie and Leslie greeted me with a flamboyant kiss on each cheek. Leslie looked fabulous in a light-coloured single-breasted suit with a pink shirt and full make-up.

"I say, ruby red." Bernie greeted me with another of his nicknames for me.

He had many, all focused on the colour of my hair. I did not mind his teasing. He was yet to use the same one twice, making me curious how long he could continue without exhausting his supply. "I cannot believe what we have heard. Are we to take it you have tamed the hitherto rampant womaniser Moorfoot? You two are a twosome?" he asked with an incredulous expression, checking we were out of Charlie's earshot.

"Well, it is rather a long story, but yes, well, I think we are." I nodded.

Bernie looked at Leslie, who raised an eyebrow to indicate a lack of satisfaction with my answer. "You think you are? My dear Scottish poppy, that is simply not anything near good enough. Either you are, or you are not."

"Well, we have seen a wee bit of each other recently."

"I see. How long have you been keeping this scandalous little secret?" Leslie asked with an exaggerated pout.

"A week, officially, although unofficially nearer six. Please don't tell Alfie."

"Why are we only informed now, so long after the event?" Leslie asked, slapping my hand. "And to suffer the ignominy of hearing it from someone else, too. Honey, if there is information of such nature going around, I absolutely must not be the last person to find out. It is just intolerable. No, it is actually well beyond intolerable."

"I am terribly sorry, but if it makes you feel any better, I haven't told many people, not being terribly sure myself.

Please don't talk about us in your column though, Bernie, we don't want to go public quite yet."

"I think it is fabulous, cherry red," Bernie said, patting my shoulder. "My discretion is assured. I am just thrilled to bits and pieces for you. Barring some royalty, he is the biggest catch this side of the English Channel. Six weeks you say?"

"Give or take," I said, nodding. He looked impressed.

"I think that definitely must be a record for him. I'm pleased for you both, chestnut, I genuinely am. Be careful with that one, though," he said in an uncharacteristic solemn voice.

"Goodness, yes," Leslie agreed with a nod. "He collects broken hearts the way young boys collect butterflies, and his is a gruesome collection of some considerable size. Be sure you keep your beady eyes on him at all times."

Before I could respond to this familiar warning, Tabby interrupted, putting an arm around Bernie and me. "Look here, there has been far too much gabbing, nowhere near enough dancing. Come on, you three. Toot suite." She offered us her silver cocaine case. We took a pinch or two each.

"There's no-one dancing, Tabs. There's no music," Leslie told her, confused.

"No, no, there isn't. So ridiculously boredom-inducing. It's such a terrible yawn, isn't it?" she said with an exaggerated sigh.

Charlie's friends were welcoming and accepting. They did not care who I was or where I came from, only that I made him happy. As I was learning, their happiness always took priority. Conformity was the greatest evil and should be avoided at all costs. Theirs proved an infectious mindset, and I found myself seduced by their thinking. Why would I not want to have the fun they were having?

We went to a few more places, accumulating more people with every stop until a happy band rolled into our final club of the night, The 43, an after-hours club. The police had raided it a few times, but that did not deter anyone from visiting. Many saw a fine from the beak under some false name as a badge of honour. I would be terrified by the experience.

Inside we were greeted by a pianist far superior to the cheap-looking instrument he was playing. The club was dingy and smoky, but I loved it. The basement boasted a de-cent-sized dancefloor and a band playing some hot jazz. They struck up the Black Bottom, and I looked for a dance partner. I caught sight of Jolly and asked him for a dance. He gave Charlie a nervous look as though seeking his permission. Charlie smiled and gestured towards the dancefloor.

"Please go on, Kitten. Dancing is most definitely not my forte. I am a complete corn-shredder. Believe me, I would ra-ther watch you dance. Go on, have fun."

I found dancing with Jolly again delightful. A curious part of me wondered what might have happened if he had not overindulged at the party.

The evening flew past. I spent it dancing, drinking, or laughing, with an occasional snort of cocaine for additional help in keeping going. After dawn, we left the club, having tucked into a tasty breakfast of overpriced bacon and eggs or kippers, although no one complained. Satisfied, we made our way into the London morning, everyone melting into the crowd of commuters. I was going nowhere except bed, feeling satisfied at having seen Tabby and Jolly leaving arm in arm. While we walked, Charlie put an arm around me and asked if I enjoyed myself.

"Yes, I did. I have experienced many enjoyable times since I came to London. Even so, this night was one of the most enjoyable," I said, giving a happy smile. Realising sex was not all he wanted from me felt fantastic. On the other hand, it felt incredible knowing he wanted to have sex with me too.

"So awfully glad to hear it, Kitten. Here's hoping we have

many more," he said, stopping me for a kiss.

The following Sunday, I walked through Hyde Park, despite knowing Charlie was not at home. For a reason I did not comprehend, I needed to lie to myself about being near him, despite his absence.

I stopped at Speakers Corner, catching a heartfelt oratory relating the plight of London's slum children. As he finished talking, a group of earnest-looking women unfurled a banner saying National Women Citizens Union. One prepared to make her speech as the others passed around leaflets. They had a sparse audience and a few hecklers. Before she opened her mouth, someone shouted, "You got the vote. What more do you want?" Others told her she should go off and find a husband.

Ignoring them, the speaker gave an impassioned, rousing speech concerning women in public life and the influence we women might have if we organised ourselves. The women distributing the leaflets had few takers, and I took one out of sympathy. Enthralled, I listened while she explained their many campaigns, including better maternity services and the nationalisation of medical care. Both these subjects were close to my dad's heart. I had heard all his arguments and could not disagree with him. The leaflet explained the help they gave women with their employment rights, health concerns, and birth control problems. Her words inspired me, and before I left, I made a healthy donation and volunteered my time.

Excited, I told Lonnie about the NWCU when I got back home. Despite my passion, she declined my invitation to accompany me. Undeterred, I attended a meeting and found myself assisting women with various problems. I offered to spend a couple of mornings a week, helping them whatever way I could. The idea that I could give something back made me feel useful, and I knew Dad would approve of helping those less fortunate than me. Meeting with these women had the added benefit of helping me remember how lucky I was. My life seemed in danger of becoming shallow. Volunteering my time and helping others would keep my feet on the ground.

Charlie and I spent all our time together until he returned to Sussex. In an attempt at keeping myself occupied, I met with Lonnie for a trip to the cinema. I chose a new film featuring a Scottish character who endeavours to ruin his former employer. I read the subtitles in a Scottish accent, although it would have been nice hearing one. Tabby loathed the cinema, declaring reading pictures the last thing she would do in a darkened room with men present. We met at Claridge's afterwards, and she was waiting when we arrived.

"Where have you been? Waiting for at least a hundred years," she announced to the room as we sat. "Am hopelessly in love, absolutely must tell you about him."

Having heard this proclamation several times, I was sceptical yet held my tongue. "Is there some spark between you and Jolly?" I asked, teasing her.

"What? No," she looked confused. "Oh, him, yes. He was last week. Must say, he proved an impressively well-endowed yet surprisingly tender shag but found conversations rather one-sided. Bit of a flat tyre who is some way from being the brightest bulb ever to burn. No, we must drink and celebrate the newfound paramour."

I must presume I proved agreeable as I have little recollection of much after that.

I spent the following day feeling wretched, although my mood improved when I received a telephone call from Aunt Violet. She talked at length before arriving at the point, asking if I would like to spend January visiting her villa in France.

My first thoughts were of how I would miss Charlie. I ached at the thought of being separated from him again. If this invitation had come earlier, it might have been a welcome distraction. Now, it was an inconvenience. I suffered a horrible flashback to my month in Hampshire and worried this trip might be a repeat experience in a foreign land. As if reading my mind, Aunt Violet explained Alfie and Lonnie would be accompanying us. I accepted, admitting that I loved the idea of drinking cocktails in the opulent casinos and nightclubs she described.

Charlie and I spent every minute together, making amends for our long separation. Taking Christmas into consideration, it would be forty-five tedious days before we could be together again. Alfie asked him to join us, but he had pressing family commitments.

December brought Charlie's birthday, and I worried about what gift I could give him. He could afford anything he wanted. What could I buy him he would not buy himself? Having thought it over for a while, I made a decision and approached Lonnie for help. When I explained my idea, she giggled, told me he would love it and agreed to help me find what I needed. Our subsequent shopping trip in an anonymous wee shop in Soho proved an educational experience.

Chapter Twelve: Mystery Guest

Charlie suggested we go for a drive on the day itself, so we jumped in the car and drove where the mood took us. It was a chilly December day, with a few fluffy clouds in a bright blue winter sky. We ate lunch in Richmond, sitting beside a cosy fireplace in a charming wee hotel.

"I have a surprise waiting for you back at my house," I whispered, leaning over my dessert.

"You do?" he asked, raising an eyebrow.

"Yes, although Aunt Violet is entertaining, so my house is not the best place for making immediate use."

He settled the bill with indecent haste. Before long, we arrived home, and I rushed inside to retrieve the parcel. He took a good look at it as I got in before driving to his house in record time.

As we got nearer, I worried the contents might fail to bring on the reception I hoped for. Feeling nervous, I presented it to him and waited while he opened it. His smile grew wider as he removed a crop, paddle, several thin velvet ropes, and a blindfold. He looked at me with an intrigued look.

"This is for you to use in whatever way you wish. You can use everything at once, or you can select one or two items. We can do so now, or if you'd like to think about it or involve someone else, I can wait. Whatever you plan to do with them, I will play along. It is your birthday, which means what happens is completely up to you," I told him with a shrug and an attempt at a sexy smile.

Staring into the box, he thought for a minute or two,

leaving me hanging. A suggestive smile and a familiar twinkle told me he did have a plan.

"Kitten, this is a fantastic gift. Thank you. Please wait in my room. I will be with you imminently. Why not play the new gramophone while you wait?" He kissed me and winked.

I went straight to the gramophone and selected some records. To kill time, I read a P.G. Wodehouse book I found on the bedside table. The music stopped, but engrossed, I hadn't changed the record for some time. I found myself absorbed in the stories, losing track of time passing. Judging by how much of the book I had read, an hour passed before Charlie returned.

"Oh, splendid, you've found something that has kept you entertained. Forgive me for keeping you waiting."

"Don't worry, I found this, and I am rather enjoying it. May I borrow it?"

"Feel free. If you don't mind?" He raised an eyebrow.

"Oh, yes, where would you like me?"

"Over here, please," he said, indicating the floor before him. I walked over, and he kissed me on the forehead before turning me and tying the blindfold over my eyes. I didn't know what he planned yet gave him complete control. Whatever he decided, I knew I'd enjoy it.

For a spell, nothing happened. I heard footsteps, then the door opening. I thought he had left the room, although it closed again seconds later. Footsteps approached me as unseen hands undressed me, piece by piece, until I stood naked. It proved a sensual experience, and I found myself getting more excited with every item. When I was naked, a hand led me towards the bed, pushing me on my back with my legs overhanging the edge. My body was caressed while my breast was sucked hard then given a gentle nibble. The riding crop traced its teasing way around my other nipple, which grew firmer in response.

My thighs were covered with tender kisses until I tingled with anticipation. A tongue made its way towards my pussy, and I enjoyed the sensation as it stroked and licked me. When it reached my pearl, it was a different technique from usual, the tongue alternating rapid taps with licking it as though it were a lollypop. The crop stroking my breasts, combined with the intense licking of my pearl, brought me to a climax. I lay, enjoying the pleasant afterglow, thinking it was time to ask the question that troubled me.

"That was delightful, although it wasn't you, Cluitie. Will you introduce me to the owner of this talented mystery tongue?"

A few seconds of silence were broken by laughter reverberating around the room. Other than Charlie, I heard an unfamiliar laugh.

"Correct, Kitten. Well done. You will be formally introduced later. I merely want you to lie back and enjoy the experience."

I lay back, loving the delight of two mouths sucking, licking and biting my breasts and two sets of hands stroking me.

"Now, Kitten, a test. My friend and I will take turns in pleasuring you. You can guess which one is which. Does it sound exciting? Do you want us to proceed?"

I uttered a long, low moan and gave an enthusiastic nod. Every inch tingled as a cock pushed its way past my lips. At first, I could not be sure, although I licked and sucked the head until I tasted a few drops of that familiar seed.

"It's you, Cluitie," I mumbled, with my mouth full.

"Correct." The cock withdrew from my mouth. My body was explored and stroked in a slow, sensual way, with occasional teasing slaps with the crop.

Soft hands turned me, placing me face down on the bed. The paddle struck me with a powerful slap on my bottom, causing a long groan, making me tremble as the waves subsided. Strong hands spread my legs apart, and a cock slid between them, exploring my pussy and pressing upon my pearl. The head slipped inside me. I found it impossible to tell if it was noticeably different to Charlie's. It pushed in further, and I felt the shaft narrow. I opened my mouth to say the cock belonged to our visitor but closed it, not wanting him to stop. The encounter was so enjoyable I felt certain I might climax any second and decided I should wait until the waves hit before speaking.

"I believe this is our intriguing guest," I said, breathless and tingling as the waves subsided.

"Very impressive, you are correct again."

The cock withdrew, and I heard some rearranging. Someone guided my mouth onto the cock of a man sitting on the bed. I took a long lick of the uneven surface and knew this cock was not Charlie's. The tell-tale taste of my juices gave the game away. It felt satisfying to discover I had been correct about the proportions. It was shorter and narrower with an enormous head. Exploring it with my tongue, I took my time before declaring my conclusion.

"Hello," I said, giving it a lick. "Again." Another lick. "Mystery." One more lick. "Man." I took the entire head in my mouth again. Charlie's cock entered me from behind while I sucked and licked the anonymous cock before me.

"A perfect score. Congratulations."

I adored the idea of pleasing two men at once, and I found it a powerful, sexy experience. The feelings set off by the man I loved thrusting himself inside me were delightful. After a few more enthusiastic sucks, the mystery cock stiffened and twitched as it shot its seed into my waiting mouth. I climaxed, grateful for the hands on my hips, holding me as my legs became jelly. I welcomed the thrust signalling Charlie's climax, feeling sure I could not take any more. In one quick manoeuvre, I was lifted, placed on the bed and kissed by lips I swear were Charlie's.

For a few minutes, I lay listening to footsteps and the opening and closing of the door. When my blindfold was removed, I looked around, expecting to see our visitor, but we were alone.

"My mystery man, you did not introduce us. Where has he gone?"

"He had to leave, I'm afraid. Duty calls."

"I have no idea who he was," I complained. I couldn't gather much about him, other than he seemed around Charlie's height but fuller around the waist and hips. His chest had been hairy, his pert, muscular bottom rather impressive.

"That is the way he prefers things, for now at least. However, he did enjoy himself very much, and he does want to thank you."

"It would be nice to hear him say so. I'd thank him myself, although I don't seem to have been given a chance. May I ask some questions regarding our visitor?"

"You may, although I might not answer," he said, enjoying the power this gave him. "I will allow you three questions." He lay back, smiling, thinking it a fascinating game.

It was fortunate I shared his fascination. "From what you said, I take it that I have not been introduced to this person. Have we ever been in the same place at the same time?"

"No."

"Am I likely to meet him?"

"You will no doubt meet him at some point, probably at nighttime. He prefers keeping to the shadows somewhat. He has his own excellent reasons for that."

"This will be strange, because one day you will introduce me to a man who knows what my most intimate places look like, and I will have no idea who he is."

"You will know how he tastes, and you can give a detailed, thoroughly accurate description of his cock. Don't you think that exciting?"

"Well, I wouldn't know what it looked like, although I have an idea of its shape and size. It is just as well I do find this exciting. I'd be very cross with you otherwise! At least I still have one more clue."

"Well, that depends upon your question." He smiled and raised an eyebrow.

"Would I find him in Burke's?"

"Yes," he conceded. "He is a distant cousin who enjoys sexual experiences of many flavours yet must remain discreet."

It seemed pointless continuing my interrogation, such as it was.

"We didn't use this," I said, showing him the rope still lying at the bottom of the box.

"Well, let us remedy that. How about you using it on me? It is my birthday, after all," he said with a wink. He picked up the blindfold. "With this."

I tied his arms and legs to the bedposts, giving him enough slack for some movement. Putting the blindfold in place with a kiss, I straddled his waist. Taking the crop, I gave a gentle swipe across his nipple. He smiled, and I hit the other one harder, causing a slight shiver together with a moan of pleasure. I kissed each nipple in turn as I stroked his chest. Insistent tapping on my back told me his cock was ready for action, but I ignored it. I concentrated on his upper body, running my nails across his chest and nibbling his nipples.

I kissed my way down his body, shuffling until I knelt between his legs. Blowing on his cock caused a twitch like a startled snake, and I giggled at the result. I ran my finger along its length as I licked the head. He gave an appreciative groan as I stroked between his balls and arse with my fingernail. Deeming him ready, I took his cock in my mouth, giving it a lusty suck, marvelling at how proud it stood, despite its previous exertions. Thinking it a criminal shame to waste this fantastic erection, I climbed on it, riding it until we both climaxed, him writhing and pulling against his restraints.

Charlie later thanked me for giving him his best birthday present ever.

The following day a servant brought me a parcel containing a beautiful silver compact with an enamel front. The card it came with had no name but was stamped with a familiar looking coat of arms, which explained the secrecy. Inside, an engraving read *To Alice, Thank you for a wonderful afternoon. G*

We visited the Kit Kat for our last evening together, making a determined attempt at keeping our mood cheerful.

"I think I have ascertained the identity of your birthday guest. Don't worry. I won't tell a soul," I said with a curtsey.

"I knew you'd be discreet. Thank you, Kitten," he said, kissing me. "He is keen to see you again."

"And you can tell his highness I am keen to actually see him. Although not as excited as I will be when I see you again, Cluitie."

I had an early morning train back home, so Charlie and I left early, not knowing our visit to that club had been our last. While we made our way home, the club had been raided and permanently closed after being caught selling booze to non-members. While disappointed that I had missed the excitement, I was relieved at avoiding a brush with the law.

We said a sad goodbye as we went off to spend Christmas with our families. The Kit Kat's closure added extra melancholy to our drive to King's Cross. It was a subdued walk towards the waiting train where we stood on the platform in a final embrace I did not want to end.

"I will miss you," I told him, feeling morose.

"And I you."

Inside my compartment, I opened the window, leaning out for one last kiss as the guard blew his whistle and the train pulled away. We shouted our final goodbyes, waving until we could no longer see each other.

I did not feel that I would cry like on the journey down, but I did feel sad to leave London and, to a greater extent, Charlie. I had no reason for tears this time. I had the consolation of seeing Dad again and being back in my beautiful homeland. It felt strange remembering how much I had dreaded leaving all those months ago. With a slight sadness, I realised how hard it was to imagine living there again. Much as I loved it, my heart was where Charlie was.

Dad met me off the train with a huge hug. "What have you done with your hair?" he asked, looking surprised.

"It was even shorter when I first had it done. Do you like it?"

"It always seemed a pity for you to tie it back. At least now it can be seen in all its full glory. Is that how London ladies do their hair now?" he asked, and I nodded. "I suppose I will grow to like it," he said with a chuckle. That was his usual answer for anything he did not feel sure about, although had he hated it, he would have let me know. "Did you meet any gentlemen in London?"

"I have met many, although I am yet to find one that is as nice as you." He gave a hearty laugh and did not ask any more questions about my love life.

Despite Dad's rejection of religion, Mum loved Christmas and insisted we celebrate it our own way. We decorated the tree, gave presents, played games, sung songs, and did everything except visit church. Dad closed the surgery for all except emergencies, which was unusual, as for many villagers, Christmas was a typical working day. As I expected, Dad had not arranged a tree, far less decorated one. Mrs. McKenzie made a herculean effort and helped me sort everything.

On an afternoon walk through the village, I chanced upon Robbie. I felt curious to see how I would feel when I saw him again. While I found him handsome, my heart did not skip the way it used to. Blushing, he informed me he had been seeing Esther since I left. I congratulated him with so much enthusiasm I worried he might think me disingenuous. We spent a pleasant few minutes chatting about nothing in particular until he told me he was saving to buy a ring so he could propose. I wished him the best of luck, and we said our goodbyes as the old friends we were.

It did not help matters, but I counted the days until I saw Charlie again. Every night I touched myself, fantasising about his hands caressing me. Every morning I woke feeling sad, remembering the hundreds of miles between us. I consoled myself by thinking of every day as one day closer to seeing him again.

Esther and I travelled to Dumfries for some Christmas shopping. Due to a chronic lack of inspiration, I had not bought Charlie a present. For some reason, I hoped a town five hundred times smaller than London might provide the answer despite reason or logic.

"Who is this friend you are buying a present for?" Esther pestered me as we walked.

I had kept quiet about Charlie, thinking I should conceal news of our affiliation from my dad for the time being.

"Just a fellow in London I have my eye on," I told her, sounding as casual as I could.

"Tell me about him."

"Well, he is a gentleman, a close friend of my cousin, Alfie. He is handsome, though not as handsome as Robbie, I suppose," I said, thinking I could divert her attention. Her blushing told me it worked, although for just a moment.

"How can I help you choose a gift if you won't tell me anything about him? Why is he such a secret?"

We passed a strange wee shop selling curios and antiques. I stopped to look in the window, avoiding her question. I saw the solution to my problem straight away.

"There, those are what I will buy him." I pointed at gold cufflinks in the shape of a devil's head with tiny ruby eyes.

"You cannot mean those horrible horned devil cufflinks, can you?" she asked, screwing up her face. "They are grotesque. What sort of gentleman would appreciate those? They are so expensive, too."

Much to her undisguised disgust, I bought them.

I returned home, where Mrs. Mackenzie presented me with a parcel from the evening post. She smiled a knowing smile but did not press me for any information. I recognised Charlie's handwriting, my face presumably telling her it was from a sweetheart.

I went to my room and opened the parcel. Inside was *The Merry Muses of Caledonia.* The accompanying letter told me he hoped I enjoyed my present and how much he missed me. I felt comforted by reading how he was also counting the days until we saw each other again.

Grabbing some notepaper, I wrote my reply, thanking him for his marvellous gift and telling him I felt the same. I enclosed the cufflinks, hoping he would appreciate them.

By the last day of my visit, I had memorised every word of his letter.

Chapter Thirteen: Greek Sex

January found me wintering in France, my first trip abroad. Aunt Violet had arranged that we would fly to Lyon from Croydon. Despite my initial excitement, I spent the entire time gripping my seat. I found the journey bumpy and noisy and hated being unable to see anything through the wee windows. Our fellow passengers did not mind or were at least much better at hiding their fear. I could not comprehend how any sane person could be anything but terrified.

Aunt Violet did her best to take my mind off the flight, regaling me with endless stories of previous family escapades *en vacances* and listing the families I would inevitably meet. Remembering Hampshire, my expectations were infinitesimal, although I gave her a few polite smiles and nods at appropriate intervals.

Free from my metal prison, I loved every second of our journey on the Blue Train. I gazed out the window, appreciating southern France's unfamiliar and delightful landscapes in the evening light. Vineyards stretched for miles, some covered with a dusting of snow, which disappeared the further south we went.

"I understand why you come here. It is gorgeous, lovely. The scenery is amazing, just beautiful," I exclaimed, exhausting my superlatives supply.

"Yes, that is what inspired us to buy a place here," Aunt Violet said with a nod that looked on the smug side. "Earnest and I came here on our honeymoon and loved the feel of the place. It was a little fishing village then. Earnest bought the land from an artist who lived there on a caravan."

"It is lovely indeed, although you must return in season, Alfie said. "Everyone is here, and the weather is glorious. We cannot visit then, as Mother insists on letting it out for the summer," he added with an innocent expression aimed at his mother.

"It pays for the upkeep and the wages of the staff. If I did not let it, we would have to sell it, and then you would not be able to visit at any time of year. It is too bloody hot during summer in any case."

"For you, perhaps, Mother. Still, winter is better than nothing. Compared with summer, it is rather bracing, although still warmer than home."

The temperature at times reached sixty degrees. Having always spent January in Scotland, I thought it felt relatively warm.

"It's quieter than Nice or Cannes, although handy for both," said Lonnie.

"That is why we bought it in the first place. It's just over an hour's drive from Cannes, far enough away to keep the Cannes set from dropping by unannounced."

"Not that distance stops them," Lonnie said with a smile. "Remember when the Brockenhams rented a villa that turned out to be miles from the sea? They came for the weekend, bringing their entire house party."

The Villa de Lumière hid behind a tall wall flanked by mature trees. My bedroom overlooked the sun terrace and stairs, which led to the swimming pool and tennis court. Trees separated the garden from the beach beyond, the sea visible on the horizon between the branches.

The following day we drove the beautiful coast road to Cannes. Our first stop was an enormous, opulent casino with high gilded ceilings and massive chandeliers. I had never set foot inside a casino, and I had no clue about the rules of gambling. Aunt Violet invited me to join her at baccarat, but I did not have the first idea how to play. She rattled through the rules, explaining about getting to nine before giving in and telling me I should just watch her. I did for a time before leaving her fully engrossed in her game. One game looked like pontoon, although lacking confidence, I left the card tables, wandering around until I found Alfie playing roulette.

I watched for a wee while until I felt confident enough to join him. I had some success playing outside bets, and feeling braver, I put a few chips on eighteen, my lucky number. Within a few turns, my gamble paid off! When Alfie admired my bravery, I realised I had staked more than I thought. Putting my win down to beginner's luck, I cashed my chips and quit while very much ahead. We met with Aunt Violet, who looked unhappy.

"Blasted baccarat, I swear I will never play again."

"Did you lose money, Mother?" Alfie teased.

"Of course, I bloody well lost money," she grumbled. "Thing is a damned fix. The house always wins. I never learn."

"Alice won four thousand francs on the roulette table. Perhaps you ought to try that instead," Alfie said with a cheeky smile.

"Did you?" she asked me, doubting Alfie's story.

"Yes, I thought my chips were six shillings, but it was bad arithmetic on my part. It's nearer sixteen." I attempted to explain, although it did not improve her mood any. She harrumphed, crossing her arms.

Leaving Violet in the casino, we met with old friends of Lonnie and Alfie. We visited a few different bars, meeting more friends, drinking new drinks. I apparently met some famous people, although I can muster no recollection of this happening.

We spent a few days visiting Aunt Violet's friends and

their children, a curious mixture of aristocracy, artists, actors and actresses, war heroes and heroines, and former courtesans. We were invited to bottle parties, dinner parties, supper parties, and one where everyone wore beach pyjamas. The older generation could be found watching their offspring from the sidelines. Although Violet claimed it was nothing more than incredulity at how the younger set were so easily amused, many eyes were rolled.

Violet frequented the casino whenever possible, trying to recoup her losses. We joined her some days but did not possess her stamina for all-day gambling. Our days fell into a languid set-up of late afternoon lunches and siestas. Some days I went shopping in the fabulous shops in Nice with Lonnie. If fair, we went for a swim and a walk to the harbour where we watched the artists. Our reward for our healthiness was visiting a cafe with a fantastic cognac selection. We made a pact that we would try every single one during our stay and were on track to achieve our goal.

I walked into the breakfasting room one beautiful, sunny morning, finding Aunt Violet perusing The Times. Fearful of missing news about events at home, she'd placed an order at the newsagents, where she had it collected every morning. She stopped spreading the marmalade on her toast and looked at me.

"Good morning. I think you ought to read this," she said, peering at me over her reading glasses. Her face was grim as she turned the newspaper, opened at the announcement page.

"There," she said, pointing at an engagement notice.

The Lord C.A.H.F. Moorfoot and The Hon Miss C.M.T. Sandow
The engagement is announced between the Marquess of Moorfoot, eldest son of the Duke and Duchess of Cyneset, of London and Sussex, and Cressida, eldest daughter of Lord and Lady Sandow, of Shropshire.

She watched me read the notice, reaching out her hand and squeezing mine. Stunned, I slumped on the chair, not believing what I had read. The newspaper was two days old. To make sure I had not misread it, I reread every horrible word.

"You are sweet on him, aren't you?" she asked in a kind tone.

"Yes, I am," I told her, gulping back the enormous lump in my throat. Even from Hampshire, she had heard we saw a lot of each other. "I thought he was sweet on me, too, although that is demonstrably not the case. Do you know this Cressida?"

"Yes. Her parents are perfectly nice although unbelievably dull, and the apple did not fall far from the tree in this case. Never mind, my dear," she said, squeezing my hand again. "All is not lost."

"I don't think so, Aunt Violet. All is looking dreadfully lost," I said, trying not to cry. Knowing he would be marrying someone who would bore him did give me some solace.

"Don't talk twaddle, girl. I have observed the way that boy looks at you. I cannot believe he possesses the same feelings for Cressida. No, I am certain I can see the dark hand of the Duchess at work. Faugh."

"He is engaged to be married," I protested.

"Engagements are not adamantine. They are broken as often as they are fulfilled. You will see when you reach my age. I was engaged twice before I married your Uncle Ernest, and he broke his engagement when he proposed to me. You young things think you invented love, and you forget us crumbly old creatures were once young and know a thing or two. Believe me, my dear, I'll be buying a dinner service for your wedding gift in no time at all." She gave me a playful wink.

I could not share her optimism. I decided it a fantastic idea to spend the day drinking, and we left for Cannes. When alone, I confided in Lonnie, asking her to keep the news from Alfie. Despite my efforts to pretend otherwise, he could tell something was amiss, pressing us until I related what I'd read. He closed his eyes, giving an audible sigh before asking me how I felt. Unable to form an answer, I donned a bogus smile and shrugged. His face remained sympathetic, although his eyes betrayed anger with his friend. He refrained from mentioning he had told me so, and I showed my appreciation with an affectionate embrace.

Alfie called over the waiter and whispered a request. He brought us glasses containing a measure of illegal and expensive absinthe, topped with a sugar cube balanced atop a slotted spoon. Iced water was dripped onto the sugar cube to mix with the green spirit. As the liquids combined, the drink clouded into a milky consistency with a strong herbal aroma. I took a tentative, wee sip, which tasted pleasant at first before leaving a burning aftertaste of aniseed, or liquorice, or some flavour I detest. I refused another yet was handed one despite my protests.

I woke unable to remember anything following my fourth or fifth absinthe. Lonnie informed me I had been utterly ossified, a delightful and hilarious occurrence for everyone who had witnessed it. It was a relief knowing I did not spend the night curled in a ball, crying hysterical tears. Now sober, that was all I had planned. I felt more than a wee bit worse for wear and declined the offer of another trip to Cannes. Before everyone left, Lonnie popped her head around my door.

"Poppet, are you absolutely sure you will be fine on your own? Are you certain you don't want me to stay with you?"

"I'll be fine. Don't worry," I insisted, trying a smile on for size. "I'll take a swim and then a wee stravaig to gather my thoughts, clear my head. Not a clever idea to be plastered every day."

"Quite," she said with a sympathetic smile. Checking there was no one in sight, she indicated I hold out my hand. As I did, she placed a cigarette, lighter, and aspirin in my palm.

"Thanks for the aspirin, but you know I don't smoke," I said, puzzled.

"It's hashish, darling. Smoke it and you will soon feel better." She kissed my cheek and left.

When I finished my swim, the housekeeper handed me a cable. I opened it, expecting unwelcome news. Instead, I saw four words.

I MISS YOU KITTEN

I stood dumbfounded, staring at the words. An endless number of unanswerable questions came to my mind. Why did he send it? Did he think I did not know he was engaged? If he missed me, why propose marriage to Cressida? Was he seeing her while he was seeing me? Had he fallen for her in the weeks since we last saw each other?

He told me he didn't want to hurt me, yet he had. Without a doubt, I deserved an explanation. I'd spent the previous day feeling sorry for myself, but the tears I fought now were tears of anger, no longer those of self-pity. Remembering the reefer, I grabbed it as I left for my walk.

I walked towards the harbour, then sat on the beach, admiring the view. Shaking, I lighted the reefer. My first few tentative attempts at inhaling brought about coughing fits. I persevered despite my misgivings, finding the rest of the experience pleasant. More relaxed and much calmer, I continued my walk with a pleasant buzzing sensation in my head.

I found myself passing the telegraph office. On a whim, I decided to send a wire to Charlie. It was far from one of my more rational decisions, but I was livid, despite telling myself I had no claim on him. The man in the office spoke no English, so I wrote down my reply for him.

BELIEVE YOU HAVE MISTAKEN ME FOR CRESSIDA OR DO YOU CALL HER KITTEN TOO

Chilled despite my woollen coat, I entered a café near the harbourside. Not feeling hungry, I ordered a large brandy. I chose a table beside a young man eating alone. He looked a few years older than me and had a handsome face, with messy sandy hair setting off his chocolate brown eyes. A tatty, paint-splattered sweater jacket hung loose over a vest and colourful tie.

"Bonjour," he said with a cute smile, catching my eye.

"Bonjour," I replied, smiling back at him. He said something I did not understand. "Je vous demande pardon," I said, searching for the words. "Mon Français, c'est tres, tres malade."

He laughed. "I do not think your French is ill."

"Oh, I am sorry, is that what I said?" I asked. He nodded. "It works in English, but not French, I think. You speak English?"

"Yes, some, I spent some time in London. You are en vacences?"

"Yes, with my aunt. She owns a villa on the other side of the harbour. Do you live here?"

"Oui, I have a studio. I am an artist."

"I presumed that," I said, indicating the various paint splashes on his jumper. He looked as if noticing the stains for the first time and laughed.

"Yes, it is apparent, non? I am the most untidy."

"You look like an artist."

"Then I am pleased to look untidy."

"I don't think you look untidy. On the contrary, you look handsome," I told him, surprised by my brazenness. If anyone told me six months previous that I would be complimenting strange French men someday, I would have laughed.

Brandy mixed with hashish clearly constituted keys to my confidence.

"Merci," he said, nodding towards me without modesty. "You are tres beau aussi. Has anyone ever painted you?" he asked. I shook my head. "Non?" His bottom lip protruded in mock disbelief. "That is the most sad case of affairs. I would like to paint you very much."

"I am here for two and a half more weeks. I can perhaps manage to get away for a few afternoons when everyone's sleeping," I said, shrugging.

"Time enough. I am done," he said, indicating his empty plate. "You want to visit my studio?"

"Yes, please," I replied, without any thought whatsoever. My need to rid myself of feelings of rejection brought about a devil-may-care version of me. He smiled another cute smile.

"My name is Georges."

"Hello, Georges. I'm Alice."

He led me along a narrow side street, unlocking the door to an empty shop. A thick wool blanket hung over the window, making the inside look dingy. The furniture consisted of a single metal framed bed pushed against the wall, a wooden chair, and a single wardrobe. Artist's materials occupied every other inch. Strewn canvases covered the floor. Embarrassed, he picked them up and piled them against the wall. I helped him, glancing at them as I did. Most of his paintings were of local landscapes. I picked one up and sat on the bed, admiring it.

"I like this one. It's enchanting. The colours are striking," I said, looking at a painting of the harbour. Its bright primary colours displayed the buildings bathed in bright summer sunlight.

"Merci," he said with a solemn nod.

He scurried through the only door to what I presumed was the kitchen, returning with a bottle of cheap cognac and two glasses wet from a rinse. Pouring two generous measures, he handed me the larger glass as he sat on the chair. We fell into an interesting discussion about art and the artists we admired.

I found him easy to converse with. Before long, we had almost finished our cognacs, and he topped up the glasses. He produced a reefer from a box, lit it, and offered it to me. I supplemented my relaxed feeling from earlier, trying to avoid the coughing fit this time. I could not fathom why I had taken so long to discover this marvellous stuff.

"I often paint local scenes because I cannot always afford a model. I create to struggle."

"Do you have one of your portraits? I'd like to see one."

He flipped through a pile of canvases. One was a stylised modern portrait of a naked lady. He flipped past it, but I stopped him.

"Is that how you want me to pose?" I asked as I pulled the painting from the pile. I had not given it a thought, but I found the idea exciting.

"That would be fantastique, if you are happy," he said, grinning. "But please do not feel that you must. You must be comfortable."

I stared at the painting as I considered the prospect. Posing nude would be daring, and I could not be sure I would be capable of mustering the confidence. I passed Georges the reefer as he sat beside me.

"Can you make me look as beautiful as her?" I asked, indicating the painting, hoping for some artistic licence.

"Ma chérie, she was a beautiful creature, but she had no soul. It was empty. I had to fight to find her beauty as I painted her. You, why you have a beautiful soul, and you can only be more beautiful," he told me with an earnest expression. I knew he was spinning me a line but took heart from the praise.

"Then I will pose like her. When would you like to start?"

"Why not now?" he asked with a grin.

"Why not?" I told him, thinking I should strike while this particular iron remained hot.

He stubbed out the reefer in the overflowing ashtray before pulling the window blind closed. A strange feeling took me when he locked the door and pulled the bed towards the middle of the room. Although I felt apprehensive, my increasing curiosity silenced my fear.

"You can hang your clothes over there," he said, indicating the wardrobe.

It contained more empty hangers than occupied ones. I hung my dress beside a dress shirt which had seen better days. Georges arranged some oil lamps around the bed, apologising for the lack of electricity.

I let my chemise fall to the wooden floor and stood naked. "Where do you want me?"

He looked me over, smiled and indicated the bed. I lay on it, leaning on one side with my hand on my hip. For a few minutes, he stood looking at me, chewing his bottom lip. He moved as if to touch me but stopped himself, his arm freezing a few inches from my shoulder.

"May I?"

I whispered my assent, and he leaned over me to arrange my arms. The back of his hand brushed my breast as if by accident, although I could not know for certain. Whatever his motivation, I could not complain as it felt good being touched there once more. I removed thoughts of Charlie touching me from my head. He had betrayed me. It was silly to think I was doing the same to him.

"I am sorry," he said, pulling his hand back.

"Don't be," I told him, looking up at him.

"You are beautiful," he said, brushing some hair from my face.

He paused before kissing me. His forceful rough lips had a

vague taste of hashish mixed with brandy. It felt strange being naked and kissing someone I had known for a few hours, yet I found it an incredible thrill. I helped Georges remove his clothes, scrutinising his thin, wiry body as he kneeled, lifting my foot and sucking my toes, which I was surprised to find rather pleasant. At a languid, teasing pace, he kissed towards my inner thigh. I expected his tongue would meet with my pearl, but it deviated, kissing my stomach, then my breasts.

Pulling his head up, I kissed his neck, placing minute kisses on his collarbone. I worked my way towards his chest, as he caressed my back. I kissed my way to his hip bone, lingering there, before removing his trunks. At its firmest, his cock was a wee bit shorter than Charlie's, narrower and not as smooth. I licked its length before taking the head in my mouth.

I was thinking of having his cock inside me when I remembered I had left my diaphragm at the villa.

"Shit, or merde, if you prefer. I have no birth control with me," I admitted, hoping he would have a French letter. It would be appropriate, I suppose. He had a solution, although not one I expected.

"Have you tried Greek sex, ma chérie?"

"I don't think I have, although I must admit I have no idea what it means."

"You will love it, c'est fantastique. Do you trust me?" he said with a smile.

"Yes," I told him, without stopping for thinking. "Although that seems a peculiar thing to say as I have just met you."

We had gone too far to turn back, and I could not pass on an experience this exciting. I'd told Charlie I intended to try everything, and this encounter promised a delicious possibility of a new lesson. With him no longer in my life, I needed other tutors in the ways of sex. Here was a perfect opportunity presenting itself.

He went into the kitchen, returning with a bottle of what I took to be olive oil. He kissed me and opened my legs, kissing my inner thighs before caressing my pearl with his tongue. I climaxed, falling back in disappointment at its ending. He poured oil on his hand and rubbed it onto his cock. It grew more erect, curving more prominently towards the left.

Without pausing, he poured more oil onto his finger before inserting it up my bottom. I opened my mouth in complaint, but it felt so good I found myself giving a deep moan instead. He pushed his finger deeper before inserting another. With some manoeuvring, he arranged me to hover over his lap, facing away from him. When he removed his finger and placed his cock against my backside, I realised what Greek sex meant.

He pulled me towards him until the tip of his cock pushed past my arsehole. I dropped myself on with too much enthusiasm, finding it bloody painful. Swearing to myself in agony, I pulled myself off and caught my breath as I held back until the stabbing pain receded. He waited with forbearance, sensing my discomfort. The pain faded, and I eased myself onto his cock, more patient this time. After a few gradual pushes, I sat on his lap with his entire cock inside me. I relaxed and enjoyed the intensity.

He grabbed my hips and made sure his cock remained in place as he flipped me, putting himself on top. He quickened his thrusting, which felt remarkable, setting off all sorts of unexpected sensations. I had always been reluctant when discussing this possibility with Charlie as I did not think I would enjoy it much. I owed him an apology, but it was too late for that.

When settled in a rhythm, Georges reached between my legs and stroked my pearl. My climax built inside me, and I emitted a loud, passionate groan, culminating in one of the fiercest orgasms I ever experienced. I hit a solid wall of pleasure, tingling everywhere. It felt delicious! He thrust hard into his climax before withdrawing, collapsing beside me. I enjoyed the experience, although deep down, I wished it had been Charlie's cock inside me.

"Well, that was rather intense," I exclaimed.

He laughed. "Oui. Exquisite," he said, kissing me and caressing my side, causing a shudder. He jumped from the bed and took a couple of steps back, staring in a strange, intense way at me the whole time.

"Stay exactly that way. Do not move," he instructed, holding up his hands.

Naked, he walked to his easel, mixing paint on a pallet before attacking the canvas with a large brush. He painted me for an hour or so until I stiffened and had to stretch.

I spent as much time as I dared in Georges' studio. To my chagrin, spending time with him did not always distract me from thinking of Charlie. He would chat with me while he painted for a few minutes, then stop talking for hours at a time. I had to stay dead still, and it proved difficult to stop my mind wandering as I lay in silence. To keep my mind occupied, I worked through my times tables or conjugated some irregular French verbs.

Having given it some deliberation, I told Lonnie what I was doing, and my revelation tickled her. The painting was taking some time, and I had no idea how Georges would finish it if Aunt Violet questioned my absences. By a happy chance, she hit a winning streak and did not ask where I went every day. I relied on Alfie, Lonnie, and the baccarat table to continue distracting her.

Towards the end of our stay, I spent my last afternoon in the studio. I thought the painting looked complete, although Georges asked to do more work on it. I suspected it might be an excuse for fucking one more time. If it were, complaining would be churlish.

"Can I buy the painting once you finish it?"

"It will be tres expensive. I think it the best I have ever done."

"Please don't sell this to anyone else. You understand there are people who must never see this?" I told him, hit by a sudden nervousness at the thought of someone I know seeing it. In my excitement, I had not considered the possibility.

"I promise I will be most careful. I will negotiate a price if you visit one more time."

I promised I would and returned to the villa. Madame Boutin, the housekeeper, met me at the door, looking relieved.

"Oh, Mademoiselle Alice, it is you," she said, looking over my shoulder. "A friend of Monsieur Alfie is waiting in the drawing room, but he is asking for you. He has waited for some time."

I went there, telling her to make sure we were not disturbed. There was one friend I hoped it would be, but what would he be doing here?

Chapter Fourteen: The Visitor

Crossing my fingers and telling myself I must be strong, I entered the drawing room. Charlie stood beside the window. Despite my previous anger, the smile that emerged as he turned to face me made me melt inside and my heart pound.

"Hello, Kitten. It is so good to see you."

Seeing him felt good, too, although I felt no desire to disclose that fact. I was angry with him. He looked as striking as I remembered or more if that was possible. I fought the impulse to run over and slap his face or kiss him or hit him while kissing him? At the thought of a kiss, my stomach flipped, my heart performing a treacherous jig.

"Hello, Charlie. What brings you to St. Tropez?" I asked, mustering a casual air.

"That is a foolish question, Kitten. You do," he responded with a screwed-up expression. "I received your telegram and came as soon as I could. I arrived in Saint-Raphaël first thing and came straight here."

"Oh," I said, feeling overwhelmed. While this was what I hoped for, it was not what I had expected. I thought I deserved an explanation, and he appeared to have come a long way to provide one. I knew I must give him an audience, curious what he could possibly say.

"The housekeeper said you were visiting a friend."

"She did?" I asked, surprised. I had not told her where I was going. It might be a guess, but I worried she knew the reason for my daily walks. "Yes, I was."

"A male or female friend?"

The question made me angry again. How dare he ask. He was engaged to someone else! How dare he pretend that he cared!

"Georges. He is my lover. He is an artist, and he is painting my portrait," I said, affecting nonchalance.

He looked pained, although my anger made me drive the knife further.

"Every day, he fucks me then paints me. He has taught me many new things, wild, passionate things. We spend much time exploring every inch of each other's bodies, and we have Greek sex now and again. It has been an amazing experience. The painting is almost finished, so we spent the afternoon fucking."

He did not reply, giving me time to regret my petulant outburst. He stared at the floor before raising his gaze to meet mine.

"Do you love him?" he asked, his voice soft.

"No, I don't. Are you angry with me?" I asked although he looked more relieved than angry.

"How could I be? I have no right to be. I presume you saw the notice and believed we were no longer together?"

"Aunt Violet showed me."

"I can only apologise. You must have felt I betrayed you and thought me incogitant. I assure you I am not engaged, although I cannot blame you for finding another lover. I regret my absence. It would have been quite something to witness, I am sure."

"Well, I was hurt, yes." I lost my chain of thought while my brain assessed this latest information. How could he assure me he was not engaged? Might it be true? With these thoughts whirring around my head, realising what he had said took a moment. Confused, I looked at him. His face had a lascivious expression. I knew that look well and also knew the effect that look had on me.

"I'm sorry, what did you say? The last bit."

"I wish I could have been there. I would have liked to watch," he repeated, staring at me without blinking.

"You enjoy watching other men fuck me?" I asked, raising an incredulous eyebrow. The idea aroused him! I would tear my eyes out rather than watch him have sex with another woman.

"Well, I enjoyed watching another man fuck you on my birthday."

"Yes, but you took part in that, would it not be different if you were there merely to watch?"

He did not answer, merely biting his bottom lip. The beginnings of a tell-tale bulge in his trousers proved the truth of what he said. The thought of what that bulge contained aroused me, though I told myself yet again, I must stop falling for him every time I saw him.

Despite my doubts, I knew I must take advantage of this situation. We had been apart for weeks, and I had no idea how much time we would have together. Without thinking, I dropped on my knees before him, unbuttoning his trousers. He wore boxer trunks, allowing me to pull everything to his ankles and free that gorgeous familiar cock. Looking him in the eye, I took it and licked the head.

With my other hand caressing his inner thigh, I licked the entire length towards the base. I nibbled his balls, flicking them with my tongue before making my way back. Looking to see his reaction, I took his cock in my mouth, probing the tip with my tongue. He gazed at me with a serene expression.

"You do realise the housekeeper could enter the room at any time," he said with a raised eyebrow I found sexy.

I removed his cock from my mouth to tell him, "I don't care." The family were due home at any time yet, caught in the moment, all I desired to do was what I was doing.

He looked at me and pulled me to my feet into a kiss. I lost myself, remembering how wonderful kissing him felt. He broke the kiss and pushed me onto the sofa. Kneeling before me, he yanked my underwear aside, licking me as if washing me clean. I had not freshened up since leaving Georges, and he had to taste him on me, although he pushed his tongue deep inside me. When it met my pearl, he took his time as though savouring every moment. I built to a rather luxurious orgasm that instantly replaced all the tension in my body with myriad effervescent bubbles.

He lay on top of me, shoving his cock deep inside me in one delicious thrust. We both groaned, making us giggle. Kissing each other with longing, we pushed into each other harder. We rediscovered each other's bodies with a renewed hunger. My climax built, and for the first time, we came within seconds of each other, collapsing with an intense kiss.

Breaking the kiss, he admonished me. "Now, Kitten, there you go again, making it absolutely inevitable I fall in love with you all over again."

"That is hardly an appropriate way for a betrothed gentleman to talk," I replied, having difficulty sounding as angry as I wanted, distracted by him saying he loved me! Pushing him off me, I drew my underwear back in place while he replaced his trousers. "At least, not when he is addressing someone other than his fiancée."

"That is why I am here. I must talk with you. Please, will you hear me out?"

I fetched drinks, sitting on the sofa furthest from him.

"I will listen. Please continue."

He sat beside me. "Kitten, I must explain everything. I will start from the beginning if I may. I was not born the Marquess of Moorfoot. I was Lord Charles Fyffe and glad of it. Moorfoot was my brother, and from the moment of his birth, constantly under the scrutiny of my mother. My sister Louisa, also, as she is the eldest. Have I told you about my sister?"

"No, but Lonnie did. She misses her."

"I miss her, too," he said with a sad smile. "Her husband heard of his appointment in Persia the day before he proposed. He worried it might make her reject his proposal, but it only made her more enthusiastic. I cannot be certain she loved James, but marrying him gave her freedom she could never have in England. My mother controlled every aspect of Moorfoot and Louisa's lives. As the youngest, I had a freedom they did not enjoy. When Moorfoot died, Mother fixated on me instead, though our views have long been incompatible. To make her happy, I attended all the deb balls, meeting endless eligible girls in the name of finding the perfect wife. I needed a suitable companion, or Mother would find one for me. Cressida's parents are old family friends, and I knew Mother approved of me courting her, although I never loved her. I took her everywhere my mother would be or would hear of, and I suppose I always assumed I would marry her someday. The prospect of there being a match Mother might approve of more are slim. I resigned myself to that until I met you. You intoxicated me before we even met, from the moment I saw you watching at the first party."

"Why did you send me away then?" I interrupted, confused.

"Believe me, I kicked myself for the remainder of that evening and quite some time after. I looked into your ingenuous eyes and saw only innocence. Perhaps I would normally take advantage, but I felt frightened lest I caused you harm. I wished to protect you, which included protecting you from me. You were a little drunk. Taking advantage of that would not be right."

"How horribly honourable of you." I tried my best to maintain my stern expression, struggling to hide my excitement.

"Thank you, yes. Uncharacteristically so, some would say,

and with some justification. I did not know your name or who you were. You were there like some real-life Cinderella, but you left without leaving as much as a shoe. Although I cannot understand how a shoe would help me find you, I am sure you own more than one pair, and your feet are neither ridiculously large, small, or misshapen."

"No, that part of the story never made sense to me either. I never understood why he could not recognise her without a shoe," I said with a giggle, annoyed that I had let my stern expression slip. "You looked for me?"

"Every time I left the house, I found myself scanning the crowds, hoping to bump into you. I told Alfie about the beautiful Scottish girl I met, and he accused me of imagining you. I did not dare tell him how obsessed I became with you as I thought he would make fun of me. I could not believe my luck when I saw you at Alfie's house that day, and I felt certain it was a sign that we were meant to be together. My heart sank when he forbade me from seeing you. I wanted to argue, although everything he said was perfectly true. He warned me he would murder me in ridiculously complex ways if I so much as touched you. I knew I should send you away the day you visited. My conscience failed me, and I just could not bring myself to do it. I found it strange, yet I felt so nervous it was like my first time over again."

"I felt nervous as well, although it actually was my first time," I said, unable to believe my ears. He was nervous!

"Yes, I have no excuse on that front. I was afraid you'd realise I was concealing my erection when I half-heartedly attempted to send you home."

"I am sorry I missed that. I was most likely captivated by your eyes."

"When growing up, I never learned about love. The love my mother expressed was no more than an extension of her expectations. Her speeches of responsibility are the most reliable emetics around. Growing up, I thought love was no more than duty, constraint, and obligation. What I feel now has taught me that I have never known love. People talked of love, and I dismissed them as easily as I would dismiss a conversation about vampires, or fairies, or Father Christmas. Some have professed the deepest love for me, and I treated them like they were a deranged fool. If they felt even half of what I am feeling, then the pain I caused them is unthinkable. I ought to seek their forgiveness on my knees. I cannot define what I feel, yet I cannot dismiss it either. You make me want to become the type of person who might deserve you. I love you, of that, I am sure. You are my one and only Kitten, I promise you."

While I longed to speak, no words would leave my lips. I doubted anything I would say could match the beauty of his words. Instead, I took his hand, unable to believe how good I felt hearing them.

"Why the engagement, the notice?"

"It was not my decision, I assure you. I told Cressida about you when we first met and explained I would not be proposing marriage."

"I see. How did she take that particular piece of news?"

"Relatively well, as it goes. I cannot be sure she expected I would marry her. She did not seem the slightest bit upset. I am not sure she loves me either. I think her parents may be more upset than she is. Noblesse oblige and all that. She kindly agreed to accompany me to my father's birthday party last month. Mother saw us together and marched over, telling us Lady So-and-So had mentioned our engagement. At an indecent volume, she congratulated us, scolding me for keeping it secret. I would have corrected her, although with a crowd gathering—all congratulating us—I couldn't reject Cressida so publicly."

He stared into my eyes. I felt confident he was telling the

truth.

"I did the decent thing," he continued. "Thinking we would wait a few weeks before breaking it off quietly. The notice appeared with such indecent haste I knew my mother planned the whole thing. She has long been guilty of ipsedixitism."

"Of what?"

"She will make blatantly untrue statements, yet the very fact words have passed her lips make them absolute gospel truth. I confronted her, and she admitted forcing my hand. I told her a few long-overdue truths, then left, telling her I was off to break my non-existent engagement."

"Can I presume she was not pleased?" I asked, sure I could predict the answer.

"She was beside herself. She threatened all sorts, mostly having me disinherited, left without a penny, ruined, stoop, and roop. I heard language I never thought she knew."

I laughed, and he joined me. "Does she know you are here?"

"No, I thought refraining from mentioning it would be best. I did not think she would take it well. She has a rather unfavourable opinion of your father."

"So I believe," I said with a nod. "They clearly have a history, although I don't know what happened between them. Your mother most likely has an issue with his socialism, although I have no idea how she knows about that. He has many opinions about the aristocracy. The mildest involves you working for a living rather than living off the blood, sweat, and toil of the working man." I paused for his reaction.

He merely shrugged. "I can see why they wouldn't get along." He laughed, but his face grew grave as he stood. "Never mind our parents. I love you." He dropped on one knee and looked up at me. "Will you marry me?" he asked, his face earnest, pleading.

My first reaction was saying yes and throwing my arms around him. A nagging voice prevented me. I loved him, although it would mean agreeing to the impossible. It appeared keeping our feet on the ground was my job.

"I'd like that more than anything, but you know as well as I do that it isn't possible," I told him, biting my bottom lip so I could keep myself from crying.

"What? But . . ." he objected.

I stopped him. "I would hate for you to go against your mother's wishes. I could not forgive myself if I split your family and left you penniless. I will not be your wife, but I will be your mistress, Cluitie. After all, I will never mix in the same social circles as your wife. It should be simple to avoid meeting each other publicly. That way, at least I might still have you in my life."

My offer was genuine and heartfelt. I could not bear the thought of being without him.

He stroked my face before taking my head in his hands. "No, Kitten. I adore you more for your offer, although I have no wish to participate in any circle that excludes you. I abhor the idea that I should spend time with, wake up with, or make love to anyone but you. Without you, I have become a dedicated onanist because I want only you. I merely think of you, and I grow hard. Until I met you, I had never associated sex with love. Now I have experienced it, I want no other type. I need you, not as a courtesan, but as my wife."

"I don't wish to see you marry anyone else, although I don't see how we can be together if you are cut off. I have no money, and my savings would last us a few months, perhaps a year. I believe I will inherit Mum's money when I am of age, but I cannot imagine it will be worth very much."

"I hate seeing you frown. It does not come easily, as even in repose, you are always smiling. Let us not worry about the future. It would be a pity to tarnish our reunion and the time we have together," he said before kissing me.

The door opened, and we jumped apart. Alfie and Lonnie walked in, followed by Aunt Violet, who took in the scene before giving her smuggest told-you-so look.

"Charlie," Alfie exclaimed, unsmiling. "What the devil are you doing here? I heard you decided to tie the knot with Cressida. What is going on?" he asked, looking at us with a quizzical expression.

"Ah, therein lies the story that leads me here," Charlie said with a smile. "If you ply me with some more hooch, I will tell you the whole sorry tale."

He told his story again, reassuring Alfie that removing a vital part of his anatomy would not be necessary. Aunt Violet invited him to stay, and we spent every minute of our last few days in St. Tropez together. I felt ashamed I had doubted his feelings, although he bore no grudge. After discussing it for some time, we decided we would try keeping our affiliation a secret to stop the news from reaching his mother.

Our last few blissful days flew past. The weather turned warmer, and whenever we had guests at the villa, Charlie and I explored like carefree tourists, doing our best to avoid crowds. Unable to book a seat on the aeroplane we flew on, he stayed in St Tropez for an additional day. I felt envious, wanting to go with him or even swap methods of transport, although I knew Aunt Violet would have none of it.

Chapter Fifteen: Scavenger Hunt

Back in London, I immersed myself in my work with the NWCU, making up for the time I had missed. My first day back started with a meeting with Olive, a nippy at the Lyons in Coventry Street. Eighteen shillings had been docked from her pay because a large group absconded without paying. Two weeks before, another group cost her fifteen shillings, vast amounts from her wages of twenty-five shillings a week. In tears, she explained her troubles after borrowing money from the wrong person to meet her commitments.

My final client was Maisie, one of our regulars. Her cheery disposition disguised her troubles, which included a big family and an unemployed husband who had lost both legs in the war. Her youngest was a few months old, and she was expecting again, only for her landlord to issue an eviction notice. As we finished our meeting, she leaned over my desk.

"Thank you for your 'elp, Miss Fraser. I am so awfully glad you are back. I 'onestly don't know what we'd do without you. You know, you are awful easy to talk to. I mean, you're educated, but you ain't all posh or anything, what with you sounding Scotch an' all."

Unsure how to take this attempt at a compliment, I thanked her without correcting her. Like most Scottish people, calling me Scotch raises my hackles. Despite my irritation, I smiled my thanks, and she left unscolded.

I stopped in a bookshop on my way home, where a snooty woman mistook me for an assistant. I could not understand the reason for her confusion, as I was not wearing anything resembling a uniform. Despite me telling her I was not an employee, she stood with an expectant look, waiting for me to fulfil her request. The annoying part was that I knew where to find the book she wanted and turned to follow her instruction. After a few seconds thought, I stopped myself, and walked away, paying no heed to her thunderous complaining.

Later, I met with Lonnie and Tabby, who announced herself in love again.

"His name is Laurence, a rather hip fellow who also happens to be an absolute Adonis."

"Tell me more about this Adonis."

"What do you want to know?"

"Well, the usual, you know, his hat and shoe size, inner leg measurements, what school he attended, and his mother's maiden name," I said, although all I received in return for such prime sarcasm was a nonplussed expression. "I mean, where you met this Adonis, where he's from, what he does, that sort of stuff."

"Met him at a remarkable little Berlin club, as it happens. Crying shame there is nothing like it here. Fascinating place, Berlin. It is just divine. You must go. You will adore it."

I waited for the detail, although nothing more was forthcoming.

"The rest? You know, about Laurence himself?"

"He is heavenly to look at, he drives cars, and he's the second son of some factory owner who comes from Stockport, or Stonehenge, or somewhere," she said with a dismissive wave of her arms.

It was foolish to expect exact locations from Tabby. For her, the geography of any area outside certain parts of London remained a complete mystery.

"Stonebridge, sweetie," Lonnie said, smiling.

"Surely, you must give Tabby some credit for

remembering he comes from somewhere beginning with S. You've met him, I take it?"

"Yes, he is as handsome as you'd expect and entirely charming. Tabs is right. He drives racing cars. His father makes bespoke motor cars. Nice chap, I will miss him when you inevitably grow bored with him."

"Does Lonnie knowing more about your current paramour than you do bother you?"

"Not in the slightest. Such detail is irrelevant flim-flam," Tabby said, shrugging.

Charlie joined us the following day in a new Indian restaurant Alfie recommended. It was my first experience with Indian food, so Lonnie helped me select a dish. I loved the flavours and exotic spices until I bit into something with a ridiculous level of heat. Gulping my water, I struggled to manage the ludicrous burning sensation, imitating an overheated dog. My expression made everyone, including Charlie, crease with uproarious laughter, unsympathetic to my predicament. Laurence sought to help, offering me some iced water. An adorable waiter saw my plight, giving me a delicious yoghurt drink, which helped soothe the burning.

Laurence was handsome, witty, and fun. Tabby has excellent taste in men. I give her that. If he had a downside, it would be his fascination with cars. He and Charlie discussed the subject long after we moved to a club near Leicester Square. By then, everyone else had grown more than a wee bit bored.

The club lay behind an anonymous-looking door with a burly commissionaire, the lone clue to what lay behind it. It was located in a loft accessed by climbing many narrow winding staircases. I was told there were over two hundred members, but I was sure they could not be accommodated if everyone appeared simultaneously. The small dancefloor made dancing a challenge, although we gave it a good try.

When I re-joined the party, plates of congealed corned beef hash sat on our table.

"Are you hungry?" I asked, confused. The food looked inedible and lay untouched.

"God, no." Charlie shook his head with a grimace. "I am not sure I'd eat that even if I were."

"It's in case of a raid," Laurence explained. "Clubs can stay open till half past midnight if they serve food, as this one does."

"Don't think I'd eat that, though," I said, turning up my nose.

"Can't say I blame you," Laurence said, smiling, "but you might need to. Place was raided last time I was here. We claimed we were diners, so we were obligated to eat the plates of cold slop, picking out the cigarette ends. The coppers knew but got such a kick out of watching they let us stay. I have a proposition. How do you two fancy watching me race this weekend?"

"Sounds like a great idea. What do you think?" Charlie asked me, his face showing delight. I didn't have the heart to refuse.

"Yes, that sounds great," I told him with an attempt at an enthusiastic smile.

Rain poured from the pewter sky on the day of the race. This weather was the last thing I wanted if we were outside spectating an event I hadn't the slightest interest in. We went over to Laurence's car on our arrival. To my dismay, it sat out in the open, not in a warm, dry garage. Undeterred by the foul weather, the men popped the bonnet and stared at the engine. Their discussion was focused on endless topics I did not understand, like torque, horsepower, and other incomprehensible gibberish.

Laurence's sister, Charlotte, shared my disinterest in matters automotive, so Lonnie and I chatted with her while car talk continued around us. Our umbrellas proved no use against the horrible wind blowing rain everywhere.

"I'd give absolutely anything to be in a nice warm—" I started saying.

"Whatever it is you were about to say, I will join you," Lonnie agreed through gritted teeth.

"Shall we visit the beer tent?" Charlotte asked.

"What a fantastic suggestion," Lonnie said with a hint of sarcasm. "I do wish you had mentioned it somewhat sooner."

We left Tabby feigning an automotive interest. Standing in a deluge watching cars race for hours on end lacked any appeal. Confident we would not be missed, we remained in the beer tent until Laurence's race. His was last, and he won by a considerable margin. The race was over before I discovered I had been cheering the wrong car. One racing car looks like another to me in mud and pouring rain. If I were responsible, I would insist cars be painted assorted colours, making telling one from the other much more straightforward.

Laurence's prize included a case of champagne, and a group descended on his house to help him drink it. As he was about to open the first bottle, he proposed a scavenger hunt with the champagne as the prize. The resulting cheer saw the challenge accepted.

A hush overtook the room while the competitors agreed upon the rules, every suggestion deliberated and voted on with a serious air. Reference was made to a previous hunt involving the prime minister's pipe where arguments raged over the authenticity of the pipes submitted. For avoidance of dispute, a complicated points system applied to each item based on the provenance provided. After a prolonged debate and many more drinks, everything was agreed upon. We arranged ourselves into nine teams, each with twenty items to collect before noon. Still drunk, we ran to our various cars, driving off into the night. It had stopped raining, yet one poor chap with a roofless roadster was forced to hire a cab for an hourly rate. His companion refused to countenance losing her hat and would not remove it.

"This list looks a mixture of rather simple and downright impossible," I told him, looking it over. "I don't know Lady Trevelyan, but don't you think she will mind drunken gangs descending on her garden collecting her lilies? Won't they be in a glasshouse? What if it is locked? It's quite dark. I do hope everyone is careful."

"They had better be, or Lady Trevelyan will arrange some nasty surprises. That might be tricky. As will the Martinware bird from Lord Young's collection. Well, it will be for me. That was Alfie's suggestion, purely vindictive on his part. Lord Young would have me whipped from his premises if he knew I was within a half-mile."

"Does Lord Young have a daughter?" I asked, guessing the reason he might feel that way.

"Two, in fact," he told me, tight-lipped.

"I see. Is there a chance we might borrow a Martinware bird from somewhere, then just say it came from Lord Young's collection?"

"Perhaps. Do you know anyone with a Martinware bird?"

"No," I admitted. "I don't know what they are."

"Porcelain birds, hideous objects. You would certainly know one if you saw one. Never mind, Watkins is friendly with Lord Young's valet. With most of the London valets, if I am truthful. I will stop here and make a call." He parked and ran into a telephone box.

"I know where to find an old newspaper and a hard-boiled egg," I told him when he got back into the car. "The multi-coloured candle shouldn't be too difficult, but where will we find a professional sporting trophy? Or a policeman's helmet, for that matter?"

"Well, I have some ideas, although right now, my thoughts are of a stuffed badger. I reckon a couple of chaps will have had the same thought. How about heading there first?"

There was Bacchants, his gentleman's club. I raised an eyebrow when he first mentioned it, but he claimed it was nothing like the Drones because it had no swimming pool. We cheered at the lack of opposition vehicles parked in the vicinity. He abandoned the car at the front door, running inside at full pelt. A few minutes later, Alfie's car flew into view, and he followed Charlie with a loud curse. I chatted with Lonnie on the steps while we waited for the boys.

Lonnie smoked two cigarettes before they reappeared, the flea-bitten mangy badger tucked under one arm declaring Charlie the victor. He ran to the car, where he handed me the spoils. For some long-forgotten reason, it wore cricket whites. I deposited it in the back, glad it was out of sight. He'd paid the steward to let him borrow it and would have been outside in minutes, but for the time it took to locate the key for the case. A bidding war erupted when Alfie arrived, won when Alfie conceded at a price Charlie would not disclose. I was not sure how much a case of champagne cost, but I could imagine him paying more. Not wanting to spoil the fun, I left the issue unpressed.

"Where next, Kitten? One of the high-value items?"

"How about the sports trophy," I told him, looking over the list. "Have you ever won a professional sports trophy, Cluitie?"

"No, my sporting prowess is average at best. However, I do know a chap who has, although he is most likely asleep." I looked at my watch. It had gone one. "His name is Sam Harding. He's a golfer. Have you heard of him?"

I shook my head.

"Golf isn't your thing, eh? He has won a few trophies.

Hopefully, he will loan us one. We can go there before it gets any later."

Sobering, we made our way to his friend's house, leaving with an impressive looking cup, promising we would look after it. We also borrowed some red and white candles we spotted on his chimneypiece.

"I have an idea about the jardinière," I told him as we returned to the car. "Three, in fact, although all currently occupied by some enormous aspidistras. We can try uprooting one, but if anything happened to any of Aunt Violet's houseplants, I think she would have us massacred. At the absolute least, we will hear it for the rest of our lives."

We went to my house, discovering Lonnie and Alfie had clearly had the same idea, as the smallest jardinières were missing. In a sporting fashion, they had left us the enormous mass of greenery that remained.

After some thought, we left it to last as I rushed to the pantry for an egg to boil, and Charlie went off to the coal store where old newspapers were kept for kindling. While the egg cooked, I retrieved a black feather from one of Lonnie's hats. Not wanting to waste time seeking the missing plant pot, we grabbed the monster one. We carefully placed it on the floor behind my seat in the car, the largest leaves alarmingly bent over at the top.

Lady Trevelyan had somehow caught wind of our treasure hunt, arranging for a servant to stand with a bucket of lilies at her front gate. Wanting to prevent foul play, or worse — damage to her remaining blooms — she gave strict instructions that he could provide a maximum of one flower for each team. I had not met her, but I loved how she accepted the spirit of the occasion. I felt sorry for the fellow, although while giving a cheerful smile, he informed me he received some handsome tips for his troubles. Other servants were patrolling the garden with no additional financial compensation. There were five left, leaving the flush chap with some waiting. The flower was beautiful, and I regretted not having any water for it.

We made some hours of satisfactory progress before realising how hungry we were. One of the items we needed was a tram ticket, and half an hour remained until they started running. Grateful for a rest, we went to a Corner House while we waited. The night-time basement crowd proved different from the daytime one, actors and musicians mixing with the area's well-known shady characters. The area known as the lily pond was busy, nippies deflecting couples towards different parts of the restaurant. We finished eating and jumped on the first tram we saw. We paid our fare, disembarked at the next stop, and walked back towards the car.

Despite having been awake for most of the night, the food gave us a much-needed boost to our energy. We spent some time crawling under bushes looking for a snail using the approaching dawn light and a cigarette lighter. We crawled about on hands and knees, lifting stones, and poking around piles of leaves. I was on the verge of admitting a grudging defeat when I found a sizeable stripy specimen, raising it in triumph. Muddied and tired, we made our way to the car, counting our efforts.

Pleased by our progress, we visited an address in Kensington to see another of Charlie's friends. He hoped he would provide us with a signed photograph of a West End actress, along with a corroborating programme. His valet showed us into a drawing room where framed pictures of actresses covered every wall. After five minutes, a young chap wearing a dressing gown over striped pyjamas joined us.

"Well, Moorfoot, what can I do for you at this unholy hour?"

His smile betrayed the ill-temper of his greeting. Charlie introduced us, him apologising for his pyjamaed state with a smile.

"I apologise for the rude awakening, old boy. I need to borrow one of your photographs, one of the signed ones."

"Borrow one? For how long?"

"Just for today, I will return it tonight, unharmed and unscratched."

"My photographs are incredibly precious and quite valuable. I don't think you are prepared to give me what I'd want for one," he said with a laugh.

"Surely you will not charge an old friend an arm and a leg for borrowing a photograph?"

"I must consider rental costs, and then there is the matter of a deposit. And, of course, insurance. I mean, look at the state of you both. You look as though you have been digging up potatoes. If there is so much as a dirty fingerprint, it will be ruined. God forbid, but if anything happened to it, how could I possibly replace it?"

"Fine," Charlie said with a sigh, reaching for his wallet. "How much do you want?"

"Come now, dear chap, what would make you think I want anything so gauche as money?"

The way he stared at me made me realise I might be what he wanted. I approached him and gave him a long, unhurried kiss.

"I believe that covers any rental fees," I told him. I placed my hand on his groin, giving a gentle rub through the thin material of his pyjamas, sparking an instant reaction. "Here is your deposit. You have my solemn word that if there is as much as a smudge on your photograph, then I will pay you in full at a time of your choosing. Is that agreeable?"

Without letting go of his cock, I looked him in the eye to see who would blink first. He did, nodding his agreement with a lascivious smile, on the proviso we both cleaned ourselves first. When scrubbed enough to pass inspection, I took a photo of Edna Best from him with care. We left, breaking into a run when the front door closed.

"Well done, Kitten."

"Thank you, but for goodness' sake, take care of that photo. Your friend seemed nice, but I'd be loathed to owe him anything."

"I will guard it with my very life," he said, kissing me with such passion I doubted his mind was on the treasure hunt anymore.

"Do we have time for this?" I asked, worried.

"Ah yes, you see, I have a confession. The remaining items are lying around my house. How about going straight there?"

"Sounds fantastic," I said with a smile as we ran to the car. I reread the list as we drove back. "Wait, how come you possess a policeman's helmet? Not to mention a street sign from the City of Westminster?"

"Signs of a misspent youth, I'm afraid."

We went to Charlie's house, finding that Watkins had done us proud. The Petty France street sign sat beside the helmet and a Martinware bird. The bird was a curious item, an ugly thing with a ferocious-looking beak that did not resemble any bird I knew. I could not for the absolute life of me see why anyone would want a collection of them.

Satisfied at completing our task with three hours until the deadline, we fell in each other's arms in a congratulatory embrace. We climbed the stair, kissing and undressing each other on the way. When we entered his bedroom, I became preoccupied with unbuttoning Charlie's trousers, so it was some time before I noticed Georges' painting hanging on the wall.

"Bloody hell, Cluitie. It's my painting. How the hell did you ever manage to get your hands on that?" I asked with a gasp.

"It's marvellous, isn't it? Are you surprised to see it? After you left, I spent the afternoon tracking every artist in St.

Tropez until I found the place. The fellow forced me into some hard bargaining, at first he was not for selling at any price." He stood behind me, an arm squeezing me as he kissed the top of my head. "I had no idea what to expect, but when I saw it, I was blown away. I locked myself in my cabin on the train home and just stared at it. I barely made it out for meals."

"I intended to go back and see Georges one more time. Your arrival put my promise clean out of my head. Poor Georges, he must think I abandoned him. I did, I suppose."

"He did seem disappointed you never came back. He hoped you still would. I had to convince him that you had already returned to England."

"I've never seen the finished painting. It was dingy in that studio, so this is the first time I have seen it in a good light. It is stunning. Even though it is quite stylised, you can plainly see that it is me with no clothes on. I cannot deny that no matter how beautiful it is. Georges told me he'd be incredibly careful whom he sold it to if I did not return for it."

"He was careful. I had to swear that I would remove body parts rather than cause you harm before he would agree to sell it. It took some persuasion and a few francs on my part. It was of no concern as I'd have paid whatever he asked."

"How much did you pay?"

"That is between Georges and me, but such beauty is worth every last penny."

"It is beautiful, isn't it? I cannot believe it is me."

"It is beautiful, yet it is nowhere near as beautiful as the real thing." He kissed my neck, slipping the strap of my slip over my shoulder.

"You do say the nicest things, Cluitie, but wait a minute, is the painting here permanently? What if the servants see it?" I said, having a sudden rush of embarrassment. "I could never look Watkins in the face again. Please tell me Watkins hasn't seen it."

"Don't worry, Kitten," he said with a conspiratorial smile. "I promise you it is our little secret and will be kept under lock and key in my chest."

He put his hands on my hips, running them up and down.

"I admire the way he captured your hips. How I adore these hips. I would willingly spend the rest of my life walking behind you so that I can observe those hips swaying. It is the absolute epitome of poetry in motion."

I liked hearing him talk in an appreciative way of my body, more so as it was a part I had always disliked.

He sat on the bed, pulling me across his lap with my back to him. He reached around me to take my breasts, flicking the nipples with a finger as he planted kisses on my neck. His cock grew harder, and I stroked it until fully erect, pressing myself against his lap while pushing him inside me.

Welcoming the fantastic experience of having him inside me again, I rocked myself back and forward on his cock. I arched my back, increasing the intensity of his thrusting to an electrifying level, making love under the watchful eye of the painting.

Fighting the temptation to sleep when we finished, we collected our items and headed to Laurence's house. We arrived with five minutes spare. Alfie greeted us, making no attempt at hiding his disappointment.

"What ho, old chap. For a time there, I thought you might not make it in time."

"Are you kidding? Not a chance would I miss this. How are things playing out?"

"Well, one team haven't returned to base yet. Word is they spent the night in the Vine Street cells after an unsuccessful attempt at stealing a street sign became an unsuccessful attempt at stealing a policeman's helmet."

Everyone made no secret of comparing their hauls, and we stood an excellent chance of winning. Tallying everyone's items proved a lengthy and solemn procedure, necessitating several drinks. Some submissions were rejected when they did not pass muster. A couple of eggs proved raw, and a shell contained mud but no snail.

With some gravitas, Laurence announced it a close-run race, a mere point between those at the top. He called the teams in reverse order, our names in second place. We lost to Charlotte and her partner by one point, which was a relief, although I pretended otherwise. I did not want to mention it, but while I like champagne, it gives me a horrendous hangover.

Considerable consternation erupted when a black feather submitted by Charlotte left tell-tale black stains on someone's fingers. A swift recount saw Charlie and I declared winners, with Tabby and Laurence promoted to second place. Charlotte had a sheepish expression when handing me the winner's bouquet made up from Lady Trevelyan's lilies. To my relief, Charlie insisted we open and share the champagne. Taking tiny sips, I made sure my glass lasted an absolute age as I celebrated our win.

Someone suggested we race the snails, everyone rushing to construct a racecourse on the wooden floor. The couple who submitted the empty shell hurried to the garden to find an inhabited replacement. They took some time, and when the course was completed, everyone piled outside to help them.

Finding a replacement became another game, punctuated by some cursing and scrambling in hedgerows. With a jubilant yell, Tabby waved her treasure. We rushed inside and released our snails. Rowdy spectators coaxed them on, some waving lettuce leaves. It was a slow yet tense race, with Alfie and Lonnie's snail declared the winner. Ours had no chance. The randy bugger deviated from its course from the off, busy attempting to fuck the snail on its left.

Chapter Sixteen: The High Life

One afternoon Bernie telephoned, asking if I would meet him for lunch. He told me he had to talk with me and insisted it must be done in person. We arranged to meet in a Wardour Street café that had resisted becoming a dress shop like many others in the street. I presumed they stayed because Bernie's patronage brought in considerable sums. His bills were extravagant and always charged to his newspaper. I arrived in good time, knowing he would most likely be late.

"Hello, gingersnap," he greeted me, not acknowledging the fact he had arrived twenty minutes after our appointment. "I presume you know why I asked to see you, apart from the added benefit of spending some time with my favourite red-head."

"Thank you, although I haven't the first idea why you want to see me."

"Why, it is all down to you, red riding hood," he said with an incredulous look. "You are quite the celebrity. You do realise you are the constant talk of the society columns? You have been for days!"

"Days? As long as that?" I asked, although my sarcasm was wasted. "Why are the society columns talking about me?"

"You don't know? Don't you read the papers?"

"Nobody does, Bernie. You know that." Experience told me the only people who cared about these columns were the people least likely to feature in them.

"Ouch, harsh but not true," he deadpanned, giving a nonchalant shrug as he lit a cigarette. "There are agencies who collect newspaper cuttings for the scrapbooks of those who desperately crave a feature in those papers. If your fame continues, you should consider enlisting the services of such an agency to ensure you are not being libelled without you noticing."

"Wait a minute," I said, spluttering. I had a sudden realisation. "Do you mean the columnists know I am with Charlie? Oh, please tell me they don't."

"Don't worry, autumn leaf, they have absolutely no idea who you are. All the talk is of the mysterious, beautiful red-headed stranger spotted at some recent social events. The problem for you is that every paper will want to be the one that unveils you, exclusively, of course. No doubt some will resort to no end of skulduggery if necessary."

"Oh, please no, if columnists start poking about, then they might find out . . . ." I paused while deliberating what I could say.

"You don't want the Duchess hearing about you two?" he asked, lowering his voice. I nodded, and he put his hand on my arm. "You don't want to upset the most high Duchess of Prigdom. I understand completely."

"Do you think they really don't know who I am?" I asked, concerned.

"Oh, copper kettle, it would be all over the papers if they knew. I am surprised the columnists have not followed you home so they can discover where you live. You haven't found yourself followed around by shadowy characters recently, have you?"

"Not that I know of."

"Sir Scuttlebutt started it, and everyone jumped on. I can't believe you haven't heard."

"Do you reckon someone found out about my affiliation with Charlie and are planning for a big revelation, having given me a great build-up first?"

"You are bloody perfect, spitfire," he said, giving an

approving look. "I admire the way you think. Have you ever thought about becoming a newspaper columnist? I do not think anyone knows just yet. With everyone on your trail, they'd be too worried about sitting on such juicy information as then there is the risk that someone else gets there first. I have a proposition for you. What do you say about me doing the great reveal and stealing their thunder? The Periodical gets the scoop, my position will be secured until I finish my novel and interest in you will die down a shade."

"It sounds a clever idea, but you do know you can't tell anyone about Charlie and me."

"My little damson in distress, I solemnly promise you, if anyone does get wind of what goes on between you two, they will not have heard it from me. I am not doing this to ruin anyone's life."

"I don't know. There are still people I would hate to think badly of me. If they read about me attending nothing but fancy parties and balls, they might disapprove."

The newspapers Dad read did not contain society pages. Despite that, news of my high living might still reach his ears, and I worried he would be disappointed.

"You don't want the strict Presbyterian father hearing about your lapses in propriety, eh?" he asked, his eyes springing open at the sniff of a story.

"Dad hasn't set foot in a church for years. There's no story there, Bernie."

"Don't worry, strawberry shortcake, I am discretion incarnate. Once the piece is out there, then everyone will be forced to look elsewhere for their next salacious tittle-tattle."

Dawson brought the Periodical to my room when the article was published. I flicked through until I found his column, which included my photograph. I had no idea where he acquired it from, although it was a flattering one.

The Mysterious Redhead

The Periodical can exclusively reveal the identity of the mysterious redhead who has stolen the hearts of London society. The flame-haired beauty is Miss Alice Fraser, daughter of Lady Mary Fraser and Dr. Alasdair Fraser. The answer to where she has been hiding until now is Scotland!

The Scottish air clearly did wonders for her as this bonnie lass has many admirers vying for her attention. All in vain, it seems as no one has yet claimed this fair maiden's hand. It appears she is too busy enjoying the culture London offers. She is a close friend of Tabby Harrington and, of course, possesses her invitation to the incredibly exclusive Gothic Ball next week. The lucky invitees are in for a treat, as with her wit, charm, and stunning beauty, she is undoubtedly an asset to any party she chooses to attend.

I liked reading these lovely things, although I blushed at the exaggerations he made for his readers. The mention of Tabby's ball made me smile. Having spent a whirlwind few weeks following Laurence around Europe, Tabby announced she and he were no longer a thing. The time he spent racing did not leave enough time for her. I was disappointed, although Charlie could not understand what she was thinking. In an attempt at recovering from the loss and rediscovering her misplaced effervescence, Tabby decided she would host a spectacular gothic ball.

Invitations were rare and highly prized. Each one featured a personalised entrance number and was hand-delivered. The unsuccessful could not admit failing to feature on the guest list, citing previous unescapable arrangements. The gossip columnists fell over themselves for an invitation. Numerous tricks, some Machiavellian in their deviousness, had been pulled in vain. No one possessing an invite would relinquish it at any cost. Bernie was the only columnist invited, and he did not turn down any opportunity to let everyone know.

On the night of the party, a few photographers waited at the gates outside Tabby's house. Thinking on his feet, Charlie instructed the driver to turn into a side street and got out. He remained there until I had been dropped off at the house, and the driver returned for him. He found the attention bothersome, although I thought it exciting, feeling a bit like a film star.

Bernie devoted an entire column to Tabby's party, occupying the whole page. Gloating, he described the attendees and a few publishable events. The article was littered with photographs, including a nice one featuring Charlie and Tabby standing together. In a clever bluff, he invited his readers to consider their financial worth if they married. I owed him a huge thank you for his valiant attempt at throwing fellow journalists off our scent.

Invites for various functions dropped through my letterbox. I could choose from balls, exhibitions, opening nights, and many parties, each with a theme or location more outlandish than the other. I worried they came because of my affiliation with Charlie, despite our efforts at secrecy. News of our reunion had been kept to a select group. We could not attend public events together, although some invitations proved too good to miss.

While the great revelation reduced the articles, columnists continued reporting on me. They claimed to have seen me on many occasions, some of which were genuine. At times, I attended two or three on the same evening. I made sure I was seen arriving at events with a succession of men. Various friends escorted me to the door, handing me over to Charlie once inside, making me feel like a hostage in a spy story.

On a few occasions, I found myself across the room from him. Pretending we did not know each other became a game, avoiding anyone catching us making eyes at each other. We developed secret signals we performed so we could let the other know our thoughts without drawing attention. A scratch of the nose meant the person we were with was boring us, rubbing the right eye indicated time for bed, and tugging the ear meant let's go home and fuck.

One afternoon Charlie decided he would teach me to play tennis. I proved hopeless, no matter how I tried. Laughing, he told me teaching me to drive had been less painful. It was a relief when I was finally able to make contact with the ball during my serve. No matter how he instructed me to return a ball with my racquet, I considered merely reaching it in time a massive achievement. I remain a dedicated, loyal spectator. I still adored the sport and had gained an increased admiration for the skill of the players. By way of making amends for his failed attempts at coaching me, he announced a surprise. Rather delightfully, he hinted it might be a new lesson.

I squealed on hearing this thrilling news, excitement building as we neared his home. He told me it was certain he would learn more from the experience than me but gave me no more clues. A sizable amount of time had passed since our last lesson, and I felt sure it would be good.

As I entered his bedroom, I was greeted by Jolly, my erstwhile dance partner. He was waiting in the middle of the room, completely naked. I presumed Charlie had something other than us dancing together in mind. Now I could see Jolly unclothed, I considered the possibility. His thickset muscular body looked as though he played much sport.

"Why, it is you, Jolly. I see you are — I mean, hello," I said, not being in the habit of addressing nude men in my lover's bedroom.

"Oh, erm, er, I mean, what ho. It's terrific seeing you again." He gave a nervous, self-conscious laugh, unsurprising considering the circumstances.

"It is good seeing you, too," I said, stopping myself from

giggling.

I could not help staring at his cock. Tabby had not conveyed quite how well he was endowed. Despite its relaxed state, it looked enormous. He saw me looking, and his cheeks reddened.

"Jolly here is rather taken with you, and he has told me how he very much regrets sleeping through his opportunity to make love at the party. I benefitted greatly from that and owe him a huge debt of gratitude. He would like a second chance at the experience, and I cannot get the idea out my mind of spectating while you make love to another man once more."

I considered it for a moment. At first, I felt cross at not making love to Charlie, although Jolly looked at me with a pleading expression, resembling a human Labrador puppy. Telling him he must dress and leave would be cruel. After all, he had gone to the bother of undressing, allowing me to give the prospect a thorough evaluation. It did look an interesting one.

"I think, under the circumstances, it would be rude not to."

Giving Charlie a kiss, I turned my back, allowing him to unzip my dress. It fell to the floor, Jolly's cock responding with a definite twitch. I grew wetter and wetter contemplating what we were about to do. As I removed my slip and stood naked, I took in the beautiful and rather impressive sight of his cock reacting to the view.

Giving him a smile, I took his hand and led him towards the bed, pushing him flat on his back. I straddled his waist, and he sat up to bury his face between my breasts, kissing each one. He massaged my bottom in a gentle way that came as a surprise. All the while, that enormous cock continued growing at an alarming rate. While sucking my breast, he moved one hand up my thigh, instigating a pleasant sensation by rubbing the side of my pearl with a thumb.

Curious, I stole a glance at Charlie, who sat on an armchair at the end of the bed. He stared, fascinated at the scene unfolding before him. Giving him a wink, I pushed Jolly back and shuffled down the bed until I could take his impressive cock in my mouth. I'd choke if I even attempted accommodating it, so decided I would concentrate on the head as it grew more substantial.

Moving back up, I guided him inside me, easing myself on his cock, scared that going too quickly might hurt. Jolly provided a welcome distraction by leaning forward to nibble my breasts. Taking my time, I slipped down at a comfortable pace until he filled me to absolute capacity. I felt no pain, although Jolly gave a low groan that made me worry that I was hurting him. I loved the sensation of ampleness, convinced I could not accommodate a fraction of an inch more.

He fell back on the bed with another pained groan, grabbing my hips. We lay thrusting into each other for a few minutes until he palmed my cheek and turned my face towards Charlie, who watched us with an expression of intent, rubbing his cock through his trousers. I bounced upon Jolly's cock, reaching to stroke his face.

Jolly took my nipples between his fingers and thumbs, squeezing them hard. My climax engulfed me, and I yelped at the suddenness. I grabbed his neck as he ejaculated inside me, staring at Charlie the entire time. He looked back with a lust-filled look and a captivating smile.

As Jolly withdrew from me, I collapsed onto him in a happy stupor. He lifted me off him and kissed my cheek, giving me an earnest look.

"Thank you for an amazing experience. Laid an egg at the party, think that jolly well makes up for it, what?"

"Thank you, too. I enjoyed myself immensely."

He blushed again as he jumped from bed and started dressing.

"Are you leaving us so soon?" I asked with some surprise.

"Why, yes. I have played my part. Thanks again, by gum, you are such a good sport. You really are the bee's knees, you know."

He nodded at us both and left the room.

Charlie lay beside me, taking me in an embrace. "Did you enjoy that Kitten?" he asked, nuzzling my neck.

"Yes, it was completely delicious. And you, Cluitie?"

"Goodness, yes. Absolute privilege. While I watched, I felt myself getting so aroused I had to remind myself I could not take part," he said with a faraway look at the recollection.

"You should have," I said with a wink.

"No, going by what you said, the point was to be a spectator rather than participant. Besides, I promised Jolly, no matter what. It seemed the only way I could persuade him."

"You know what they say about promises and piecrusts. Ah, well, perhaps next time," I said without thinking.

"Ah, there may be a next time? In that case, I might teach Jolly a little of the art of seduction. I told him he should be ready to make love to you. I had no idea he'd be naked."

We giggled as he kissed me. Before I knew it, we were grinding our bodies against each other. We kissed with a new hunger until he deviated to kiss my stomach all the way to my pearl. I shivered as he applied his fantastic light touch, lapping with increasing ferocity until I found myself climaxing with a violent shudder.

I pondered what tasting another man on me would be like, yet again, he did not mind. He lay on top of me and took my arms, pinning them above my head with one hand, using the other to penetrate me. Without warning, he withdrew his fingers, sticking his cock inside me with some power and great urgency. He thrust into me with full force as I raised my hips to meet him. We held hands from beginning to end, my legs wrapped around him, sharing long kisses, holding each other close. It became our steamiest sex ever.

Chapter Seventeen: Separation

Blinded by my happiness, I could not foresee anything going wrong. I knew from the warnings I had received from the beginning that our affiliation would have to end before it became too serious. For the moment, I was keeping that prospect out my thoughts. This strategy proved a glorious failure, as I discovered earlier than I expected.

I was playing a gramophone record when my world fell around me. Jenkins informed me that the Duchess of Cyneset was asking for me. I jumped up and switched off the gramophone while she swept into the room as a queen surveying her kingdom and finding it wanting.

"Miss Fraser," she said, looking as though articulating my name engendered pain.

"Good evening, Your Grace. I had no idea you would be paying me the compliment of a visit. May I get you anything, some tea, perhaps?" I blurted.

"No, thank you, this is not a social visit. One will not be staying long," she said with a grimmer expression than the first time I saw her. "It is our manner to get straight to the point. It has recently come to our attention that Charles has been walking out with you," she said with unabashed asperity.

"Yes, in a way, but . . ."

"That was not a question. It needed no affirmation. One will continue without hindrance, if you please. Now, it would be an affront to your intelligence, which we assume you are in some possession of, not to be completely frank with you from the off. One would think you aware that your familial relations leave you far from worthy of any connection with Charles. Your father surely cannot approve of any such pretension on your part. Is he aware of the ridiculous association between you two?"

"No, Your Grace."

"That you would conceal this from him shows you understand how poorly this connection would be seen. This would certainly be one of the very few times one would be in accord with your father."

Her mention of Dad and presuming to speak for him awoke my forthright side. My body tensing, I found I could not let her continue unchallenged any longer.

"I believe my father would tell me I should follow my heart to be with the man I love. He married my mother purely because he loved her. He cares not for ideas of rank and nobility."

"The wife of the Duke of Cyneset must care about ideas of rank and nobility. You may think such an attachment will increase your social standing. Those who are aware will realise your inferiority immediately. You will never find yourself accepted in the circles that matter. Nobility comes with responsibility, something your kind does not appreciate while always having a good time and letting others brunt the cost."

I wondered if *your kind* meant socialists like Dad or women like me, although I decided against asking for clarification. Long before I met the Duchess, I expected someone would tap me on the shoulder and explain that a terrible mistake had been made. My remarkable life belonged to someone else and must end without notice. This was my fear, alive in living and fire-breathing reality.

"If you care for Charles, you will end this ridiculous affiliation and allow him to devote his attention towards finding a wife worthier of his station."

She paused, and I took my opportunity to speak, trying to stay calm. My fingers clenched so tight my nails stabbed my palms. I did not draw blood, although the indentations remained visible for some time after.

"I am the daughter of a lady, and I believe I am worthy of his attention. Charles clearly believes so, too. He loves me, and I love him."

"Love," she said with a laugh and a horrible sneer. "What Charles feels for you is merely a temporary infatuation. You are far from his first, and you can be certain you will not be the last. Your sort is good for nothing more than allowing nobility the opportunity to sow their wild oats. Do not think this shabby affiliation could ever be anything more. You may have enchanted Charles into thinking he will be with you, even marry you, although he will recover his senses long before that ever happens. It will leave you quite publicly jilted. Is that what you want? One will take one's leave. One has made our feelings extremely clear and cannot expect any rebuttal worthy of attention. Goodbye, Miss Fraser."

She left me reeling as I considered her words. Dismissing her as a crabbit old witch was tempting, although I recognised some truth in what she said. I was not good enough for Charlie, and that was something I could never change. Despite what I'd told the Duchess, I doubted Dad would give his approval. I was inhabiting a Jane Austen novel, although I abandoned hope of seeing the happy conclusion that awaited Elizabeth Bennett.

An hour later found me playing records and drinking large measures of gin. I replayed the exchange, thinking up all the things I wished I had said. A footman interrupted my melancholy to inform me Charlie was asking for me. We had no arrangement to meet, although I knew why he was here. Being prewarned did not make things any easier. Charlie entered wearing a grave expression. "Always" was playing on the gramophone, setting a sombre mood for a song I loved.

"You look solemn. Whatever's the matter?" I asked. I did not know if he knew that his mother had visited me and felt in no hurry to relate the details. He kissed me in a perfunctory, distracted manner.

"Please sit down, Kitten. I have something I must ask you."

I could not understand why he said ask me when he meant tell. I sat beside him, trying to keep calm, knowing this conversation would be unpleasant.

"My mother has discovered we are together. She looks unfavourably on your family and even less favourably upon us being together. Her quest for a way to separate us appears to have resulted in the perfect plan. She has decided we will spend time with her sister, my Aunt Catherine, in Southampton."

"That is not far from Foxcotte House, isn't it?"

"No, Southampton in New York State—my Uncle John is an American. My aunt is recovering from terrible injuries suffered in an accident. My mother will be visiting them. It was made quite clear that if I do not accompany her, I will be left penniless."

"How long will you be gone?"

"Six months, I'm afraid," he told me, and my heart sank. "We leave next Monday, at noon."

"So soon? Your mother is determined to separate us, isn't she?"

"Yes, I am afraid she is," he said, giving me a sad smile. "She insisted I stop seeing you immediately or else permanently forgo my allowance. I was left in no doubt whatsoever that her threat will be carried out."

Here it was, the ending I knew would come. I'd hoped this particular day would be some way away. Swallowing the growing lump in my throat, I gathered myself to say the

185

words I had to say so I could avoid prolonging my agony.

"I think it would be for the best if we permanently parted," I said, to save him having to.

"Why on earth would you say that?" he asked with a confused, wounded look.

I could not understand why he was making it difficult. We knew our affiliation was ill-fated, yet had hoped avoiding any discussion would make our problems go away. The strategy failed, and this was clear and painful evidence. I took a deep breath and swallowed, fighting the lump forming in my throat.

"The most dreadful wrong I could possibly commit is coming between you and your mother. The tie between mother and child is imperative. I wish more than anything Mum was here. I miss her terribly. The idea that someone could come between us is unthinkable. I have no idea what I would do if she told me to stop seeing you, although I think that is a moot point. She would be fond of you, I am sure. I never heard her speak ill of anyone. Nevertheless, if you disobey your mother, it will drive an irreparable wedge between you. I could not live with knowing I were the cause."

"No, Kitten, please. I love you, and I know now that I always have. I suppressed my feelings before, but it made me miserable. Every time we met, I fell deeper and deeper for you. Eventually, I realised I would continue to be miserable if I did not spend every last minute that I have on this earth with you. I tried staying away and turning you away, but I could not. You captured my mind and my heart, and I surrendered completely. I cannot enjoy myself if I go anywhere and you are not there. I see beautiful women, and I have no thoughts of bedding them. You have domesticated me, and I believe the effects are permanent. I came to ask if you will reconsider my offer of marriage."

He looked pained, his eyes brimming with tears, as were

mine. What he said moved me, but I had to harden my heart to harden his. Taking a deep breath, I readied myself for what I was about to say.

"Please do not, because it is time you knew that I do not love you. I have great fun with you, and I will fuck you again and again at the drop of a hat. Let me know where and when you desire me, and I will be there. I will always want you, but I cannot and will not marry you, so there is no point in you giving up anything for me."

I looked him in the eye, thinking it might disguise my lie, but saw nothing but pain on his face. He looked as though he had received an unexpected stomach punch, stunned and perplexed. I looked away, unable to bear seeing him upset. Blinking, I hoped he did not see the tears I held back.

"You do not love me?" he asked, his voice unsteady.

I detested myself for causing his pain. I longed to stop the lie, hug him, and tell him the truth. Despite my doubts, I knew I was doing the right thing.

"No, Charlie, I do not. I never told you I did." The last part was genuine. Although I'd yearned to say it, those words would not pass my lips. It might have been because, deep down, I knew this moment would come. His look of betrayal broke my heart.

"I see I have misread our situation terribly. I had the damned silly idea you felt the same way I do. I did not realise the idea of marrying me without money would be so abhorrent to you." He stood. "I must thank you for your honesty. I should go before I make even more of a fool of myself than I already have. I will trouble you no more. Goodbye, Alice."

"Charlie," I called. He was already opening the door. When it closed, I walked to the gramophone. The record had long ended, the stuck needle hissing and clicking. I took the record and smashed it against the cabinet, certain I would not want to hear that song again. Unable to believe what I had done, I rushed to my bedroom and fell apart at the seams. The pain on his face etched itself onto my brain, and I could not stop seeing the hurt in his expression. I cried myself to sleep, feeling lost and confused.

The next thing I knew was Lonnie entering my room the following morning.

"Is it true?" she demanded, with a horrid, angry tone in her voice. "Did you really tell Charlie the two of you are finished? Did he really ask for your hand in marriage, and did you really turn him down?" Her face showed total confusion.

"Yes, it's true. I did." I sank into my pillow at the horror of the memories.

"Are you screwy? Off your nut? Have you gone insane? Lost your fucking mind? What the fuck were you fucking thinking?"

"I think I have lost my mind," I told her while the horrible events of the previous evening marched back into my mind. "Wait, how do you know this?" I said, sitting up.

"Because Alfie and I spent the entire night trying our absolute damnedest to comfort an utterly inconsolable Charlie."

"You have? Really? I didn't think he'd take everything so badly."

I knew she must be exaggerating. He had looked pained, although, in the cold light of day, he should see it was necessary.

"Badly? He is beyond shattered, heartbroken. We have never seen him like it. To think Alfie worried that Charlie would break your heart, and you have gone and broken his."

"Do you think Alfie will cut off my testicles?"

"I will repeat my question. What the fuck were you thinking?" she asked, ignoring my attempt at a terrible joke.

"The Duchess is determined that we must be separated. She paid me the honour of a visit yesterday."

"She did? Damn her bloody eyes. What did she say?"

"She made it incredibly clear that I was not fit for her son. She is taking him to America for six months."

"You will not fight for him, wait for him? I do not understand." She looked incredulous.

"Of course, I'd bloody wait. I would wait forever, but I cannot. She told him he would be cut off without a penny. I cannot be responsible for coming between them."

"Oh, sweetie, you must stop putting others before yourself. If Charlie decided you are more important to him than his mother or allowance, then why the hell would you argue with him?" She put her arm around me. "I thought you were happy together. He is undeniably devoted to you, and you are obviously besotted with him. I do not understand. Isn't you two being together what you wanted?"

"Yes, it is. I have been deliriously happy. He has been all I ever wanted since the first time I saw him. He is all I want."

"It is impossible to roll my eyes high enough to express how stupid you are being right now. Why the hell would you pass up this chance of happiness?"

"Lonnie, I am a doctor's daughter who attended the village school with the children of farmworkers. I was brought up thinking that being rich was a sign of excessive greed and something people should be ashamed of. Dad will disown me if he thinks I am even entertaining the idea of marrying someone with a title. I have a Scottish accent. I use Scottish words no one understands and regularly make grammatical errors. I never came out. I still have no idea what cutlery I should use. I am constantly petrified I might call things by the wrong name. I am unquestionably not cut out to be a marchioness, far less a duchess someday. I am the type you are supposed to fuck, not the type you marry. As I am constantly reminded, I lack the necessary pedigree for that."

"Some of that nonsense can be learned, some no longer

matters in this day and age, and the rest? Who honestly gives a fuck?"

"Her Grace certainly does. She made it perfectly clear my inferiority would make me a poor and shunned duchess, leaving me incapable of performing my duties. That might frighten me more if I knew what duties a duchess has," I said with a slight smile, despite myself.

"As far as I know, it involves getting funding for your pet projects, cutting ribbons, opening fêtes, sitting on committees, presenting prizes, attending long formal dinners, and endless waving with a fixed smile on your face. I am sure you would manage without much trouble. You get on with people, though, which might be considered an impediment. Aloofness is an essential quality. You must learn the ways of the utterly bogus. You then engage in massive one-upmanship, having the biggest occasions with the most impressive guest lists catered by staff you poached from your competitors. The smug sense of certainty of your superiority would definitely be a problem for you."

"None of that sounds like me. Charlie and I are from two completely different worlds."

"Now that is absolute bollocks, and you know it. Look at your mother and father. They came from vastly divergent backgrounds and loved each other deeply. Were they not happy together?"

"Totally. They were devoted to each other. Dad has still not come to terms with Mum's death. I cannot help thinking that if they'd never married, I wouldn't be in this mess."

"Sweetheart, if they'd never married, you wouldn't be here to be in this mess or any mess, for that matter."

"Perhaps that might be for the best."

She pulled me towards her. "Darling, don't say that. Do not dare even think it. You are a gorgeous person, and we adore having you. You are a breath of fresh air around here, and we all love you. Regardless of you thinking yourself unworthy, Charlie loves you very much."

"I know he does, and I love him very much too. You know that is why I must let him go." The tears I was fighting won the battle, and I burst out crying again. Yet again, the tears came without stopping until I was a pathetic, weeping wretch. Lonnie handed me her handkerchief, holding me until I sobbed all the fluid out of my body.

CHAPTER EIGHTEEN: SUBMISSION

When Monday arrived, my mood kept fluctuating between extremes. At times, I felt relieved that Charlie was out of the country, and I would be at no risk of encountering him by accident for six months. At other times, I felt heartbroken that Charlie was out of the country, and I would be at no risk of encountering him by accident for six months.

For a fortnight, I spent every day alone in my room, leaving only to fulfil my NWCU obligations. I saw no good reason for altering this arrangement.

Lonnie had other ideas. For a few days, she left me alone as I requested, but she decided one afternoon my moping must end. Trying her utmost to occupy my mind, she planned an extravagant evening on the town for us. Any other time I would leap at the chance. I did not feel up to it now. I told her I thought I might be coming down with something, but she was having none of it.

Tabby arrived, declaring herself famished and insisting on whisking us off for lunch at Primo, her favourite Italian restaurant. Unable to comprehend why I had never been before, she professed it the most authentic Italian food outside Italy, assuring me everything on the menu was both ingenious and delicious. Despite her praise, I felt disinclined to join her. The louder I protested, the more she would not take no for an answer. Defeated, I prepared for socialising.

Primo was in Greek Street, and Luciano, the owner, greeted Tabby as though long-lost family. He walked with a distinct limp, which was the result of an injury sustained fighting for the British army during the War. Smiling, he kissed us on each cheek, whisking us upstairs to a private alcove. The rooms on that floor had only been open for a few weeks. Until he acquired them, they had been hired out to ladies of the night, morning, or afternoon.

"Never mind the food. He is quite a dish himself," Lonnie commented as we followed him. Our group, Tabby in particular, considered war veterans prehistoric. I saw why she might make an exception. He was a handsome man with a happy smile, his jet-black hair flecked with grey at the temples.

"Don't go getting any ideas," Tabby whispered. "He is tragically devoted to his wife and not the slightest bit interested in assignations behind her back. That is accurate information garnered through a combination of first-hand experience and repeated reports of failure. Confounded luck in finding the world's solitary monogamous Italian."

He showed us to our seats, smiling the entire time. "Now, fanciulle," he said, clapping his hands. "Welcome to Primo, where you will find the finest Italian food in London. Real Italian food now, not French food masquerading as Italian," he said with a grimace, placing our menus in our hands with a flamboyant wave.

"Such a pity," Lonnie murmured, watching him leave the room. "If the sway of those hips is any guide, then I bet he is sheer dynamite between the sheets." We watched him in appreciative silence, considering the possibility.

Tabby winked at me as he took our order and asked him in an innocent tone when he would put spaghetti Bolognese on his menu. He moaned and clutched his heart in response, a pained expression on his face.

"Now, Signorina Tabby, why do you upset me so? You know, no matter how many times I am asked, I refuse to add such a dish. Doing so would only insult my Bolognese mama, may God rest her soul," he said, crossing himself.

We shared a fonduta, one of the most delicious things I ever tasted. With delightful food and company, I started feeling human again.

As we ate, Tabby gently asked if I wanted to talk about Charlie, curious about why I ended things. I related the Duchess' visit and the aftermath in all the horrible detail I could remember. I did get a wee bit maudlin when describing how I denied loving him, although I explained everything without crying.

"I believe I understand your motivations, although I still think you didn't need end your affiliation quite so bluntly," Lonnie said, shaking her head.

"Perhaps you are right. I hate myself for having done it. I did not know how else to end things. Everyone kept telling me that he would become bored with me eventually. I suppose I wished to end things before he did. I do think I might have acted rather hastily, though. I do miss him. We were never going to be together forever, although we might have had a few good years, I suppose. Also, I resent doing what his mother insisted. She won, as she had her way. That is annoying."

"Part of me wants you two to marry so you can spite the old dragon," Lonnie said, smiling at the idea.

"Part of me wants that, too," I confirmed.

"Understand completely, heard she is a horrible piece of work, and this confirms it." Tabby nodded.

"You've never met her?"

"God, no," she said, shaking her head. "Not in the same circle at all, no title, new money, as Father come from absolutely nothing. Staff did not always live in. The family were wrong religion, although they never set foot in a church. She has no time for my type."

"You have no idea how envious I am," I said with a

genuine smile.

"As am I, believe me. Any antipathy you feel towards her is richly deserved." Lonnie nodded her agreement.

"Sorry to bring you both down with talk of my worries." I apologised.

"Don't worry," Tabby said, putting her arm around me. "No doubt roles will be reversed someday. May well need you for the same one day. Are you going home and moping or staying out to let loose?"

"I think I might go home," I told her.

"Oh, no, poodle, you absolutely must come," Lonnie insisted. "The gang will be there, and it is so wrong seeing you staying inside pining. Bugger that. Besides, Layton and Johnstone are playing tonight. Need I say more?"

"Layton and Johnstone, how could I possibly say no?" I said, trying to sound enthused, although doing a terrible job. The thought of them playing *Always* saw a horrible panic set in. I did not think I could listen to that song again without awakening many awful memories.

"You have locked yourself away for long enough. I know you want to go home and wallow in your sorrows. Why don't you try drowning them in alcohol instead?"

"At least take them for a bloody good swim?" Tabby added.

"I know you're right," I said with a sigh.

"You are bloody right we are right. There is no acceptable reason why you ought not temporarily lose yourself in an orgy of sex, drugs, booze, and dancing, not necessarily in that order. You absolutely positively must get back up on the horse, metaphorically speaking."

"Yes, think it is well and truly time you acquired yourself a damn good fuck. Last thing you want is becoming a cancelled stamp," Tabby agreed.

They had a point. I did miss having sex. That was

undeniable. Pursuing a new lover might prove a good distraction from contemplating what I'd thrown away. Georges proved an exciting diversion when Charlie and I were separated. Despite myself, I smiled at the idea of having sex for the first time in an age.

"A good fuck does sound incredibly inviting right now," I conceded. "I might be doomed to live a life without love, yet I cannot and will not live without passion," I exclaimed, posing with my wrist on my forehead mimicking a ham actor from a bad movie.

"Exactly. Let us go and procure you an umbrella before you change your mind," Tabby said, standing.

"Procure me a what?" I asked. It had not been raining.

"An umbrella, a fellow you can borrow for the evening," Lonnie explained.

"That sounds fabulous. Why not?" I said, enthused at the idea and apathetic about whom they paired me with. I acquired a new determination to fuck someone, no matter what quantity of booze or coke I needed to manage it without thinking about Charlie.

We paid Luciano a reasonable four shillings each, leaving a good tip. Despite myself, my excitement built while we waited for Layton and Johnstone. Tabby excused herself and was away so long I worried she would miss the start, but she returned with a smile and minutes to spare. I attempted to enjoy it without worrying what songs they might perform. They did not play *Always,* which was quite a relief. Lonnie confessed later that Tabby visited them backstage, tipping them a considerable amount to drop the song from their set.

The show ended, and we headed into darkest Soho to a club in Gerrard Street. The street was full of revellers and the ladies who plied their trade there, everyone ignoring the old man with the placards saying Hell awaited them. We received a few propositions before we reached the front door, Tabby informing potential customers they could not afford us.

My recollection of subsequent events is hazy. However, I do remember dancing with any man who asked me. Towards the end of the evening, spurred on by Tabby, I talked to a stranger I found attractive. He was tall, with honey-blond hair, a short moustache, and incredible deep brown eyes. He did not remind me of Charlie in any way, and I aimed to make the most of this fortuitous opportunity.

"My dear, I have just realised I do not know your name," he said with a charming smile as we walked towards the door at the end of the night.

"It's Alice, Alice Fraser."

"Hello, Miss Fraser. My name is Edmund Clevedon." He held out his hand, shaking mine in a formal manner.

"Hello, Mr. Clevedon. Please call me Alice. May I call you Edmund?"

"Of course," he said, giving me a strange half-smile.

"Do you have arrangements for the rest of this beautiful evening, Edmund?"

"The rest of the evening? The rest of this beautiful evening is this morning."

"It is only just past three. The night still very much lies before us," I said, waving my hands in an attempt at indicating the endless possibilities.

"I fear you may already have consumed enough for one evening. May I see you home?"

"I'd prefer seeing you home," I told him, trying to sound seductive, my drunken mind devising a plan of seduction. I needed to feel desired by someone, and this gentleman might be persuaded to help fulfil my need. We continued our conversation on our way outside. The night air gave an unwelcome reminder of the amount I had drunk. I wobbled, although my companion held my arm to steady me.

"Whoops, my brain has lost all idea of the geographical

location of my feet," I said with a giggle. He gave me a polite smile, which faded in an instant as he strode along the street to hail a cab. He asked where I lived, although I did not plan to tell, compelling him to take me home with him.

It became evident my plan worked when I woke in an unfamiliar bed. Lifting the covers, I found I was wearing my slip, although I had no recollection of much beyond entering the cab. The light was dim, and I struggled to distinguish the time from the clock on the bedside table. I opened the curtains, screwing my eyes as bright daylight hit my eyeballs. Blinking, I peeped outside again. The window overlooked the backs of whitewashed terraced houses with well-tended yet tiny gardens. My bag and shoes had been placed on a chair, and my dress hung in an otherwise empty wardrobe. I would be incapable of this tidiness without help and presumed my host had helped me undress. Judging by the bedclothes, he did not appear to have slept there with me.

I dressed and checked my appearance in the looking glass, setting eyes on a tired, hungover woman. Combing my hair and rubbing at mascara smudges with my handkerchief did not help. I had no thoughts of what I would do, although my initial reaction was running away and hiding in my bedroom for a few years. My plans were dashed when I reached the landing and encountered a footman standing at the foot of the stairs.

"Would you like me to send some hot water up with a maid, miss?"

"Yes, please," I said, retreating into the room.

Escaping unnoticed was no longer an option. If I had no choice but to face my host, I felt I must look presentable, if possible. A maid entered the room, asking if I would like some aspirin and a glass of water. I accepted with gratitude. When she returned, I washed my face while she brushed my hair, offering me a loan of a dress to wear so she could press what I had on. I agreed, even though my dress did not look too crumpled, and she brought me a dainty blue day dress. I wondered how Edmund possessed such a thing, although I thought remaining ignorant would be best. Having my needs met in this way did look like a well-rehearsed scenario. I presumed I might not be the first unaccompanied female guest to stay overnight.

I reached the stairs and found the valet standing in the same spot.

"Mister Clevedon is in the dining room. He would be delighted if you would join him," he stated, his face impassive.

"I'd be happy to." What could I say?

Edmund stood as I entered the room. "Good afternoon. How are you?"

A footman stood beside him, causing me to hesitate before answering. "Good afternoon. I am well, thank you, and you?"

"I am in fine fettle, thank you. Please join me," he said as the footman moved the chair for me. "Are you hungry?"

I asked for toast and jam with some tea. The footman disappeared to fulfil my order, and I decided to come clean.

"You are a perfect host, but I fear I am a poor guest, and I am a little embarrassed."

"Now, why would you be embarrassed?"

"I am afraid I might have made rather a fool of myself last night."

"Not at all. You were most charming."

"Did we, you know?" I asked, uncertain.

"Why sadly, no," he said with a smile.

I gave what I hoped was an internal sigh of relief that further elaboration was unnecessary.

"You enjoyed yourself a fair bit last night, and it would be most ungentlemanly for me to take advantage."

"I should thank you. Not everyone would be so chivalrous, I think."

"Perhaps, perhaps not." He smiled, but it had no warmth.

"I hope I didn't say or do anything inappropriate. If that is the case, then I apologise unreservedly."

"You have nothing to apologise for," he said with a smile, but I could not be sure I believed him. A slight raise of an eyebrow made me presume it was unlikely that was the case. In all likelihood, I'd said or done something. I assumed him too much of a gentleman to say.

The toast arrived, reminding me how hungry I was. After I had eaten a few bites and sipped some tea, I felt more relaxed. Edmund proved more interested in asking me questions than saying much himself. Questions, however innocuous, were batted away with a retaliatory question. His neutral expression was disconcerting, neither frowning nor smiling at any point.

After I had changed back into my own freshly pressed dress, he offered to drive me home, refusing my objections. The silent journey back was broken when he reached my house. He stopped the car and told me he had enjoyed my company and wanted to see me again. While surprised, I agreed, and we planned for him to collect me the next day.

Seconds after closing the front door, I regretted making the arrangement. Drunk me had thought bedding him a promising idea. Sober me felt unsure I wanted this second chance. He had been pleasant, although I sensed a darkness I could not put my finger on. I had to go through with it. We had made arrangements, and I had no way of letting him know that I had changed my mind.

Edmund collected me at the exact time he said. He drove me to a French restaurant where we had a lovely meal. We talked while we ate, and he again proved a listener rather than a talker. After, he invited me back to his home for drinks, and I found myself agreeing.

We had a few drinks, although I made sure I avoided overindulging. Edmund sat beside me on the sofa before kissing me. I disliked how it felt when his trimmed moustache brushed my lips, although I attempted to enjoy my first kiss for some time. As my lips met his, a hand travelled up my dress. I let it, relishing a lovely shiver of anticipation.

"Shall we go upstairs?" he asked with an intriguing look. I let him lead the way.

In his bedroom, I unbuttoned his shirt, revealing a chest with a surprising amount of hair. I rejoiced, as it meant no chance he would remind me of Charlie. He unzipped my dress and carefully removed it to avoid creasing before placing it on a chair. Without me noticing, he pulled off my slip, revealing my breasts, cupping them while kissing my neck. I relished the experience of being touched again, my body tingling. Taking my nipples in his fingers, he squeezed them hard, causing a delicious sensation. Without warning, he thrust his fingers between my legs in a sudden, forcible movement that took me by surprise.

"Yes, you are quite wet. I think you are certainly a bad girl . . .," he said in a cold, emotionless tone I found intimidating, "and bad girls must be punished. Is that correct? Are you a bad girl?"

"I am a bad girl, yes." I hung my head. It was true in many ways. He pulled my slip to the floor, hitting my bare bottom with his hand. It was a light slap, yet sufficient to make me jump. I found myself astounded at how much I enjoyed the aftermath of the warm glow it implanted.

"Do you deserve punishment?"

He opened a box and produced a riding crop. I found it weirdly exciting when I would expect to feel scared.

"Yes."

I deserved punishment more than he would ever know. What he proposed would doubtless be nowhere near enough.

"If you desire for me to continue, you will call me sir or

master. Is that clear?"

"Yes."

"What did you say?" he asked, holding the crop against my bottom.

"Yes, master," I said, sounding timid. The word felt strange, and it took an effort to bring it to my lips. Having come this far, I knew I had to stick around and see where it would go. He hit my bottom with the crop, which stung at first before fading to a strange, pleasant glowing sensation.

"Better. Shall I spank you again?"

"Yes, please, sir."

While more natural on my lips than master, it felt as though I were back in school. I was a well-behaved pupil, fortunate in avoiding finding myself on the wrong end of the belt. Considering it, I do not know why we called it a belt. It was a tawse, several stiff leather straps sewn together. I had seen it delivered, and it looked unpleasant. On one occasion, the unfortunate recipient, an innocent soul, wet themselves. His was an unusual case, as most recipients deserved their punishment.

Taking the crop, he hit me with more force this time. I gasped. Smiling at my reaction, he grabbed my bottom, parted my cheeks and teased my arsehole. He alternated hitting me with the crop and stroking me. I'd heard talk of exquisite pain and thought it a stupid oxymoron. For the first time, I understood what that meant. I felt alive for the first time in weeks.

He removed his clothes and stood before me, running a finger along the crop. I had my first glance at his cock, a vivid purple-red specimen covered with prominent veins. Calling it the nicest or largest I had ever seen would be a downright lie, although I cared more about what he would do with it. He caught me looking and smiled a sneering smile.

"You want this inside you, don't you?" he asked with an

aggressive, arrogant tone.

Despite my reservations, I grew wetter at his words. Denying it would be a blatant lie. "Yes, sir," I replied with a nod.

"Suck it and make me good and hard."

I did as he instructed. This was a strange, unusual game, yet I was willing to play along. Kneeling before him, I took it in my hand and stroked it. Without looking up, I leaned forward, flicking the end with my tongue. His cock grew harder, my head jerking as he grabbed my hair with a firm, although not painful, grasp, pushing my lips along his shaft. The unexpectedness meant I struggled to breathe for a second or two. He released his grip, and I took a deep breath before sucking again. This continued for a few minutes until he pulled himself from my mouth, telling me to stand.

He tied a scarf over my eyes so I could not see anything. Walking around me, he hit my bottom with the crop again. I gasped. He slapped my breasts with his open hands, taking them in his mouth as he sucked and bit them. This experience had none of the gentleness I was familiar with, although I moaned at the sensations. Sneering, he put his fingers between my legs again.

"This is making you incredibly wet. You are a dirty, little slut, aren't you? You want me to fuck you, don't you?"

"Yes, sir, I do."

"Good girl, I will, but not yet. You must be patient."

He pushed me towards the floor, so my hands were almost touching my toes. It felt uncomfortable until I became distracted from my discomfort by him tracing my exposed pussy with his finger. He shoved a finger deep inside me before withdrawing to give my pussy a slap. While I recovered, he licked his way towards my pearl, which he nibbled. When I was on the verge of climax, the licking stopped abruptly. I gave a disappointed yelp.

"Spread yourself for me," he commanded.

I opened myself for him, spreading my legs. In response, he stuck his fingers inside me, then placed them in my mouth, making me lick my juices, which I lapped with enthusiasm to his obvious delight. He pulled my hips, driving his cock hard inside me, meeting no resistance, thrusting hard. Every now and again he would pull himself out and smack me on the bottom again. I whimpered with anticipation, encouraging him to continue. He grabbed my hips, pulling me upright, driving himself hard. I grasped his bottom, pushing him deeper. Another smack followed before his fingers made their way towards my pearl. It took only a few strokes for me to climax with a loud moan, trembling all over.

I received another smack as he withdrew from me, shoving me onto my knees as he pushed his cock into my mouth. Holding my head in a firm grip, he thrust himself without pause, fucking my mouth. At times I struggled to breathe, my saliva and our juices running down my chin. When approaching orgasm, he pulled himself from my mouth, and I felt his ejaculate spurt over my breasts. I licked his cock clean, swallowing his salty ejaculate. He pulled me onto my feet, giving me an unexpectedly gentle kiss.

"Extremely stimulating. You did well," he told me while he removed my blindfold. My cheeks flushed upon hearing this praise, and I wanted more.

"Thank you for the fascinating experience, sir."

"The bathroom is through there for you to refresh yourself."

I collected my clothes and went to clean myself up, wondering what the hell I had just done. It had been far from unpleasant and fitted the criteria of different from the familiar, although I could not be sure I enjoyed myself. On returning to the bedroom, I found Edmund fully clothed as if nothing had happened. He offered an arm and escorted me downstairs, asking if I wanted a drink. I felt convinced it would not be anything but awkward and asked him to call me a taxi.

"I would like to see you again. Would you be available to come for supper on Friday, at seven o'clock?" he said, opening the cab door for me.

"Yes, sir, I am available, and I look forward to it," I told him without thinking.

Did I? My quick reaction surprised me, but I had agreed. Changing my mind would be rude. I reminded myself I had not thought about Charlie once, the longest I had managed for some time.

CHAPTER NINETEEN: THREE'S A CROWD

When I arrived at Edmund's house, he took me into the drawing room. A beautiful woman was sitting on the sofa. He had not mentioned anyone joining us, although, being fair, he had not said we would be alone. Edmund took my hand, leading me over to her. She was beautiful, with golden-brown skin, mahogany coloured hair, and eyes so dark I could not see where the pupil ended, and the iris emerged.

"Alice, meet Inés. I have promised her a reward, and I hope the reward will be joining us for the evening. However, that very much depends on you. The decision is yours alone. If you think she should leave us, I will fetch her coat, and she will leave this very minute. What shall it be? Would you be happy for her to join us?"

He raised an eyebrow, daring me to say no. Inés looked at me with a pleading look, although silent. I saw no reason for turning down the opportunity of spending some time with this gorgeous woman. If he planned for us to make love, all the better.

"I would, sir," I answered, intrigued.

Inés clapped her hands, giving a happy yelp.

"Excellent," he said with the closest approximation to a smile. "Shall we go through to the dining room?"

I had forgotten the supper and felt disappointed that whatever he planned would have to wait. Edmund sat at the head of the table between us. Looking from her to me, he gave a self-satisfied smirk.

"Yes, tonight will prove interesting, most interesting, but

first, we must fuel our bodies."

During the meal, he asked us many questions while diverting discussion about himself. Inés was from a small village in Granada, and she described the mountains and Moorish architecture with enthusiasm in her gorgeous accent.

Edmund had me describe Scotland for Inés, and I tried portraying my homeland in an equally enchanting way. During the meal, which we ate at a languid pace, our conversation remained light. No mention was made of what he had planned for after we finished eating. My curiosity built with the thrilling suspense. When finished, we returned to the drawing room, where Edmund dismissed the footman. Inés and I sat side by side on a sofa. Edmund handed us each a drink and sat opposite us.

"Inés, do you think Alice is beautiful?"

"She most certainly is, master."

"Alice, do you think Inés is beautiful?"

"Stunningly beautiful, sir."

"Excellent. I am in the presence of two incredibly beautiful women who appreciate each other's beauty. I cannot describe how I am looking forward to seeing what you will do with each other. Alice, you possess a gorgeous tasting flower, and I am sure you will appreciate what Inés can do with her tongue. Inés, if you are good, I will let Alice give you your reward. Inés, are you aroused?"

"Yes, sir. I am very aroused," she replied, her eyes open wide.

"Let me see."

She parted her legs and pulled her dress around her waist. As her skirt lifted, I could see she wore nothing underneath. Edmund pushed a hand between her legs, nodding in appreciation. "Ah, yes, good. Incredibly good."

Her thick black hair glistened, making me long to stick my tongue inside and lap her up. I was desperate to discover how her beautiful mound tasted.

"How about you?" he asked me.

The discussion, combined with Inés' nakedness, had affected me. Feeling nervous, I lifted my dress so he could pull my slip aside, hoping I met his approval. His fingers traced my lips, parting them with a fingertip.

"Excellent. You are evidently both ready. Shall we retire upstairs?"

Edmund offered us an arm each, and we went upstairs. In his room, he had us undress each other. I removed Inés' dress, and she did the same until we were both naked, her skin making mine look even paler than usual. Her breasts were petite, although beautifully pert, with dark nipples.

He handed Inés a silk scarf, telling her to tie my hands. She pulled my arms behind my back and tied my wrists together. On Edmund's instruction, she kissed me. Her nipples rubbed against my chest, mine hardening further in response.

Meanwhile, Edmund ordered her to undress him. She removed his shirt, dropping on her knees and pulling his trousers to the floor. When given permission, she grabbed his cock, sucking it with enthusiasm. With my hands tied, I stood immobile and watched, squirming at how wet I was getting.

"Poor Alice is feeling neglected. Go over and do what you did to me."

She kneeled before me, parting my lips with her hands before placing her tongue on my pearl. I quivered as she licked a lazy figure eight. Edmund was right. She possessed a delightful touch. She licked, edging me nearer my climax until my legs gave a tell-tale tremble.

"Stop," he commanded.

On his command, she withdrew her tongue! The suddenness shocked me. I was furious he had made her stop when I was so close.

"Apply your tongue to her bottom," Edmund directed.

My disappointment faded when she moved behind me and her tongue made its way towards my back passage. It circled around a few times before darting inside, making me gasp at the delicious feelings. Edmund watched with a lecherous expression, snapping a fringed strap on my nipples. I moaned as I experienced pleasure and pain at the same time. The way he denied my orgasm made me want it more.

"Kneel," he directed me. "Inés, stand before Alice so she can return the favour."

She did, although with my hands tied, I could only burrow my mouth deep in her bushy mound. I explored until I found what I sought. Her delicious pearl felt engorged, and I lapped with my tongue, building pressure until she moaned. Again, Edmund made us stop.

"You want to come, don't you, Alice?"

"Yes, sir, I do. Very much, please," I said through gritted teeth.

"Very well, Inés, please untie Alice." He lay on the bed, head on the pillow. "Come here," he said, patting his stomach. I straddled him, sliding down his cock without difficulty. As I rode his cock, he beckoned the watching Inés, commanding her to straddle his head, facing me. She kissed me while Edmund licked her pussy, still not allowing her to come. Speeding my pace on Edmund's cock, I caressed her breasts, and she nibbled mine. This tipped me over the edge to my much-delayed climax. I trembled with each wave that hit me, collapsing into Inés' arms.

"Thank you, sir," I said, panting.

"You are welcome," he said, withdrawing from me. "I think it time for us to give Inés her reward for being good."

"Gracias, master," she said, sounding excited.

"Alice, do for Inés what she did for you earlier."

She climbed off Edmund's face, kneeling alongside him, and lifting her bottom in front of me. I licked around the rim the way she had done. Curling my tongue, I wiggled it, spreading her bottom further apart as I pushed my tongue inside. She moaned and trembled when Edmund had me stop not very far in. He beckoned a disappointed looking Inés towards him, and she sat up, moving over to sit on his lap, facing away from him. Her bottom hovered over his cock as she guided it inside her.

Curious, I shuffled until I could see Edmund's cock pounding into her arse, glistening with their juices. Finding it fascinating, I extended my tongue, applying it to her pearl between each bounce. She climaxed, shaking and moaning. My tongue found the base of Edmund's cock and I licked his balls until he twitched and thrust with his orgasm.

We cleaned ourselves without conversation. Feeling discomforted, I longed to leave, finally doing so after an interval I thought appropriate. We said our goodbyes, making no arrangements to see each other again.

Back home, I poured myself a large gin and orange as I contemplated my experiences with Edmund. While fulfilled sexually, I still felt empty. The catharsis I sought evaded me. Sex with Charlie and Jolly had been acts of love, sex with Georges an act of passion, yet sex with Edmund no more than an act of contrition. I decided I enjoyed my experiences to an extent, although I needed tenderness. More than anything, I yearned to make love rather than be fucked.

I threw myself into meeting with old friends, thinking the Kit Kat's reopening the perfect opportunity. To my complete annoyance, it had converted into a restaurant, the new management's attempt at getting around licencing rules. The cabaret remained first-rate, yet it was not the same.

I insisted on visiting numerous clubs until the following afternoon. This became my routine, spending days taking as much coke and drinking as many cocktails as possible.

This practice continued until I woke in a strange bed with no idea where I was. My head thumped so much even thinking about moving was agony. Confused, I considered going home, although merely opening my eyes proved an arduous endeavour. I concentrated on the impossible task of keeping my head as still as possible.

My recollection of the previous evening proved hazy. I remembered a club, although I was unsure which one. The more I struggled to remember what happened, the more difficult it became. I retained a vague recollection of feeling joyous when I realised the effects of cocaine lasted longer the more I drank. My mind appeared to be trying to wipe my slate clean. If I could make it erase more time, I would stay drunk forever.

Blinking heavily, I went to fetch a remedy for my head, realising my strategy of lying still and merely hoping the pain would go away was failing. Sitting up, I realised my surroundings were more familiar than I thought. I was in Lonnie and Alfie's room. I had made it home, albeit to the wrong bed.

I went to my room to take some headache powders from my drawer, lying on my bed until my head started clearing. The clock chimed nine as I passed, and I presumed I crawled into bed at a ludicrous time to wake at such an early hour. I went to the drawing room and poured myself a large brandy for its restorative powers.

I drank the brandy, feeling more restored with every sip. The door opened as I poured myself another, and Lonnie walked in.

"You're still with us? How are you feeling?"

"Rather rough."

"That is only to be expected."

"I do think I must have overdone things last night. I can't remember much."

"Last night? And the rest, darling."

"The rest of what?" I asked, having no idea what she meant.

"Honey, what day is it?"

"It's Tuesday, isn't it?"

"No, sweetie, it's Wednesday."

"Wednesday? Are you serious?" I asked, stunned.

"Yes, God's honest truth."

"So that's why I couldn't find Dawson. It is her day off. I thought she must be buying us stockings in Berwick Street or something."

"At nine o'clock at night?"

"It's nighttime?"

"Haven't you noticed it is dark outside?"

"I haven't opened the curtains. I did not even wonder why they were closed, now I think about it. How long have I been sleeping? What the hell happened to Tuesday?"

"You don't remember?"

"Bits, not much, well nothing, really."

"Think you need to knock the gross intemperance on the head for a time," she said, pointing at my brandy.

"That is what gets me through my day," I argued, knowing I sounded pathetic.

"The way you have been staying permanently stoned, you won't have many days left to get through. You do know the idea is burning the candle at both ends, not burning the entirety of the candle?"

"It hasn't been that bad. Without booze, I always feel such a pill."

"I have not long returned from the NWCU, where I went in your stead, helping out the best I could. I am utterly quanked."

"What?"

"Quanked, exhausted, my vigour has been drained. Did you forget the important preparations for the rally on

Saturday? Perhaps because you were unconscious after consuming your body weight in alcohol. Do not worry. I told them you had a bug. Everyone missed you and felt just awful about you being ill. They sent their best wishes for a full recovery."

"You did? Thank you, Lonnie. I am sorry you had to lie for me and for letting everyone down. I promise it will never happen again."

The remorse was genuine. I hated disappointing people. From an early age, Dad had instilled the importance of meeting my responsibilities.

"Alice, you are a charming drunk, but recently you are getting so tight you are practically comatose every night. I can tell when it is happening. You can hold a perfectly coherent conversation for perhaps ten minutes or thereabouts. Then your eyes glaze over, and if I ask you what we just discussed, you have no idea. It usually ends with you going somewhat berserk. Do you have any recollection of last night, or the night before?"

"I was . . . wasn't I with you? I have no idea where we were. I cannot remember. I can try to tell you, although I fear you'd find me an unreliable witness." I endeavoured to dredge up some memories, although it felt like holding onto sand. The more I tried, the blanker my mind became.

"Do you remember suddenly taking up smoking and stealing my gaspers?"

"I did? No wonder my throat is rough."

"Or meeting with Effy Evesham?"

"Oh, now I do remember talking with him about his very rosy cheeks."

"Rosé cheeks more like," she said, laughing. "Do you remember entering a laughing fit that went on for at least ten minutes? Then crying hysterically for a time then laughing again when you forgot why you were crying?"

"I hope never to meet him again. I should make sure to remain here at all times to ensure it never happens," I told her, considering the possibility.

"Decidedly cringe-making. I think he probably will not remember much about it either, if that is any consolation. Do you recall having to be all but rugby-tackled by Tabby in an attempt at preventing you from kissing the policeman you found irresistibly handsome?"

"I don't think you will be terribly surprised by this, but no, I don't. Might he have been, in any way, irresistibly handsome?"

"He was fifty if a day. I didn't consume anything like enough booze to find him either irresistible or handsome."

"It appears drunk Alice is terrible at making decisions."

"That is unquestionably safe to say. I presume you do not recall Alfie holding your hair while you threw up in the coalscuttle?"

"No."

"Or you getting into bed with us?"

"That explains why I woke in your bed. I'm sorry, please don't tell me more."

"Alfie slept in your room. I thought it best to stay with you so I could keep a concerned eye on you. I understand what you are doing, but this will not replace Charlie. Nothing will, and you know that."

"I only want it to stop hurting. I can't deal with the pain sober."

"I know, darling, but it turns out drowning your sorrows in booze is not the way to do it. You are obviously desperately missing Charlie, and Alfie reports he is uncharacteristically quiet. Why don't you write him a letter, let him know your true feelings? Alfie can address the envelope to avoid the Duchess seeing it. No matter how he replies, or even if he does not, how could you feel any more hopeless?"

"It is too late for that now. He must despise me for being so cowardly. I cringe when I remember my craven spineless behaviour. He offered to give up everything for me, and I sent him away because I feared his mother? I cannot bear the thought that he might hate me. If he does, I don't think I want to know."

She was unaware of my numerous attempts at writing that letter. The words conveying the sorrow and misery I felt eluded me.

Chapter Twenty: French Fancy

Once again, I invested my efforts in getting Charlie out of my head. Doing so sober was more challenging than I imagined. Time proved negligent in fulfilling its function of mending my broken heart. The more time passed, the more agonising it became.

While sure I had no room in my heart to accommodate love for another, I did want someone to touch and hold me again. On occasion, I would meet a gentleman who I thought might prove a worthy distraction before a smile, a laugh, or a look would bring Charlie back to mind. These reminders made me unable to look at my prospective partner the same way again. I bedded one or two gentlemen who bore no resemblance to him, yet found it an empty experience. The short-lived satisfaction served merely to remind me how much I missed him.

I missed more about him than making love. There were many simple joys. The way he held me, our conversations, or how he would stroke the fine hairs on my neck until I shuddered. I longed for his touch. Knowing I would never experience it again was agony to bear. At times, the despair grew so intolerable I wished for death to end the agonising omnipresence of his face in my thoughts and dreams. Some days I would be able to function until the slightest thing reminded me of him, then I would find myself fighting despair once more.

I considered if it would be better if I had never met Charlie before deciding that too stupid an idea to contemplate. Despite the pain caused by our separation, I could not wish away our time together. I considered myself fortunate to have experienced such love. If I could, I would give everything to turn back the last year to relive every single moment.

Every day I plastered on a smile, facing the world as life and soul of each event I attended. Every night I went to bed disconsolate, knowing with a horrible certainty I would wake wanting and longing for him again. It was inevitable I would spend all the days I had left feeling this way, and I endeavoured to become accustomed to the idea. I garnered some consolation in having reached my lowest point. Nothing outside losing anyone else I loved would cause more pain, and I would get through it as I was getting through now.

Tabby decided the thing to cheer me would be a party. She chose a film studio in Wardour Street for the venue as it was somewhere I had not visited with Charlie. The gesture was thoughtful and gave me no excuses for non-attendance.

At the party, she introduced me to someone called Ainsworth with no trace of her usual warmth. I took her unenthusiastic introduction as a warning, although I had no idea why she would invite someone she did not like. He was a handsome young man, dressed in an immaculate, yet even for our crowd, extravagant style. With a beguiling smile, he asked me to dance. I looked at Tabby, who shrugged, but the way she pursed her lips made me wary. I could not think of a reason to refuse, so I accepted. He proved a decent dance partner. We danced together for a while then agreed to stop for a breather.

"I say, I am famished. Shall we go grab something to eat?" he asked as we sipped our drinks.

"There's a huge spread next door. Do you want to go through?" I pointed towards the food Tabby had provided. The food at these parties made me feel guilty. The amount wasted could feed a family for a week.

"Nah, not in the mood for party grub. Could go a plate of steak and kidney pudding and some pud with custard. How does that sound?"

"If you like," I said with a shrug. His menu suggested school dinners to me, although I had no objections. "Where do you want to go? There's a Lyons not far from here."

"Best avoiding it for the time being," he said with a smug smile.

"Why?"

"The chaps have been carrying out a terrific wheeze there. We eat the most expensive thing on the menu, before making a sharp exit without paying. Done it a few times recently, so I should avoid the place for now at least, I think," he said with a snort and a chuckle.

"You think that is funny? It is stealing. That money comes from the wages of the nippy."

"So? It's only a few shillings."

I slapped his face with some force, vanquishing the cocky smile, which was replaced by a confused expression. I doubt he had been slapped often, certainly not often enough.

"You heartless bastard. You can afford it, and they cannot. A few shillings here and there are nothing to you but a huge loss for her. Now, if you will excuse me, I think I'd rather stand somewhere else on my own than continue this conversation with someone so lacking in empathy for your fellow human beings."

I joined Tabby, who witnessed the slap, finding it hilarious. I explained my reason for hitting him, and she gave an approving nod.

"Marvellous work, good for you. Rather envious, always wanted to give him a good slap. Invited him against better judgement, only did so as a favour. Ought to have warned you, although you sized him up incredibly quickly. You do realise you just slapped one of the most eligible bachelors in England?"

"I have?"

"Yes, dear, you have. That man is Lord Ainsworth, otherwise known as Viscount Ainsworth of Mirlton, eldest son of the Duke of Dorset, one of the richest men in the country."

"Well, it proves what my dad always says, money can't buy class."

"Correct. However, the inverse is often also true. Why not talk to those incredibly handsome guardsmen over there? Ran into them on the way over."

The soldiers proved fun companions. As we were leaving, we spotted an inebriated Ainsworth propped against a wall. Laughing, we hailed a passing cab and helped him inside. Tabby retrieved his wallet and removed enough to reimburse Olive several times over, giving the driver what remained to drop him at Hampton Court Palace.

Having experienced a few tedious, dry evenings, I decided moderation must be the key to my enjoyment. I allowed myself a few cautious drinks on my next night out. I aimed for no more than two sheets to the wind, not fall-down drunk. More than anything, I wished to dance, yet not the limited, confined dance of the nightclub, packed like sardines on tiny dancefloors.

For a change, we visited the Palais. I watched a rather handsome professional dancer perform a steamy tango with a customer. After enquiries, I discovered it cost sixpence a dance, so I negotiated with the master of ceremonies to engage him for the rest of the evening. I tipped my new dance partner two guineas, even though only half an hour remained until closing time. We danced two dances before retreating home so I could get my money's worth.

One evening I bumped into Simone in the Shim Sham. She was in town discussing Vérité de la Beauté, her upcoming exhibition. Advance word had been hyperbolic, and it had shown in Paris to rave reviews.

"Bonjour," she said, kissing both cheeks. "I have not seen

you since the evening with Charlie. I hear you and he is no more?" she asked with an exaggerated frown.

"I am afraid so," I said, nodding my head.

"Ah, c'est très, très triste, you two were so beau ensemble." Her pout was charming. I could not fathom the reason I found French artists so sexy.

"Are you seeing someone?" I asked, changing the subject. I did not see why my love life should be our sole conversation topic.

"Non, I am . . ." she said, waving her arm as she sought the term, " . . . between lovers. My time, it is spent here, there, everywhere. I am not a one to be tied down because I stay and poof, like that I am gone." She snapped her fingers.

"That must make affiliations rather difficult."

"Mais non, c'est pas de problem finding suitable ladies when I need them," she said without modesty. I wondered how she found these women. The lesbian world appeared a secretive one. Until that moment, I had not considered sleeping with just women as a possibility. I was contemplating the prospect when Tabby interrupted my reverie.

"Penny for them," she asked.

"I was considering having an affiliation with a woman."

"Oh, good for you. Anyone in particular?"

"Well, no, although I am rather excited by the idea that if I made love to a woman, there might be no chance she will remind me of Charlie."

"Very little chance, certainly. You will not be comparing their cock sizes or anything. Whatever it takes, darling. It is all the rage, quite the thing. Quite honestly, never been tempted."

"What, never?"

"Father was scared his daughters would end up lesbians like Aunt Bernadette, his younger sister. Difficult for the family, being Catholic. Do you know what happens to Catholic lesbians?"

"No," I said, shaking my head.

"They become nuns. Father refused to send us to all-girl schools. He thought them breeding grounds for lesbianism. Even stipulated it in his will. Know how hard it was for Aunt Agatha to find a mixed boarding school? Have attended them all at one point or another. Seems to have worked, though. Sexual experiences with women have been exceptionally disappointing and entirely last resort."

"That is a pity. I always enjoy the experience. How do women find other women for romantic involvement? I know men hang around Covent Garden and some places in Soho to find other men, although I am unsure where women go to meet women. Do they have special places like men do?"

"Believe so, though no idea where. Never been interested in finding out. Why not ask Simone?"

I approached Simone later.

"If you do not mind me asking, how do you find these women you are involved with? Do you have clubs and suchlike you can go to?"

"There are certain places, oui, not as many as the men, but we have some."

"Would you take me to one of your clubs one day?" I asked, my curiosity piqued. The idea of finding one of her suitable ladies proved a fascinating one.

"Are you thinking you will submit to the sapphic side? I always hoped zat you would," she said with a sexy smile. She phrased it as a straightforward proposition, giving the impression she was keen. The invitation proved irresistible, although I tried playing flirty yet far from easy.

"Ah, no, not quite Simone, you see, while I am somewhat keen for some lesbian love, I do appreciate the penetration of a good hard cock."

"Zat is pas de problème." She winked at me.

"Show me," I said, my intrigue causing me to drop my act.

"What, now?" she asked, her eyebrow raised.

"Why beat around the bush? If you pardon the expression," I said with a smile at my joke.

We left without delay, walking the few streets to her apartment on Soho Square. The Bohemian interior had been decorated with fabrics and throws. She fetched us drinks while I admired some of her sculptures, mostly figurines of the female form. They were beautiful, although one in particular caught my eye, an alabaster portrayal of a seated woman's torso and bottom. Five or six inches tall, it looked so tactile I fought to resist stroking it.

"Do you like it?" Simone asked, handing me a glass of a delicious red wine.

"It is absolutely stunning, just gorgeous."

"Merci. It is a prototype of a piece entitled Grâce Voluptueuse. It will be exhibiting in London. You must come see it."

"I'd love to."

"Bon. I will put your name upon the guestlist for the grand opening."

She showed me to the bedroom, kissing me as she closed the door. I removed her shirt as we undressed each other. Half-dressed, I followed her, admiring her gorgeous curves and beautiful round bottom. We sat on the bed, her sitting on my lap. As we kissed, she made sure her nipples brushed against mine, generating a delicious tickle. We caressed and kissed each other's bodies, grinding our hips against each other.

With a smile, she took a box from a drawer and produced a dildo attached to a leather belt. I helped her step into it, tightening the straps as she oiled the length. Excited, I kissed the end and climbed onto my hands and knees. She placed the dildo between my legs, rubbing it against my pearl before inserting a finger inside my pussy. Satisfied, she pushed the dildo inside me. I gave a happy groan when it entered. In response, she grabbed my hips and started thrusting.

"Merci," I cried, pushing against her to let it go deep inside me. She grasped my right nipple and switched to quick, shallow strokes. I made an appreciative moan when her hips hit against mine, as she pushed herself as far as possible. She increased the speed, building my climax. I collapsed my head in the pillow so I could muffle my moans. Encouraged, she thrust faster, slapping herself against me. Pushing into her until my climax came, I quivered and groaned until the waves subsided.

She withdrew from me, and I fell on the bed, watching her unbuckle the strap-on.

"Do you want me to use that on you?" I asked, unsure if I wanted to, scared in case I hurt her.

"Mais non, not for me. C'est trop masculin, I cannot climax zat way."

I smiled, pulling her towards me and parting her legs. She moaned as my tongue met her enlarged pearl. I teased her, enjoying the noises she made combined with her sweet aroma. She gave another moan, purring something in French, some of which I did not understand. I built the pressure until her legs trembled to the accompaniment of another soft moan. She climaxed with a shriek, clamping my head between her legs.

We lay for a while until she got up to pour us some more wine and light a thin cigar. She finished smoking it and kissed me. I enjoyed it, though I struggled to ignore the taste of her cigar. As we kissed, she placed her leg between mine, manoeuvring herself so her pearl and mine met. I lay on my side as she straddled my leg, grinding herself against me. Loving the sensation, I rubbed myself quicker and harder until I climaxed, an incredible rush of electricity overcoming me. I held her hand as her climax hit with another yell.

We spent the night playing records until we returned to bed, making love until we fell asleep.

I woke alone the following morning. After I remembered where I was, I dressed and walked to the kitchen, where I found Simone drinking coffee. She kissed my cheek as she handed me a cup.

"Bon matin, darling. Sorry, but I have no breakfast for us. I return to Paris this afternoon, so alas, I have nothing."

"Please do not worry about it. I'll get something on my way home. I'd best leave you to your packing."

"Merci, I have still some errands before I leave. I very much look forward to seeing you at the exhibition. If I am over before then, I will be in touch. I want you to have this," she said, handing me the model Grâce Voluptueuse.

I thanked her and drank my coffee. When I finished, I kissed her goodbye, leaving clutching her beautiful but weighty gift.

It felt different being with Simone, and I enjoyed it. I felt fond of her, although she would not be in the country long enough for an affiliation. Delightful though it might be, that option was a disappointing non-starter. It had been a successful liaison in one way, as Simone did not remind me of Charlie in any way.

My love for Charlie meant there was no chance of loving anyone else, although I considered doing as Simone did. Experiencing numerous fleeting encounters with lots of women sounded an interesting prospect. I knew a few lesbians, although most of them were attached. I needed someone who wanted a temporary affiliation with me. Lonnie and I had made love a few times, and while I enjoyed being with her, it had always been for fun, and we would hate it to get stale. I regretted missing the opportunity for visiting one of Simone's clubs. One thing I wished I had asked her. Were the women she slept with happy with her arrangement? Hurting anyone was the last thing I wanted.

A gilded envelope arrived for me containing an invitation for the opening night of Simone's exhibition. Invitations became prized in the best circles. Alfie and Lonnie were unfortunately busy and received many offers of considerable sums and various favours for their invitation.

I went with Tabby, who had no interest in art but hated missing a party, the more exclusive, the better.

Grâce Voluptueuse was the first exhibit, sitting five feet tall without its plinth. I thought it breath-taking. Tabby left me admiring it, going off on the arm of someone who caught her fancy.

I wished everyone would go away so I could run my hand over the sculpture. Despite my temptation, I resisted, feeling sure someone would scold me and ask me to leave despite the fact no one paid me any attention. I heard a cough behind me and turned to see Simone. She gave me an embrace, kissing each cheek.

"Do you like it now you see it in full size?" she asked, taking a long drag of her cigar.

"It's wonderful," I told her, nodding. "Although I am very fond of my version."

"Thank you. I like zat you appreciate it. What does it declare for you?"

I stood contemplating her question.

"Many things, but mostly it talks of the strength and elegance of the feminine form," I said, and she nodded thoughtfully. "I do so want to touch it."

"So, go on."

Despite having the artist's permission, I wondered if I should. I extended a tentative hand, caressing the sculpture's cool smooth curves.

"It's beautiful," I said, enthused.

"Merci," she said, putting her hand on mine, stroking it

with an almost imperceptible touch. I looked at her, wondering if she would kiss me. She stubbed out her cigar, nodded towards a door, and moved towards it, still holding my hand. I walked close so that our handholding would be less noticeable.

We walked through a door with a sign saying staff only, revealing a staircase leading to the basement. The basement door slammed closed behind us, leaving us in a dingy light. I could discern many chests and rows of metal shelves which contained junk and cleaning materials. She led me towards some tea chests placed in front of a few chairs stacked in a corner. Taking one, she put it on the floor, indicating that I sit. Kneeling before me, she slid my underwear aside, applying her tongue to my pearl. I sat in the dark between crates and mops, enjoying the delicious sensations.

As I approached climax, the overhead light flickered on as a gallery employee entered the room. He stopped in the middle of the floor, checking something. We were partially hidden behind the crates, but he could hardly fail to see us if he looked over in our direction. The interruption proved no deterrence to Simone, who continued her pace unconcerned. Maintaining my silence to avoid detection became unbearable. I came without making a noise, biting my lip to make sure. The light dimmed, and the door slammed shut, allowing me to release the moan I held in.

Giggling, we swapped places, and I teased her with my tongue before bringing her to a quick climax. My pace was swift as I worried that she might be missed, although she did not care. She came with a squeal, and we cleaned ourselves best we could before re-joining the party.

CHAPTER TWENTY-ONE: DOMINATION

As I walked from the NWCU one beautiful sunny after-noon, I thought I saw Charlie walking across the street from me. I knew I must be mistaken, as September was four months away. Various thoughts catapulted themselves through my mind. He could not have returned without me knowing, could he? It was possible. If he returned home, look-ing me up would be the last thing on his mind. If Alfie or Lon-nie had heard he had returned, they might think it best to keep that information from me.

I abandoned my usual route to follow him, crossing the street to take a better look. He walked towards Piccadilly Cir-cus, and I quickened my pace so I could close the gap between us. I got within a few feet from him before realising he was not Charlie. The resemblance was striking from a distance, although at close range, subtle differences became apparent.

He entered the Maison Lyonses, and I followed him, afraid I would lose him in its vast interior. He took a seat at an empty table, and I wondered if he planned to meet someone. For some strange reason, the thought made me feel envious. The only way I could be certain was taking a seat nearby. After negotiating with the nippy, I took a table where I could watch him without appearing obvious. His navy-blue wool double-breasted suit jacket looked a trifle big for him and too warm for the weather. He removed it before he sat, carefully placing it on the seat beside him.

I had already eaten, so ordered a pot of tea and a cream scone. He did not look in any hurry as he pulled a paperback from his jacket pocket. I wished I had brought a book with me so I could feel less conspicuous. Besides the odd old lady, he and I were the lone solitary diners.

The nippy brought him something from the fixed price menu and a cup of tea. The time he took to eat gave me the chance of considering my options. He was not Charlie, although the resemblance was undeniable. Might the similarity fool my growing libido? I tried avoiding people who reminded me of him. Might I do any worse with someone who resembled him than with people who did not? Despite everything, my worries might be irrelevant. He could be married, attached, homosexual, or simply not find me attractive. I spent some time considering which was the likeliest option.

When he stood to leave, I did the same, following him as he walked into a bank near where I first saw him. I watched him through the window as he disappeared through a door beside the counter before reappearing at a teller's window.

I walked towards the door, although unable to muster the confidence to enter. After a few minutes, I went home, considering my options. I could not be sure pursuing this stranger would bring about a happier ending than my last dalliance. Despite my concerns, I felt bored, lonely, and horny.

The following day I walked to the bank, looking for my Charlie replica. A peer through the window revealed him sitting at the counter again. He had no customers waiting, so I took my chance. Walking up to his desk, I asked if I could cash a cheque, smiling my brightest smile.

"Of course, miss." He smiled. Taking my chance at a close look, I liked what I saw, although comparing him with Charlie was hard to avoid. His smile, although nowhere near as captivating, looked friendly and open. He had blue eyes, although a much lighter shade with greenish-gold flecks. His hair was straighter, shorter, and deep brown rather than black. In an added bonus, that I had not noticed from a distance, his chin had a cute, wee dimple I found attractive. I wrote a cheque for a guinea, collecting my money with my friendliest smile. Taking my time, I walked into the Maison, sitting at a table facing the door. As I hoped, he arrived at the same time. I stood up, forcing him to pass me. He gave me a smile and a slight nod of recognition when passing me.

The following day I repeated the process, making sure I arrived a few minutes before him. I requested a table near the door, hoping he would walk past me. Having brought a book with me, I feigned reading, glancing up every time someone entered. I had almost finished my scone when he walked in. I looked up and caught his gaze.

"Hello again." I tried looking surprised, not as if I planned it to the minutest possible detail.

"Oh, hello, Miss Fraser." At first, I did not understand how he knew my name, but I remembered the cheques.

"You possess an excellent memory and the advantage over me, it seems," I replied with what I hoped was an alluring expression.

"I am sorry, Miss Fraser, my name is Ashley Williams."

I told myself to be careful in case I called him Charlie by accident.

"I am pleased to meet you, Ashley. Please call me Alice. Why don't you join me?"

He looked shocked at the invitation. I worried I had scared him with my forwardness until he nodded, sitting across from me.

"It really is a lovely day, isn't it?" he asked, looking nervous and reluctant to look me in the eye. I found it rather cute.

"Yes, it is. I take it you lunch here often since I keep bumping into you?"

"Yes, every day. I can read my book in peace here." He pulled a library copy of *The Murder of Roger Ackroyd* from his pocket.

"Ah, I'm sorry, if you'd rather eat alone . . ."

"No, not at all," he said with a nervous smile.

"I see you're a fellow Agatha Christie fan," I said, closing the cover of *The Big Four* I was re-reading and showing him.

"You like Agatha Christie, too?" he asked, smiling. "I haven't read that one yet. I have a copy reserved at the library."

"It is a good one. I must lend it to you."

"Thank you, that would be kind."

We chatted about books until we discovered a mutual love of movies. He mentioned a new film he wanted to see, some American film about two men in love with the same woman. Despite not having heard of the film, I declared it an incredible coincidence as I also wanted to see it. The following silence continued for an age. Realising my hints had not been taken, I asked him if he would like to go with me. His gaping mouth and wide eyes indicated his unfamiliarity with such a proposition, although he flustered an agreement. We arranged to meet at the Royal Cinema on Kensington High Street the following day. We made our plans, and he announced his lunch hour had almost ended. He left with my book under his arm.

Ashley looked offended when I offered to pay my share of the cinema entrance fee, refusing any money, even though he chose the expensive seats. Despite his description, the film was a melodrama. I would have preferred a romantic flick so we could set the scene, yet I enjoyed it. We went into a nearby café where we discussed the film over some cocoa, for which he insisted on paying. He raved about it, and I adored seeing his excitement. His enthusiasm proved infectious, and it was a perfect, enjoyable evening. He inquired if I would permit him to walk me home, despite it taking him further away from the bus stop taking him home to Acton. I felt sorry for him when he saw my house, mouth agape as he gave a visible and audible gulp. He walked me to my door, thanking me for a lovely evening as he turned and walked away.

"Will I see you again?" I called after him. He spun on his heel.

"You want to see me again?" he asked, looking surprised.

"Yes, I would," I said, nodding.

"How does Friday suit you? We can meet at the Corner House on Coventry Street for dinner, same time?"

"Yes, please," I said, running over and kissing his cheek. His eyes grew wide, a lovely if dopey, smile coming across his face.

We sat on the mezzanine level of the Corner House, the orchestra playing a selection of slow waltzes while we ate. He ordered pickled herrings, although I wondered if the cheapest item on the menu might be a practical choice. I ordered chicken cutlets on buttered toast. It is not what I would usually have chosen, but it was only a penny more than the herrings, which I detest. My choices were thrifty on purpose, as I suspected he would insist on paying.

During our meal, he told me about his family. His father had been a schoolteacher, rejected for service on medical grounds, although his religious beliefs meant he would refuse combative roles anyway. Feeling the need to help others, he volunteered as a fireman. He died during the Liverpool Street Station bomb attack when a wall collapsed while trying to free someone. His mother had been pregnant with his younger brother at the time. Since leaving school, Ashley provided for his mother, sisters, and brother. He expressed no self-pity, feeling it his responsibility as the oldest.

I found him a kind, modest gentleman with perfect manners. He confirmed my suspicions about his financial situation when he blanched while looking at the bill, which was no more than five shillings. I wanted to offer to pay my share, although I knew he would be horrified at the suggestion, and I was reluctant to offend him.

We saw each other a few more times, although he showed no interest in kissing or touching me. I decided I would force matters by meeting at a less public location, inviting him to my house for supper. He hesitated yet accepted my invitation.

From the beginning of our supper date, Ashley looked intimidated by his surroundings. He was wearing his best suit. I wondered where he told his mother he was going, although I thought it best not to ask. For the first time, our conversation was peppered with pauses, which I filled with talk about films. When we walked into the dining room, he looked confused.

"Is anything the matter, Ashley?"

"I expected I would meet your family, your aunt."

"Aunt Violet is at Foxcotte House, the family home in Hampshire. She spends the largest part of her time there. She hates London. I live here with my cousin Alfie and his wife, Lonnie."

"Then they will be joining us?"

"I'm afraid not. They are visiting friends this evening."

"You mean we have no chaperone?" He looked alarmed.

"Why no, I never even considered that. It is not a problem, is it? Does being alone with me make you feel uncomfortable?"

"Of course not," he stammered.

I adored how it was apparent when he was lying. I longed to kiss him, although I worried that he'd run away if I did. There was a grave danger I could scare him into running away without looking back.

When we finished eating, we went into the smoking room to play some gramophone records. When I sat beside him, he moved away, although he had not got far before hitting the arm of the sofa.

"You are what my mother calls a modern girl, I think." He looked at a fixed spot before him.

"Quite possibly. I presume she warned you should stay away from girls like me?"

"Yes, she did."

I admired his honesty. "And yet, here you are."

"I . . . I enjoy spending time with you," he told me, meeting my gaze. His cheeks went a violent red.

"I am extremely glad to hear that, because I also enjoy spending time with you, Ashley. Did you tell your mother you are seeing me?"

He paused before answering. "No, she thinks I go to the cinema with a friend from work."

"Are you concerned I might somehow corrupt you?"

"Honestly? Yes, I am a little," he said, looking at the floor, blinking.

"What are the consequences of this corruption?" I asked, intrigued.

"I will lose my immortal soul and my place with God in the afterlife."

"Do you believe that?"

"I do, I mean I did. That is what I grew up believing, although now I am less certain than I was before. I want to kiss you, but I fear what that might lead to."

"You can kiss me, or you can go home if you wish. The choice is yours alone. I'd hate you to feel I am forcing you into something you are uncomfortable with," I told him, crossing my fingers behind my back.

He sat pondering his options. Competing with an eternity in Heaven was a new challenge, and I thought it was inevitable I would lose. To my surprise, he leaned forward and kissed me. I leaned into the kiss until his quivering lips met mine, hoping he found it as thrilling as I did. While we kissed, I wrapped my arms around him, pulling him towards me.

The pleasing bulge in his trousers convinced me I should take control of the situation.

"Ashley, I'd like you to make love to me. I can see you'd like that too."

Too late, a hand moved to cover his erection. His face took on a guilty expression as he realised I was aware of his proclamation of arousal.

"I am going to go upstairs to my room. I would be thrilled if you came with me. If you do not want to, I understand completely. If that is the case, I will thank you for a lovely evening and wish you goodnight."

I left the room, crossing the hallway and walking towards the stairs. I turned to see Ashley standing stock still. He first looked at the door, then at me. He stood for a few seconds, came to a decision, and walked towards me. Finally exhaling, I took his hand, leading him into my bedroom. I closed the door and kissed him. His lips responded while he stood, frozen and unsure.

"Take off my dress, please, Ashley."

The realisation he required constant instruction hit me, and I found the idea rather exciting. I turned so he could unzip me, a shaking hand gradually revealing my brassiere and panties. He scrutinised my body with an appreciative smile. I pulled his wool pullover vest over his head while he fumbled with his shirt buttons. As he did, I helped remove his trousers. He stood in his union suit, uncertain about removing the last item that stood between him being clothed or naked. I helped him remove it, and it fell to the floor. His was an attractive body, his cock standing proud and looking promising.

I removed my brassiere, took his trembling, hesitant hand and placed it on my breast. He gave it a tentative stroke until becoming more confident and taking them both in his hands. Being the recipient of this cautious exploring was a lovely experience. I took his hand, leading him onto the bed.

"Please, sit down," I said, patting the bed.

He did, and I sat across his lap. My breasts were at eye level, and he stared at them with an incredulous expression.

"You are wondering how my breasts taste, aren't you, Ashley?" He nodded, mouth agape. "Then why not find out? Take one in your mouth, lick it, then suck it."

He leaned forward and did so with increased enthusiasm. I stroked his cock, which had reached a pleasing size.

"Oh, that is incredibly delightful. I am about to take you inside me. Would you like that?"

"Yes, please," he said, his voice a hoarse whisper.

Pushing myself forward, I guided his cock inside me, loving how fantastic it felt. He groaned a soft growling noise as he pushed himself further. Riding his cock with slow, steady strokes, I made sure I was careful. I guessed it would not take much to bring him to climax.

He groaned, and I slowed my thrusting. "Do not come yet, sweetheart. Wait for me." His eyebrows knitted in concentration as he attempted to defer his building orgasm.

Knowing time was short, I leaned towards him, rubbing my pearl on his pubis until my climax neared. "Now, darling," I whispered, nibbling his neck while the waves took me. His face contorted, with a look of sudden surprise turning into a look of pure joy when he came. "Well done."

"Thank you," he said, panting, although it was unnecessary. Gratitude was written over his face.

For a few weeks, we saw each other every opportunity we had. He fulfilled my every request without question. One afternoon, he came to visit, although far from his usual enthusiastic self. I sat beside him, placing my hand on his.

"Sweetheart, what's wrong?"

"Nothing, there's nothing wrong."

"Now, that is clearly untrue. You have been quite distrait

this afternoon. Ashley, we both know you are the most terrible liar. Please do me the courtesy of not lying to me." I turned his head, making him look me in the eye.

"The thing is." He looked pained, although he maintained his gaze. "There is a girl, Ivy, that I have been sweet on for a long time. Ever since Sunday School, in fact." He gulped. "She is a nippy."

"At the Corner House, where you take lunch?" I asked. He nodded. This confession distressed him.

"She's never shown me any interest at all until fairly recently. She saw us together, and word reached her that you are, em, well off, and you and I are seeing each other." He chose his words with care.

"She came to you professing her eternal love?" I suggested.

"Why, yes." He looked surprised, yet it seemed evident. Nothing in life is as desirable as that which has recently become unavailable. "My pastor tells me I should stop seeing you and marry her instead."

"You discussed our affiliation with your pastor?" Knowing I had taken part in a confession by proxy felt strange. I almost blushed to imagine what he had told him and in what detail.

"God sees all, so lying is pointless."

"I understand, I think. Why does he say we should part?"

"The Bible says it is better to marry than burn. I cannot marry you, so I must marry Ivy." He gulped again.

"Why do you think we cannot marry?" I had no thoughts of marrying anyone but Charlie, and that was an impossible dream. The idea that anyone other than Charlie would consider marrying me was a complete surprise.

"Even if I could afford it, it would be wrong for us to marry. You do not love me, and I am sure what I feel for you, while incredibly powerful, is not love either."

"Much as I hate admitting it, you are correct. I care for you very much, but what I feel for you is not love. It is insulting you to pretend otherwise. I wish I were capable of loving you, I know you would be the sweetest man to love, but it is outwith my power. I can say I have enjoyed being with you for whatever we have."

"It is lust perhaps, sexual desire, passion, but whatever it is, it is not love, and never will be. It is a craving, I think, an urge. I have a hunger for you which overwhelms me in ways that scare me at times. For the sake of my eternal soul, I should resist."

I fought the temptation to laugh, declaring such notions meaningless. There was no God, no Hell, just nothing. His expression stopped me. Silly though I thought it, for him it was a genuine concern. Dad encouraged me to discuss and debate religion, but he'd taught me I should never scorn people's beliefs. I did not know anyone who believed in it. I found the idea fascinating. "Do you believe Hell exists?"

"I don't know. While we mostly agree Hell exists, there does not appear to be much accord about precisely what it entails. I have read of Hell as a fiery place, rife with torment and pain. Others say it is more an unconscious death, annihilation, or non-existence. Some say Hell is where God is not. Although, God is everywhere, so there can be nowhere He is not."

He had clearly done some reading on the subject. I wanted to tell him that no matter which definition he took as correct, Hell did exist. I had been there for some time. "You have given this some thought." I took his hand, and he looked at me with a sad expression.

"I have come to terms with being damned because of what we, what I have done. I have no excuse, I knew it was wrong, but I did it anyway. When I talked with my pastor, he reminded me of God's mercy and forgiveness. He told me there is hope for me yet if I turn my back upon my evil ways and truly repented. What we do would not be a sin if we were married, but we are not, and we never will be."

I sat dumbstruck. No one had ever offered their immortal soul for me before. It struck me as too high a price, despite being unable to believe such a thing existed.

"Why are you with me? Why have you not gone to Ivy as your pastor instructed?"

"Because I am drawn to you like a moth to a candle. You control my every will. I cannot hear you tell me I must do something without knowing I must obey."

"Fine. Then hear me and obey," I said, turning his head towards me. "Go to Ivy, marry her, make love to her, and have a long, happy, sin-free life with her."

"Thank you," he said, giving me a grateful smile.

I gave him a goodbye kiss and watched him walk away, another man walking out of my life forever, leaving me to consider his words. We both enjoyed what we did. Why would something so natural be considered a sin? Why would a god, who was purported to love me, condemn me to an eternity of burning torment for sharing my body with others in acts which hurt no one? Although, as I considered my solitary future, I did wonder if my eternal torment had already begun.

For the first time in my life, I felt alone, and it was all my fault. I had fallen in love with the most unavailable and inappropriate person possible. Falling in love had been the easiest yet hardest thing I had ever done.

Chapter Twenty-two: New York

The rare occurrence of a letter from Dad made me homesick for Cludenbrig. News of goings-on back home made me almost wish I had never left. I reasoned if I had stayed at home, I would not have met Charlie. If I had not met him, I would never have hurt him, and if I had never hurt him, I would be feeling no pain now.

I thought leaving London a splendid idea. I would visit Dad. Seeing no reason for hesitation, I wired telling him to expect me, and hired a car to drive to Scotland. I considered going by train, nervous about driving without a navigator, but banished these thoughts as I was keen to show Dad my driving ability. The journey took longer than I thought, but I arrived as the twilight moon cast its silvery-blue light over the village, feeling incredibly pleased with myself.

Seeing Dad again was lovely, and I felt guilty for staying away so long. Spending time with him in the beautiful scenery back home made staying sad difficult. Esther and her mother invited me for tea in the front room of the manse. We had never done that before, and acting in a formal, grown-up manner felt rather strange. They told endless stories of our old friends, and I admired her engagement ring, a lovely gold band with a square ruby. When we finished our tea, Esther suggested we go for a stroll in the garden.

"Can you believe Morag is expecting? Such a quiet wee mouse, Heaven knows how Callum noticed her to get her that way." Esther said with a giggle, making sure her mother could not overhear us. "Believe me, they were the talk of the village for ages. Daddy married them as soon as they got the banns sorted. Oh, Mary and Tam are engaged, too. I meant to tell you. I'm sorry I've been terrible at letter writing."

"I'm sorry, I haven't been any better," I admitted. After the first few letters between us, they had dwindled somewhat. "It is astounding how many of our friends have a marriage or engagement to report."

"I know. Isn't it strange? You went to London to find a husband, yet you remain unattached when there is, all of a sudden, no shortage of eligible young men back home," she said with a laugh.

I gave her a bogus smile. "Yes, it is strange, right enough. So, when are you and Robbie setting a date?"

"Not for a wee while, as Daddy insists that Robbie save up a deposit for a house first. I am sure that he is putting us off because he thinks we are too young, but he will not admit it. Anyway, Robbie is hoping that we'll have enough saved so we can get married next summer."

"That's fantastic. Good for you."

"I'll send you an invitation. You will come, won't you?"

"I would not miss it for the world," I told her, and I meant it.

"It is a pity you are not engaged, too. It is wonderful being in love. What happened with that gentleman, the one you bought those horrible cufflinks for?"

"We are no longer together," I told her, hoping my tone might deter further questions.

"Pity. I bet it was those cufflinks. I told you they were awful."

Another benefit of being home was spending time riding Bertha, a gorgeous bay I had always considered my horse. Although seventeen, she still thought herself a youngster. We had grown up together, and learning to ride her is among my earliest memories. While I loved riding, my solitude gave me time to think about Charlie. Fortunately, Bertha proved an excellent listener.

"I wish I could have taken you down to London with me, Bertha. I have missed this so much. Still, it is nice being home. I am glad I have nothing here that reminds me of Charlie. In London I have put everything that reminds me of him in a chest. It's getting rather full. Despite the luxury of a lack of aide-memoirs here, I cannot stop my mind torturing me. It feels good talking about it, and I cannot tell anyone else here."

She whinnied in response.

"I can admit this to you, Bertha," I told her, leaning closer in although miles from anyone. "I miss him. We were happy for a while, and it was the happiest I have been since Mum died. If the chance presented itself, I would happily trade all my remaining days to re-live any one of my days with him. I had no idea those days would be so few. I curse myself for not savouring them. How lightly I took them. Three months have passed since he walked out of my life. He took my heart with him, although I have only myself to blame."

She gave another whinny. I gave her an appreciative pat.

"It is great talking with you, but I do wish Mum were here. That is one of many if only possibilities passing through my head lately. If only I had not gone to London, if only I had not returned to the party. Oh yes, if only I'd listened when Lonnie warned me and not fallen head over heels for Charlie, and if only I had been brave enough not to send him away. Oh, the hardest one, Bertha, if only I could stop myself wanting and missing him."

Hearing the church bell ring six times, I turned towards home.

"I think I should never return to London. What do you think?" I waited for Bertha's reaction, although she remained silent. "September will be here before I know it. The thought that I might see him again is scaring me beyond reason. Do you think I should stay?"

Her silence was resolute.

"Ah, then you think I should go back. I know you are right. I do miss my friends, not to mention the clubs. Compared with London, things can be a wee bit boring around here. I would kill for a between the sheets. Can you imagine me in the Brig End ordering one of those at the bar? I would be the main topic of conversation in the village for months. If they knew half of what I have done since I left, I could never show my face again. Having some fun again would be great, but I will miss you if I go, Bertha."

On my birthday, Mrs. Mackenzie handed me a letter from Lonnie that had arrived in the morning post. Inside was my present, tickets for the All England finals. If anything was going to drag me back to London, it would be tennis. I would hate to miss the championships. After giving it some thought, I told Dad over breakfast.

"I've had a letter from Alfie and Lonnie with their birthday present, tickets for the tennis championships. I went last year and loved it. It is a thoughtful gift. They know I love tennis, although I cannot play for toffee."

"You'll be wanting to go back to London then?"

"Yes, although not until next weekend," I told him with a nod. "Is that all right with you?"

"Well, although I have appreciated having you here for these past few weeks, you are clearly missing London."

"Yes, a wee bit, although I have loved being home," I told him, scared he would think me ungrateful.

"To think you didn't want to go in the first place," he said, looking smug. "Then you must go. Goodness knows there is not enough going on here to keep you occupied. It will also provide you with a chance for meeting the young gentleman you are pining for."

"Oh no, Dad, there's no gentleman," I said, although his disbelief was apparent. "Well, there was, but it is over."

"I see. Did this gentleman end things between you?"

"No, I did. It seemed the right thing to do."

"You are a grown woman who is more than capable of making her own decisions, but I must ask. If you are confident that you did the right thing, then why are you so unhappy?"

"Is it that obvious?" I asked, and he nodded. "It's a long story."

"Not one you want to share with your old dad, eh? He isn't married, is he?" he asked, his forehead creased with concern.

"No, Dad, it's nothing like that."

"I understand. Believe it or not, I was young once. Remember, you can talk to me anytime you need to. I will always be here, and you are welcome home any time you like."

Despite him being with his mother, I had convinced myself Charlie was living it up in America. Meanwhile, I was alone, regretting my choices. I longed to see my friends again, knowing spending time with them without having fun was impossible.

Back in London, I found an answer to whether Charlie ever thought of me. A parcel with a New York postmark had arrived on my birthday. The handwriting was his, although messier than usual, as if written inside a moving vehicle. Inside I found an unmarked wooden box containing a beautiful gold locket with a thistle intertwined with a rose engraved on the front. The evident symbolism was not lost on me. It had no note, yet I knew who sent it. Goodness knows how he found it in New York.

The glorious conclusion I drew was that Charlie retained some feelings for me. He remembered my birthday, bought me a meaningful present, and sent it with perfect timing. There might be a chance he would forgive me if I could show him how repentant I was. I would walk barefoot across broken glass if it helped convince him. I wore the locket every day. It brought hope along with some painful memories.

The tennis proved a fantastic diversion. I found it engrossing and enjoyed every minute. Loudspeakers broadcast the umpire's calls, giving the whole event an even more exciting air. I hoped to see Monsieur Lacoste in the final but saw him eliminated in the semi-final instead. The all-French final was a joy with two of the Four Musketeers in action. Monsieur Cochet won in a well-matched competition, compensating for the one-sided ladies' match. I cheered Miss Godfree, hopeful she would retain her title, although Miss Wills proved herself a worthy champion, dropping just one set during the entire tournament.

With the championships over, I determined I would keep myself busy. I needed further distraction so volunteered for extra duties with the NWCU, making sure I left the house every day. One afternoon, I lay resting with a headache. The day had been close, with a sepia light attesting to a storm that refused to arrive. Alfie knocked on my door, entering with a grave expression. I knew it was about Charlie.

"I know you are feeling unwell, but can I have a word?"

I nodded assent, and he sat beside me with a cable in his hand.

"I think you ought to read this. It's from David, Charlie's cousin in Southampton."

I read the cable over, incapable of believing what I read.

MOORFOOT MISSING IN NY FAMILY CONCERNED ANY CONTACT?

My insides gave way, falling towards my feet.

"When did you get this, Alfie? What happened? Why is his cousin concerned?" My questions were endless. Alfie lifted his hand, indicating I must stop talking to allow him to answer.

"It arrived this morning. I have sent a few telegrams and made some calls. He argued with his mother during their journey across. He walked out when they arrived in New York and never went to Southampton. We know he sent you the locket from New York, and I have talked with friends there who have seen him. By all accounts, he is attempting to send himself into nothingness through drink and dope. No one has seen him for some weeks. I am leaving for New York to look for him."

I paused, considering what he told me. Charlie was in danger. I knew it was my fault.

"Take me with you, Alfie. Please."

"Do you think that would be a good idea? After all, it is . . ." He trailed off, trying to avoid hurting my feelings.

"My fault that he is in this mess?" I finished his sentence for him. "Perhaps it is my fault, but we have no way we can know for certain unless we ask him. I must find out, and that is why I must talk with him. Please, Alfie, you must see that I owe him that at least."

He did not look convinced, but I had no intention of letting him go without me.

"Alfie, I think, and I am certain you do, too, that he is unhappy because I concealed my feelings for him. You must allow me the opportunity to put things right and tell him the truth. When we find him, you can talk with him first, tell him I am there, then ask if he will speak with me. I will understand if he does not want to, but I must try. If you do not take me with you, I swear I will go on my own. I have some money set aside. I am sure I will have enough for my passage."

He hesitated yet saw my determination. "Fine, fine, you can come with me. I'll telephone the travel agent."

"Thank you, Alfie. I'll go and pack." I rang for Dawson.

"There is no rush. We do not leave for two days."

"I know. But packing will give me something to do."

We sailed on the Olympic, trying not to think about its sister ships. I was wee when they sank, although, like everyone, I had read about what happened. One or two nervous passengers jumped at every unexpected noise or movement. Those with a more devil-may-care attitude made jokes about going down with the ship and suchlike. Alfie explained many checks had been made and additional lifeboats added so we would be a good deal safer. I found it ironic as I would have walked onto a sinking ship without hesitation a few weeks before—now, I needed to live so I could find Charlie.

In normal circumstances, I would find an ocean crossing exciting. Any other time I would have been thrilled boarding the beautiful vessel where Douglas Fairbanks and Mary Pickford spent their honeymoon. Unfortunately, this was not any other time, meaning I endured the most tedious days of my life. Despite the marvellous attractions, I refused to leave my cabin for the first two days. I could not care how many decks the ship possessed, and I did not intend visiting the ballroom, however grand. Alfie brought me food I did not want, and I picked at it.

On our second day of the crossing, Alfie found himself reunited with Rupert Hayes, an old friend and occasional lover. He accompanied his parents, who were in the dark about their son's sexual proclivities. Alfie asked if I would mind leaving my cabin to allow them some private time. When I asked why they wanted my room, I was told that explaining sneaking into my cabin would be easier than explaining sneaking into each other's.

I did not mind the possible slight on my reputation. Being forced out of my room allowed me to spend my time hiding in the first-class library, used by only a few older passengers. Alfie was worried, too, and I liked seeing him smile again. He and Rupert spent their time in each other's company, meeting in the bar or during gentlemen's hours in the Turkish baths.

Just as I was despairing at the age we had spent at sea, we finally sailed into New York. The skyline took my breath away with its enormous buildings waking with the dawn light. I felt how Jack must have felt on reaching the summit of the beanstalk. I could not see how we could possibly find Charlie in a city so huge. Yet, despite the enormity of our task, I strove to stay positive. Charlie was out there, and we were going to find him.

We completed the lengthy customs process and made our way towards the Plaza. Alfie booked two adjoining suites, each with two king-sized beds. For the complete life of me, I could not understand why a room should accommodate so many people. They were enormous rooms for an enormous city. The window offered a stunning view looking over Central Park, which was fringed by more huge buildings.

We started our search by visiting Herbie, an old friend. Alfie introduced me as we entered the apartment.

"So, this is Alice." Herbie looked at me, raising a curious eyebrow. "I have heard so much about you."

I expected he would be American, but he spoke with an English accent. "Oh, I am sorry. There is no way what he said about me could have been good."

"On the contrary, he would not hear a single word against you."

His attempt at making me feel better only made me feel worse. I did not deserve any defence, as my actions had been no better than those of a vile stinking poltroon.

Alfie saw my discomfort, valiantly jumping in. "Have you seen or heard from Moorfoot recently?"

"He did stay with me for a few days, but I haven't seen or heard from him for some weeks. I must admit I am concerned for his welfare. He cannot have much money left, and he is becoming a real dope fiend. He was making good money playing cards for a while, but he was soon not in any fit state to win anymore. It started with him seeking a permanent state of discombobulation, some coke or hashish. Before long, his addiction became serious, with him taking opium, morphine, or whatever he could get his hands on. He took more coke to counteract the worse effects of the morphine and vice-versa, all the time getting increasingly paranoid, erratic, and distant. I must say he was hardly the same Moorfoot at all. He left one afternoon and never returned, and I haven't seen him since."

My heart sank at his report, and Alfie looked grim. Herbie gave us a few addresses to try, primarily clubs and opium dens Charlie frequented. We visited other friends, all with similar reports. It was far too early for the clubs, so we went back to the hotel to plan our stops on a map. After we had eaten, we left for an opium den, the first destination on our list. Though dusk, I found myself amazed at the brightness of the incredible city lights. The sights and smells of Chinatown were grander than those in Limehouse. Chinese signs and flags mixed with a few American ones among the lamps and lanterns.

Any other time I would love exploring the strange new streets, yet we had a mission. We pulled into a grubby side street, entering a doorway alongside an anonymous shop. It smelled peculiar, with a heady sickly floral perfume, as though someone set fire to potpourri. Inside looked more beautiful than I expected with gorgeous silk wall-hangings. There were a few chaise-lounges, covered with cushions and blankets, one in Stewart tartan. I found it a strange memento of home in such a foreign place.

An inebriated man lay on a sofa, although he was not Charlie. Alfie showed a photograph to the proprietor, who recognised him. My heart rose but sank again when he said he had not seen him for some weeks. Our lead came to nothing, although we had other addresses. It was early, no need for despondency yet. We ate at a modest delicatessen before heading to some speakeasies Herbie told us about. The first address took us to another seedy-looking side street. Nothing indicated its existence, which made sense, given its illegal status. We walked down a dirty staircase towards a door with no handle. We knew the drill from clubs back home. Having checked no one was watching, Alfie knocked on the door. A flap opened, and a bright light illuminated a face behind a metal grill. A few words and some dollar bills later, the door swung open.

We entered the smoke-filled interior, separating so we could study the people inside. I looked around, hoping to see those familiar features. Searching took an age as every square inch was crammed with inebriated pleasure-seekers, although we eventually decided he was elsewhere. We tried a few more places, with depressing results, before we lacked the energy to try anywhere else. Despondent, we ordered a drink to cover the one drink minimum demanded by the management, figuring we needed it. We both took a long sip and realised with disgust the reason locals called the stuff coffin varnish. Disgusting does not come near describing the bitter metallic taste. We put the drinks down and called it a night, neither of us wishing to consume enough to make it palatable.

On our second day, we met with a private detective, an ex-policeman called Goodwin. He was younger than I expected, and a touch on the plump side. I hoped he would not have to pursue anyone on foot. He asked about Charlie's friends in New York, although I proved useless in that respect. Goodwin spent the next few days searching clubs, opium dens, speakeasies, private addresses, and alleyways. We also checked them, as we needed to do something. At times we would find someone who had seen him, although no more recently than some weeks ago. In desperation, we checked police stations, clinics, hospitals, and morgues. We had no luck in these places either, although I would say we were more lucky than unlucky in the case of the morgue. We left there with a silent yet grateful invocation of thanks on my part.

Chapter Twenty-three: Cold Turkey

At the end of a fortnight consisting of the two longest weeks of my life, we were yet to find Charlie. Sensing my despair, Alfie attempted to raise my spirits. One morning he met me for breakfast with a smile, his first for a long time.

"Our private dick has a new lead. I know nothing came from his previous leads, although this is hopeful. He thinks Charlie is staying with a friend at an address in Harlem. He followed him last night and is fairly sure he is still there. He's watching and will follow him if he goes anywhere." He consulted some scribbled notes on hotel notepaper. "It's West 125th Street. I don't think it is anyone I know."

I wanted to leave that minute, although Alfie refused. He argued we had no idea when we would have an opportunity for eating again and insisted we order breakfast first. We left when we finished eating. Actually, when Alfie finished eating, I just pushed my food around my plate.

The taxi crawled through the traffic, the ride taking hours. I spent the entire journey trying not to get my hopes up, having had them dashed many times. I kept recalling the old phrase *it's the hope that kills you*. It was doing its damnedest to kill me.

We arrived at the address, finding no sign of Goodwin. Presuming him away somewhere following Charlie, we knocked on the door. There was no answer. Refusing to be daunted, Alfie banged harder, and this time the door swung open. The young man who opened it gave the impression of having dragged himself from bed, although he wore trousers and a vest. His pale, emaciated face suffered from pock-marked red skin and sunken cheeks.

"Can I help you?" he asked with a suspicious tone.

"We're friends of Charlie Moorfoot, sometimes known as Charlie Fyffe. We believe he is here."

"Well, you are wrong. There is no-one by that name here," he said with a sneer.

Alfie took a twenty-dollar bill from his wallet, holding it towards him.

He regarded it with greed, deciding it sufficient to justify ratting on his friend. "He's gone out."

My heart sank. Not again.

He stretched for the note, but Alfie pulled it from his grasp. "Do you know where he has gone?" Alfie asked.

"Maybe I do. Maybe I don't."

"Do you know where Charlie is?" He started returning the note to his wallet.

"He went to buy junk," he answered, scared at the prospect of losing the money. "I forget the number, but it's the brown door on the right of the Flophouse on West 123rd, apartment five. He is in a bad way, and he is already well stoned. He won't be going anywhere for some time." He took the money and closed the door.

We walked to the address, which seemed quicker than trying to find a cab, taking hope from what he told us. The shabby, run-down area looked a world apart from Manhattan. New York had been a city of contrasts. We'd visited some incredible, enchanting places and some horrid ones. A few looked so intimidating, Alfie insisted I wait outside in the taxi.

We found Goodwin smoking a cigarette near a door covered with layers of peeling paint, the majority in shades of brown. He told us Charlie had gone in twenty minutes previous and had not left by the same route. I walked with them, although they had reservations about me entering such a place. Annoyed, I let them know they were going in without me over my dead body. Leaving me outside on my own would be more dangerous, leaving them in no position for arguing. Alfie looked at the detective, who shrugged and walked to the door, which wasn't locked.

He indicated we should stand behind him as he knocked on the shabby door of apartment five. It opened a crack and a face popped up.

"Wadda ya want?" The chubby red face spat the words.

"We're looking for an Englishman, known as Charlie Fyffe or Moorfoot," Alfie answered.

"Never heard of him," he answered, looking from Alfie to the detective to me.

Alfie presented him with a fifty-dollar bill. A hand emerged round the door to grab the money, and the door opened. The detective entered, followed by Alfie, who took my hand as we walked inside.

"Just as well you came. Thought I might have to have him disposed of," the man said without a trace of guilt. "Told him he didn't need that much."

He led us along a narrow corridor towards a tiny window-less room. There, slumped on some cushions, lay a thin, dishevelled looking Charlie. My heart leapt before sinking at the sight of him. He looked horrendous. He was pale, with cuts and bruises covering his gaunt face, blood congealing in the bigger gashes. His right eye was swollen and bruised. A rough beard showed he had abandoned shaving, and his long hair was neglected. As I ran to him, I could see that his lips were tinged with blue. He was breathing, although each breath was shallow, his pulse weak. He clutched a syringe, which I took from him and threw on the ground. The man grabbed it, examining it for damage.

"These are all the rage. Nobody wants to smoke it no more. Don't suppose he'll want it back."

"No, he certainly will not," I said, discovering my voice. I stared at him, unable to digest the state we found him in.

"Charlie, can you hear me?" I asked, shaking him. He did not react, and I felt a cold feeling of dread.

"It's me. Can you hear me?" I repeated, shaking him harder.

His bloodshot eyes opened as he struggled to focus on me.

"Cluitie, talk to me," I demanded.

"Fuck, this is a new one," he slurred, his voice hoarse. He was conscious, although in a terrible way.

"What happened to him?" Alfie asked our host, indicating Charlie's injuries.

"I hear he got beaten pretty bad last night because he owed the wrong somebody some money."

Alfie and Goodwin lifted Charlie, carrying him between them. He had left his car at the first address so he could follow him on foot. Unable to find a cab who would take us with Charlie in such a bad way, Goodwin fetched his car. We got in, reassuring him we would pay through the nose if he bled or vomited. Charlie drifted in and out of consciousness the entire time. When conscious, making much sense out of him was difficult.

We walked into the hotel, the men carrying Charlie with his arms draped across their shoulders. I borrowed Alfie's hat, pushing it over his face, assuring the concerned doorman he was drunk and requiring a lie-down. They took him to Alfie's room, laying him on the spare bed. Goodwin recommended hiring a particular doctor who specialised in these matters. He went off to fetch him, assuring us he would return as soon as he could.

We undressed Charlie, exchanging horrified looks at his appearance. His ribs jutted out under his skin, leaving every bone visible. Enormous red bruises covered his chest and stomach. Getting him into a pair of Alfie's pyjama bottoms proved tricky, although we managed between us. We decided against the top, unable to solve the riddle of putting it on him without causing him pain. Alfie fetched warm water and a flannel, and I sat beside the bed.

Charlie lay awake, groaning and mumbling incoherent words.

"Don't you dare die on me, Cluitie," I whispered, unsure if he could hear me.

I had not been so scared since Mum first told me she was ill. Alfie handed me the washbowl, and I wiped the dirt and dried blood from his face and chest. Aware of his bruises, I sought to be gentle. He looked at me, although I could not be sure he recognised me. His pupils were mere pinpricks, his eyes unable to focus. A pained moan and a laboured wheeze accompanied every breath.

This continued for an excruciating hour until the doctor arrived. He gave Charlie a disdainful look while examining him. For him, Charlie was merely another drug addict, and he could not care less whether he lived or died. He saw no reason for being anything other than blunt with us.

"Way I see it, you've two choices. Option one, you can let him recover through complete withdrawal, cold turkey, they call it. Treat his symptoms as they arise, making him as comfortable as you can. It will be difficult and will not be pretty, but he is young and still has some strength. If he survives the night, then he most probably will get through this in a week or two."

"If he survives the night?" I echoed, shocked.

"It's not touch and go, maybe nearer fifty-fifty. He has made it this far, but there's still a long way to go."

"What is the other option?" Alfie asked. I was still reeling at the odds the doctor quoted. Disliking the sound of option one, I hoped option two might be a more palatable one. Something about the doctor's demeanour informed me that would not be the case.

"You monitor his withdrawal. You will need to inject him with heroin at regular intervals, reducing the dose a little each time. This method is considerably less traumatic for the patient, but it takes longer for them to recover. I can no longer legally prescribe what you need, so you must procure it some other way and be extremely careful how you administer it."

He treated Charlie's wounds, stitched some cuts, and informed us he had three or four broken ribs. Reaching inside his bag, he produced a syringe, a vial of liquid and some tablets. Handing me the pills with instructions, he injected Charlie with something, wishing us good luck.

Alfie settled the bill, and the doctor left us discussing our options. Neither of us wished to inject him with the poison, leaving us with the choice of cold turkey. We stayed with him until I insisted Alfie go to my room so he could rest. It had gone three, and Charlie was in a relatively peaceful sleep.

I sat beside his bed, staring at his beautiful, battered face. I stroked his hair, hating myself for causing this horrible thing to happen to him. Half opening his eyes, he peered at me.

"You look so like her," he mumbled, falling into a restless sleep, fidgeting, and twitching.

He slept for an hour or two while I sat beside his bed, scared to take my eyes off him or fall asleep. As I watched him sleeping, I grabbed some nail scissors and clipped a lock of his hair for my locket. If he were to die, I wanted it to remember him by, although I admonished myself for considering the possibility.

We destroyed the ripped and bloodied clothes he had been wearing, and the contents of his pockets sat on the dressing table. While he slept, I looked at the items. The meagre pile consisted of a tatty handkerchief embroidered with his initials, a few coins, and a wallet. The wallet contained a one-dollar bill, some pawn tickets, and a creased, faded photograph of me. As I picked up the handkerchief, a paper package fell from it. I unwrapped it and found a familiar pair of cufflinks in the shape of a devil. My heart swelled with unspoken hope.

Despite my best efforts, sleep overcame me. I dozed, feeling befuddled when I woke. A dawn light peeked through the gaps in the curtain. Remembering where I was, I panicked, looking onto the bed where Charlie lay twitching through a feverish dream. I rejoiced at seeing he had survived the night before scolding myself for falling asleep.

I touched his forehead. He was burning up. Panicking, I ran into the bathroom, wringing out a flannel and mopping his brow. When I did, his eyes opened again, and he stared, looking confused. He tried sitting up but winced, crying in agony, as he fell back on the bed.

"It's okay, Cluitie. You're safe."

"Hurts."

I dissolved a tablet the doctor gave me in water, helping him sit up so he could drink it. Doing so brought on tremendous pain, his drowsiness preventing him from helping me. I grabbed pillows from the other bed, propping him up with them. As he sipped the medicine, he took my hand.

"You ought to meet her."

In my tired state, the statement left me mystified. It took a while to realise he thought he was talking to someone who looked like me.

"I love her."

"I know." I mopped his brow again, tears rolling down my face. "She loves you, too."

"No, no, she doesn't," he said, his tone matter of fact, with sadness on his face.

"I do, Cluitie, I honestly do." His eyes closed, and I

wondered if he heard me. I told myself it had been the drugs talking, although it gave me goosepimples hearing him say he loved me.

When Alfie joined us, Charlie was rousing but feverish.

"How is he?"

"He has slept, although never for awfully long. Whenever he is awake, he is in pain. He has a terrible fever, one minute he is burning up, the next, he is shivering. I'm not sure he is aware of much. He doesn't have any idea who I am."

He sat on the bed.

Charlie opened his eyes, peering at him.

"How are you doing, old friend?" Alfie asked.

"It hurts," he said with a grimace.

"Yes, I am sure it does."

"I need more dope. Can you get me some?" he pleaded through gritted teeth.

"No, Moorfoot. No more."

"Please. I need it. The pain."

I looked at Alfie, opening my mouth to speak. He shook his head. I could not see him in such pain, although I had to agree. For his own good, we had to deny him what he wanted. Having Alfie's help made helping him sit up easier, and he managed another tablet.

"Are you hungry?" I asked, changing the subject.

"No." He shook his head, closed his eyes, and appeared to fall asleep.

Alfie put a hand on my shoulder. "Right, this is what will happen. You will go to your room and get some sleep."

"But . . ."

"You will go to the other room, and you will get some sleep," he continued. "You will eat something, and you will come back when you are not dead on your feet. I will stay with Charlie."

Exhausted past arguing, I climbed into bed, expecting to lie staring at the ceiling, agonising. Despite my fears, I fell asleep straight away. My first thought on waking was of Charlie. Without changing out my pyjamas, I rushed through the connecting door. My heart was in my mouth, despite telling myself Alfie would have let me know if anything terrible had happened.

Charlie was vomiting into the washbowl. It was the most marvellous sight I have ever seen.

"He's been retching like this for an hour or so," Alfie told me. "His stomach is empty, so all he is bringing up is bile and the little water he has drank. He doesn't want to eat anything, but we must get him to try."

Charlie stopped being sick and settled for a time but then suffered severe stomach cramps. Alfie lifted him as though he weighed nothing, carrying him into the bathroom. He placed him in a warm bath, where I washed him with a sponge, trying not to hurt him. When we got him back in bed, I re-bandaged his chest with the compression bandages the doctor had left. It made the pain worse, his breathing becoming more laboured. After some deliberation, I removed it, hoping it was the right thing to do, and he fell asleep again.

When he woke, I called room service, asking for some warm milk and porridge. The poor Frenchman who answered had no idea what I meant. I described it until he recognised the word oatmeal. The porridge arrived, and I mixed it with milk, putting the spoon to Charlie's lips.

"No," he refused. "Not hungry, the pain . . ."

"Cluitie, you will do as you are damn well told and eat some right now," I told him, leaving him in no doubt I would not be argued with.

He opened his mouth, taking a tiny bite. The elation this wee activity set off was overwhelming. He managed two more mouthfuls before refusing any more. I exchanged a hopeful look and a smile with Alfie.

"Why don't you let me die?" he asked.

I swallowed a huge lump in my throat as my eyes welled.

"Never will happen, my friend," Alfie answered him, putting a hand on my shoulder.

Charlie gave a violent shake, and his breathing became more laboured. I held his hand, scared I might lose him. He did not respond to me, although his eyes were open. The horrible episode lasted half an hour, ending when he fell asleep. All I could do was dab the sweat from his brow.

The attacks recurred every few hours over the following few days. I took turns with Alfie to sit with him, doing our best to help him through the cycle of cravings, cramps, and breathing attacks. He only slept an hour at a time until awakening, crying for more dope or, at times, death. We bathed him often to help with his aches and pains, encouraging him to eat and drink. For every period of progress, we suffered horrible times when he got much worse.

Days passed before I believed that he would turn the corner. The breathing attacks subsided, and he could eat a touch more, although suffering from shivering, vomiting, and stomach cramps. As another bad episode abated, I reached to mop his brow. He looked at me through half-opened eyes.

"Thank you, Kitten."

He had not called me that or acknowledged he knew who I was since we'd found him. I took his hand, my heart rejoicing.

"You need not thank me."

"I'm sorry," he added, although it was unnecessary.

"No, I am the one who should be saying sorry. You concentrate on getting better."

He gave a weak smile, trying to squeeze my hand.

By the week's end, we saw some signs of the old Charlie returning. He regained some mobility, and although nauseous and agonised at times, could keep his food down. Alfie helped him shave, and at times, I fancied I saw the twinkle returning to his eyes. He decided he wanted to leave the room that had functioned as our prison for eight long days. Sharing his enthusiasm for being free, I went shopping for new clothes for him, and we went to the atrium.

As we walked, I took his arm, and he leaned on me as he shuffled along the hallway.

"It has not escaped my notice that you are wearing the locket I sent you," he stated as we sat at our table.

"It's beautiful. I wear it every day, thank you. Did you have it made especially?"

"No, I admit I did not. I was on my way to an opium house when I saw it in a shop window on the Lower East Side. I was feeling rather flush as I had just taken some chaps at cards. For some time, I stood staring, thinking solely of you. I fought the temptation to buy the opium, but I could not walk away. I had just enough to buy it and no more. Seeing it there felt as though you were talking to me. Getting the money to send it to you in time for your birthday became my reason for living."

"Then I love it even more." I squeezed his arm.

As soon as Charlie felt strong enough for the journey home, Alfie booked us places on the Mauretania. We sent a cable home announcing our return.

I took more interest in my surroundings on the liner home than on my previous trip, although one nagging concern troubled me. Charlie and I had not yet discussed what happened between us or our feelings towards each other. I had avoided the subject for fear his feelings might have changed. His manner reassured me he did not hate me, but did he love me? He loved me at one time and did not seem to hold my actions against me. I could not bring myself to enquire about his feelings. Much as I yearned to know, I feared his answer might be one I did not want to hear.

This silence continued until the last evening when we were drinking tea in the first-class lounge. We talked about the other guests, making up silly stories about them and their reason for travelling, making each other laugh. His face took a thoughtful expression.

"Alice, I must thank you, most sincerely, for everything you have done for me." For a moment, I was stunned by how my name sounded coming from him. I could not believe how much I yearned to hear him call me Kitten again.

"No, you do not. I am sure you would have done the same for me."

"I cannot believe you would be so stupid as to do as I did." He looked shamefaced.

"No? I had a damn good go at stupid after you left," I admitted. "I missed you so much I lost entire days at a time. I became a consummate mess, which took me to some strange places. Thankfully, Lonnie stopped me going too far."

"You missed me?" He looked surprised—even possibly hopeful?

"More than anything," I answered. He gave me a piercing look, doubting my words. "Charlie, what were you thinking?"

"I cannot say I did any thinking. It proved too painful. It seemed so bleak, facing life without you. I found myself caught in la douleur exquise. I have never known such desolation. Mother confronted me about my attitude, and I informed her you had ended things. She told me you must be more intelligent than she gave you credit for and that it saved her the expense of paying you off. We had a blazing row, and when we disembarked, I stayed in New York. They say time is the healer of necessary evils, but I grew impatient, trying dope instead. I wanted oblivion, not feeling anything anymore. I took whatever I could. Every night I dreamt of you, and I tried re-creating my dreams with dope. At its worst, I kept hearing you say you did not love me. My money was soon gone, and I had pawned almost everything. If you had not found me, I fear what might have happened. I did not necessarily seek death, although I did not want to live either. I became nothing more than a suicidal coward."

"Then cowardice is something we are both guilty of," I confessed. "I did not think you'd feel my loss so badly, or I'd never have done what I did. I thought I acted for the best. You are an idiot, as I am not worth giving your life for."

"You are worth it to me." He took my hand. "You were the last person I anticipated seeing in New York. I thought I dreamt you again at first. You saved my life. I owe you everything."

"No, Alfie saved your life. By your account, I almost cost you it."

"No, that was my stupidity. You came here for me, and I have convinced myself you must care for me after all, else you would never have done so. However, I must ask you the question I am yearning to ask. You are too kind a person to hurt me consciously. If your answer is no, then please say nothing. I cannot bear to hear you tell me again. However, I need to ask, is there perhaps a chance one day you might love me?"

"Cluitie, I already love you."

"You have no idea how delightful hearing that is," he said, smiling. "Please, say it once more."

"I love you with all my heart. I always have. When I am with you, my mind lights up, and when you touch me, my body does the same. I am never happier than when I am with you. When you left, I was disconsolate. When we could not find you, I feared I would never see you again. Thinking that I might lose you scared me more than anything. The doctor told us you might die, and I despaired, willing you back to me constantly. I found myself desperately praying to a God I

263

do not believe in, pleading that he would spare you. I love you and have done since the night we first met."

"Why did you tell me you did not?" He looked relieved yet confused at the same time.

"I hated myself for saying that. It was never the case. I said that because I did not feel good enough for you. Do you forgive me?"

"Are you mad?" he asked, nonplussed. "You are, by far, the most wonderful and precious thing that ever happened in my life. Falling in love with you is by far the best notion I have ever had. You broke my heart so beautifully I cannot even be angry with you for that. All I have to forgive is your lack of belief in yourself and how much you mean to me."

"Your mother visited, letting me know in no uncertain terms that I was and will always be your inferior, and I should let you find a wife worthier of you. I believed her."

"She told me about her visit. I cannot tell you how ashamed I feel about that. No one could ever be worth more than you are to me."

"But your mother, your title, your allowance . . ."

"I'd happily give them all up for you."

"I don't want you to," I protested.

"I don't care if I do. If that is the decision I must make, I choose you. Who knows what will happen? Whatever we face, as long as we are together, we will manage."

We kissed a long kiss, not caring a jot about our fellow passengers.

"I love you, Kitten, and I will ask you this question for what I very much hope will be third time lucky. Forgive me if I don't go down on one knee, but will you marry me?"

"I love you too, Cluitie, and yes, I will marry you."

"Well, we are buggered now then," he said.

We giggled and kissed again.

ABOUT THE AUTHOR

Faye Keltie was born and raised in Fife, Scotland and lives near the water of the stunning Firth of Forth. Her job titles have included waitress, shelf stacker, and shop assistant. After a few years working as a secondary school history teacher, she took (very) early retirement for medical reasons. Although she dabbles in wonky craftwork and tries with various levels of success to keep plants alive, writing has always been her primary hobby. After conversations with friends and workmates, she turned to writing erotica after realising many of them were looking for erotic fiction that was sexy but had a tender and lightly humorous touch. The exact phrase that resonated was, "I would like something that's a bit like Downton Abbey but with shagging." The idea for the Age of Decadence came into her mind and would not leave. While The Age of Decadence is not the first book she has set out to write, it is the first she has ever managed to complete.